To Chris.

THE GREAT FIREWALL

A thriller

Michael C. Boxall

Michael C. Boxall (signature)

The Great Firewall is a work of fiction. All incidents, dialogue and characters are products of the author's imagination and any resemblance to actual events or persons is entirely coincidental.

For my beloved wife, Keiko Tsutori Boxall,
who makes all things possible

ACKNOWLEDGMENTS

My thanks to Ross Browne and Peter Gelfan
of The Editorial Department, who did so much
to bring this idea to birth.

I am also grateful to Prahlad Delaney, who designed
the cover and the website, www.thegreatfirewall.com.

Cover image courtesy of www.cepolina.com

Contents

ONE

OBSESSION

SHANGHAI, 1923, five years after Bolsheviks shot the czar and shot the empress and shot their children and their doctor and their servants and splashed their faces with acid. Nikolai follows the rickshaw and its passenger inland from the Bund, half-running, half-staggering, flapping along in his threadbare greatcoat as if blown by the wind. Ahead of him Chatwin's skull gleams pink through thinning sandy hair. The bamboo rickshaw creaks.

Scummy brown water fills the potholes on Nanking Road. The barefoot puller stumbles, almost falls, slows down.

Chatwin aims a kick. "You one damn slow Chinaman! You makee chop-chop!"

Cars sweep past, carrying foreigners away for cocktail hour. A gangster's black Crossley, bodyguard on the running board, cuts in and makes the rickshaw swerve.

Nikolai's breath comes in gasps. He reaches under his coat and shifts the Nagant revolver tucked in his belt so it no longer jolts against his hip.

By the foundlings' home, where a drawer in the wall says, "Place baby here," the rickshaw comes to a stop, angled across Wei Hai Wei Road. The ragged figure between the shafts slumps to the ground.

"No catchee sleepee on my dollar, boy!" Chatwin stamps his foot. "Chop-chop!" When there is no response he steps down, cursing.

Free of his weight, the rickshaw tips forward. The puller rolls over, face to the sky. The eyes flicker.

Blue eyes. A woman's blue eyes.

"Damn Russkies. Should throw them back in the sea. What's John Chinaman going to think when he sees white people pulling rickshaws?" Chatwin flags down a taxi.

The dying woman's lips move as she tries to whisper a prayer, a confession, an entreaty. Passers-by barely glance.

Nikolai stares at the taxi, then at the woman. He kneels beside her and murmurs words from another lifetime: "Deal not with me after my sins, but according to Thy bountiful mercy, for I am the work of Thy hands and Thou knowest my weakness." Then he takes her shoulders and brings his face close to hers.

"That man. Chatwin. Where is he going? I have to know. He killed my brother."

But it's too late.

What was it like to live like that, at the very bottom of the ladder, lower than the nightsoil carriers who emptied their reeking buckets into the Huangpo each morning? To have nothing, not even enough at the end of the day for a pipe of opium to kill the pain?

Daniel Skye had never lacked anything, and he'd seen enough of the world to realize he was lucky. Now he felt more than lucky: he felt blessed.

He pressed rewind and on the bank of monitors in front of him the animation reversed itself at speed. Nikolai sprang to his feet, Chatwin jumped backward into the rickshaw, the blue-eyed woman hauled herself up on the shafts, the gangster's Crossley backed hastily out of the frame. A spreadsheet on one of the monitors listed scenes: who was in them, where they took place, their length. Daniel scrolled through, looking for the smoothest segue, and stopped at N, C-rickshaw 2-1' 07"s.

This time the rickshaw does not slow down. Instead, it turns north and crosses one of the ramshackle bridges that span Suzhou Creek. Again Nikolai follows, along narrow streets with dank, cramped tenements on either side. The rickshaw stops outside a low wooden warehouse. Chatwin goes inside without looking back. Nikolai draws the revolver and steals around to the side that faces the creek. He edges forward and peers through a torn paper shade. The room is lined with wheelless two-man barrows, like giant tea trays. And on each barrow is a pile of black, grapefruit-sized balls of opium.

He turned to a laptop and added item number 723 to his to-do list: *find archival pic warehouse for N, C-rickshaw 2-1' 25"*. Shouldn't be hard. Long before Cartier-Bresson arrived with his Leica Shanghai had been catnip to photographers, lured by its temptations and caught like flies on paper by its feverish, churning energy.

His stomach growled. Not for the first time, he ignored it. How could he stop, when he was creating something that would change the world, as surely as the Lumière brothers changed it when they told stories in light instead of words? Piece by piece, the production was taking shape. A dark, brooding thriller, *The Riding Instructor* told of two White Russian brothers washed up in 1920s Shanghai, penniless in the world's capital of flamboyant excess. Nikolai, the older, is a former medical student who teaches riding to the wives of foreign businessmen. Petya is a gifted violinist, decorated by the czar but reduced to playing dance music in a gangster's nightclub. One morning Petya doesn't come home. *The Riding Instructor* follows Nikolai's quest through the Shanghai underworld to find him.

At times the story unsettled Daniel, for reasons he couldn't put his finger on. There was something spooky about it, something almost supernatural, as if it already existed and he was just taking it down like dictation. But that didn't keep him from the monitors; he stayed in their glare fourteen, sixteen, sometimes eighteen hours a day.

In fact, it wasn't the story itself that obsessed him. It was the way he would tell it. Or more precisely, entice viewers to tell it. To each other. He knew, in his bones and his gut and beyond the faintest whisper of pre-dawn doubt, that *The Riding Instructor*, part-computer game and part-interactive movie, was the best idea he'd ever had. It could well be the best he ever would have. A once-in-a-lifetime chance to make history. Turning it into reality was more than just ambition, more than just a dream. It was his destiny.

The animations were one level in a treasure house of every kind of storytelling device imaginable. Narration. Video. Music. Text. Archival photos. Maps. Menus. Film clips. Race cards. Old magazines. Architectural plans. Tide tables. All bundled up in SkyeWare, the application that tied the different threads together.

At its heart was the most seductive feature of all. The animations would not stay animations: they would blossom into video of real actors who played out different versions of the story. Not just any actors: Daniel, being Daniel, wanted the best. Johnny Depp. Daniel Day Lewis. Sean Penn. Actors who, simply by their presence, could lay bare characters and their tormented history. Users would create their own unique productions with their own solutions to the mystery. And once they'd made the last cut and mixed in the music? Upload it to the Web. Invite friends to watch. Post it on Facebook. Vie for advertisers, like bloggers. Enter it in a contest ... *item 724, check Sundance.*

The Riding Instructor would take the world by storm. He was sure of that, too, because he knew exactly how to market it. The timing couldn't be better. PC games were in a slump. Phones had tiny screens and not much computing power. But tablet computers like the iPad had enough muscle to use tools and material held in the celestial data domain known as the cloud. And gorgeously bright silky screens. And a boundless appetite for new kinds of content.

He swivelled in his chair and lost himself in the monitors again.

HIS TO-DO LIST reached item 1274: *Bolshevik assassinations 1923 check North China Daily News.* Then things went bad.

To get the Steinway back up the cliff his creditors brought in a helicopter, *thwacka-thwacka-thwacka* drowning out the jeers and catcalls of the assembled seagulls. As it rose above the house the gulls followed, an explosion of surf-white feathers and yellow beaks, swerving, racing, cursing. For a moment, before the helicopter turned inland, the piano hung motionless in the sky, the last drawn-out note of some brooding symphony. Then it disappeared behind the lip of the cliff, trailing its feathered motorcade toward Seattle.

He stared after it from the beach, fingering his watch strap. Going bust felt like a sudden bereavement, a loss that turned everything upside down and left an aching nothingness in the fabric of life itself. But the spiriting away of eight hundred and sixty pounds of maple and ivory should not have come as a surprise. Notice of repossession was among the letters he'd tossed in a drawer unopened, less important than the surging torrent of ideas. What was the best way to make animations morph into video? He could work backward, freezing the first frame of video and turning it into the last frame of the animation. The problem was, he still didn't have the video.

The Riding Instructor had obsessed him for months.. From when he woke up to the last moment of dissolving consciousness he thought of nothing but Nikolai and Petya. What had happened that night? How could he tell the story? What combination of elements might be possible? Then a vertiginous shock made him grip the edge of the table: *everything was possible.*

He knew his vision was expensive. He just hadn't realized how expensive. Or that the money could disappear with such breathtaking speed. When the credit crunch hit and backers backed out he cashed in his own investments: Apple stock he'd been given on his twenty-first birthday had gone up to fifty times its price over the past eight years. He used the house as security for half a million. But he was still far short of what he needed just to make a proof of concept.

He walked slowly back to the house, lips moving in a soundless conversation with himself, past the maples with their wind chimes and the cherry trees Sophie had planted when they moved in. She'd never lived in a house of her own and she'd fallen in love with this one as soon as they saw it. Designed by an architect for his parents, it straddled a cleft in the rocks like a glass bridge supported on massive timber beams. "We've got to have it," she'd said, draping a slender arm over his shoulder. "We can afford it, can't we?"

Quiet descended as the seagulls pondered what they had seen, each sudden raucous hypothesis followed by a thoughtful silence. In the hallway motes of dust drifted in a shaft of sunlight where the piano had stood. He glimpsed his face in the walnut-framed mirror, half-moons like bruises under the eyes. The last three nights he'd slept in his office, cradling his head on his arms and sinking into a bottomless black hole until he jerked awake again and reached for the keyboard to capture whatever new idea had come to the surface during his brief dip into oblivion. Which they did, constantly.

He went down the stairs. Sophie wanted their bedroom on the ground floor so on summer mornings she could jump out of bed and dash naked into the ocean. Amazing how fast she could swim. Without seeming to exert herself she slid through the water, a lean, golden blur. Faster than him.

At the end of an airy, white-painted passage stood a pair of double doors. He turned the handle. Locked. He tapped.

"Sophie, let me in."

Nothing moved.

"Sophie, open the door."

No reply. He tapped again, bone on wood.

"Open it. Please. You know you'll have to eventually."

The click would have been unnoticeable had the house not been so quiet.

She wore a kerchief of lilac and green and as she stood barefoot amid the wreckage of their lives she looked to him more beautiful than ever. The room could have been turned over by looters--drawers pulled out and their contents tipped over the floor, the brass bed covered with magazines, photos, sheet music, CDs from a Japanese language course, her original composite from Belles de Jour modeling agency.

"Sophie ..." He found himself lost for words. Like other military kids whose childhoods had been jolted by frequent upheavals, he distrusted long-term plans. He even paid for his phone by the month to avoid a contract. He preferred to live from day to day, relying on his own abilities and a measure of luck. Buying the house in the first place had gone against his instincts; he'd only agreed because he knew how important it was to her.

"You've blown it, Daniel. You really have." Her eyes were red-rimmed and he knew she'd locked the door because she didn't want him to see her cry. Like a man, she withdrew into herself for protection. Some people found her independence off-putting. Daniel found it irresistible.

"I'm so sorry," he said. "So sorry."

She blew her nose and looked around. The drapes fluttered in the breeze from an open window.

"Strip jack naked. A game for two players . Too bad we both lost." The world had been overrun by people who wanted money. It was like lifting a rock in the garden. Creditors scuttled over their lives like sow bugs, feelers probing the most intimate corners, carrying off a piano, a painting, a car. A house.

"I'll get it all back," he said. "It'll take time. But I'll get it."

"How? How y'all going to do that? Autograph these and sell them to the adoring masses?" She pulled a wicker basket from under the bed and hurled its contents at him like water from a bucket. He flinched, raising an arm to shield himself from the avalanche of sex toys.

He tried to put his arms around her. She pushed him away.

"Why didn't you tell me? Why didn't you at least warn me? Was that too much to do? Tell your wife you've lost all our money? Or did it slip your mind? You being so busy and all."

"I will get it back. There'll be a way. I know there will. I'll make *The Riding Instructor* and--"

Her grey eyes widened. *"The Riding Instructor?* Oh, Jesus. We're losing this house because of *The Riding Instructor.* And you still think it's going to make you rich." She stared, as if seeing him for the first time. "You're mad, Daniel. Certifiable."

"If you'll just listen--"

"How much do you owe? One million? Two? Or is it closer to five? And what are you going to do about it? Make the fucking Riding Instructor." In a fury she mimicked his gestures, gathering nothings out of the air and shaping them to imaginary perfection. She grabbed his arm and brought her face close to his. "Alright. You're smart. Smarter than me. But simple basic common sense? None. Nothing. Absolutely fucking zero."

"Sophie, listen. Listen! I know it's hard to understand. But I didn't choose to do *The Riding Instructor.* It chose me. I can't stop now. I have to finish it." Again he tried to put his arms around her. He caught the ghost of Chanel No 5 lingering about the scarf. Again she fended him off.

Can't blame her. Not in my right mind. Haven't been for months. It's as if someone else is in my head as well, some presence using me for its own ends. A spirit. A doctor would prescribe Zoloft. But I haven't gone crazy. I know I haven't. I've been given a gift. Something unique and priceless and astonishing. A vision.

"Mad. What are the voices telling you to do next, Daniel? Rob a bank?"

He didn't know the answer to that until he heard himself saying it.

"Pierre. He must know people with money. In Shanghai. He'll help."

She went very still. "Pierre?"

Obvious choice, now I think about it. Only choice, given the way things have turned out.

"Lots of contacts. You know how he works. Mr Sociability."

"Yes. I know how he works. Sleazeball."

"Jesus, Sophie, I don't have much alternative. He's in the right place at the right time. And I helped him get started."

"He's a jerk. An animal."

He looked at her. "I thought you liked him. Gallic charm with a Boston accent was irresistible, you said."

"It's resistible."

"What do you mean?" He took her shoulders. "Sophie. Look at me. What do you mean, it's resistible?"

"He's an asshole. Thinks women can't wait to open their legs for him. Just because he's got a camera."

"Girl talk."

She shook her head. "Not girl talk. I know."

"How?" He shook her, harder than he'd intended. "How do you know?"

She pushed him away. "I wasn't going to say anything. Your friend, right? Maybe he is. Maybe it's just a man thing, trying to stick your dick into anything that moves. Maybe you're alright with that. Y'all okay with that, Daniel? Having a friend try to get your wife drunk enough for a threesome?"

Try to get. She said try to get. Not got. Try to get. He clung to the distinction like a shipwrecked sailor to a spar.

"When?"

"Last year. Hong Kong. He turned up at the party after the shoot. Said he'd been brought over by some Chinese millionaire to take pictures of his horse at Happy Valley. Got a thousand-dollar bonus when it won. Looked like he'd spent it on booze. And blow. Things got crazy. I was very drunk. Pierre and some Japanese girl started taking my clothes off. He kept trying to make me drink more whiskey. Said it would relax me."

"Jesus." What could he do? Smash Pierre in the face and then ask for help finding ten million dollars? "Sophie, you're right. Of course.

9

He's a jerk. If there was any alternative I wouldn't go near him. But there isn't. Nobody here is going to give me money. Not now. He's the only one who can help."

She stared at him. "Help what? Fight off the creditors?" She dashed to the bathroom again. A moment later she was back, holding out a box of Tampax. She emptied it onto the floor.

"If they're taking things away they can take these. I won't be needing them. Not for a while, anyway."

He froze.

"Congratulations, Daniel. You're going to be a father."

TWO

MAYLING YU

TWO DAYS LATER, on the other side of the Pacific, the gates of a provincial Chinese courthouse swung open and a glossy blue and white Jinguan van pulled out. Squad cars turned on their sirens and formed an escort, red and blue lights sweeping over the Jinguan's darkened windows. Oversized wing mirrors that stuck out like curved arms from the front of the van made it look like a monstrous predatory insect.

With lights flashing and sirens blaring the convoy moved slowly so it made its point with maximum impact. It passed row after row of apartment blocks whose only splashes of color came from lines of washing strung across the cramped balconies. Any residents not at work putting together semiconductors or circuit boards or running shoes slipped inside when the vehicles came into view.

The cortège passed factories like vast windowless barns and headed toward a range of low hills. On the highest stood a squat, ill-favored building from whose flagstaff drooped the banner of the People's Republic of China, limp in the windless air.

In a third-floor meeting room a dozen members of the city council sat around a cherrywood table. The propaganda department had summoned them to see justice at work, and they were all turned toward a large flat-screen monitor.

The mayor raised a liver-spotted hand.

"Curtains," he said.

A skinny girl with downcast eyes who was serving him bitter green tea put down the thermos and moved to the window. Mayling Yu

11

closed the drapes as the Jinguan pulled into the courtyard below, wheels crunching on the gravel. It swung around so its back faced the building, then stopped. A man in a white coat, carrying a bag and wearing a stethoscope, got out of a squad car and walked over to the van.

The monitor showed a photo from the city's website, smiling workers beneath a sign: "Move forward together to seize the changing times!" It switched to a live video feed from the van in the courtyard of a man strapped to a stretcher.

"More efficient," the head of the propaganda department said. He lit another Hongtashan and tossed the match toward an overflowing ashtray. "See how humane we are. Even with terrorists like Shaowen Gen."

On the screen the doctor appeared and bent over the immobilized figure, whose eyes were fixed on the van's video camera.

"Excuse me," Mayling Yu said in a low voice. "Forgive me. I can't watch." She hurried from the room.

The doctor removed a vial from the bag. He shook it, then held it toward the camera.

"Cocktail hour," the propaganda chief said, eyes fixed on the screen. The mayor grunted.

In the malodorous ground-floor toilet Mayling Yu squatted beside a hole in the floor. On the other side of the low partition a round-faced woman from the accounts department turned the pages of a magazine. "Little whore," the woman muttered. "Those Shanghai sluts fuck like animals." Mayling could tell she was in no hurry to get back to work.

Gen's arm had been bared and bound with a rubber cuff. Beads of sweat appeared on his pallid, unshaven face. He continued to stare up at the camera, which showed the whites of his eyes.

"The doctor puts the needle in the vein," the propaganda chief said. "But he doesn't push the plunger. Of course not. That would violate medical ethics."

The mayor gave a short laugh. Without looking away from the monitor he reached for a cigarette. The sleeve of his fake Brooks Brothers jacket caught the teacup and knocked it over. Tea splashed the documents in front of him and dripped from the edge of the table. He cursed and glanced around for a cloth.

Three floors down, Mayling's heart was pounding so hard she thought the woman in the next stall must surely hear. Her bag, too, would make a noise when she unzipped it. But she had no choice. Suddenly the unseen woman belched, sighed, belched again. Mayling tugged at the zip. It parted with a ripping sound. She froze. The building was unusually quiet. No voices, no footsteps, no distant music from an unseen radio. Only the rustle of paper as the woman turned the page. With trembling hands Mayling took out a laptop and cuatiously opened it.

In the van Gen thrashed his head from side to side. A ball gag, held in place by thongs, muffled his shouts. The doctor held the syringe up to the light and pressed the plunger until all the air had gone. A thread of brown liquid trickled down the needle.

"How long does it take?" one of the councillors asked.

"Not long enough, for scum like that," the mayor said. Tea soaked the papers and blurred the red of the official seals. "Don't any of you lumps of horse shit have a handkerchief?" He looked around. "Where's Yu?"

She'd practiced what she had to do a hundred times. *Speaker off? Yes. Mustn't make a mistake, check again. Press the power button.* The computer started with a faint whirr. *Log onto the city's website. Check the light that flickered on the wireless card, a pinprick of green in the gloom. Click the box that said Restricted. Enter the code the mayor had put in his day planner--the fool! Click again.*

The screen went blank for a moment. Then the condemned man stared up into her eyes.

A stocky figure in olive-green fatigues appeared beside the

stretcher. In the meeting room the propaganda chief adjusted his steel-rimmed glasses and leaned forward. "The People's Armed Police give the injection," he said. "It's one of their new skills."

The mayor went to the door and bellowed into the corridor, "Yu! Come here!"

Mayling jumped. She clicked the red button that said *Capture*. Only when she was perfectly sure it was working did she rush for the stairs.

THE NIGHT AFTER Gen's execution Pierre Kennedy Mears spread a map of Thailand on a low table in his Shanghai apartment and looked for Nong Khai, where the Mekong lights appeared. Orbs of cold fire, the lights rose from the bottom of the river with the eleventh full moon of the year. Local legend said they were the eggs of a giant serpent. Others said they were an optical illusion, a reflection of the moon on the waves of the rain-swelled river. Or the spontaneous combustion of gases from decaying vegetation, like will-o'-the-wisps or corpse candles. Gallic skepticism passed down from his mother made Pierre inclined to think they were marsh gas. But whatever they were, *Skyline*, an Australian in-flight magazine, wanted pictures. His pictures.

He followed his calling—he'd known it was that since the first time he saw an image take form in the developing tray—with unstinting rigor and he'd long known that success was ninety-five percent preparation. He'd hire a boat and shoot as the lights came up out of the water. In his mind's eye he saw the image he wanted: a ball of fire glinting on the stubbled, upturned face of the boatman. That and the moon, if indeed there was a moon, would be the only sources of illumination. If the river was swollen it would run swiftly. The boat would rock, so he'd need a fast shutter speed to keep the images sharp. But shooting fast in the dark meant having the aperture wide open. There wouldn't be much depth of field. If the boatman's face was in focus the lights would just be a distant blur.

He was mulling over combinations of lenses and ISO settings when the house phone rang and a voice barked in guttural Chinese,

"Golden Lotus--reservation for four tomorrow."

"*Da cuo le*," Pierre said after a moment. "Wrong number." The caller snarled and hung up.

Pierre felt a hollowness in his stomach. He took a tumbler of whiskey onto the balcony, which overlooked a park. The city's feverish churn produced a never-ending growl, like some insatiably hungry beast. Shanghai's pace and aggression and swaggering cash-fueled braggadocio grew more strident by the day and made New York seem dull in comparison.

A sliver of moon climbed up the eastern sky. Twelve days to full. Plenty of time to arrange the trip to Nong Khai.

Golden Lotus, four o'clock.

He just had to get through tomorrow.

THREE

PICK-UP ON A LAKE

"I SEE YOU'RE STILL clocking up decisive moments," Daniel said as he studied the photos on Pierre's wall. Some he'd seen before. The haggard woman and two children, each staring fearfully in a different direction as they crossed a bombed-out street, had been nominated for a World Press Award. The conclave of vultures waiting in a gaunt and twisted thorn tree in Mogadishu had picked up a Hearst. And the grizzled veteran in a wheelchair, eyes closed as he rested his forehead against the marble and trailed his fingertips over a name incised in the Vietnam memorial wall, had graced the cover of *Newsweek*.

But the file of kimono-clad women picking their way by moonlight across a wintry landscape was new. Each carried a bundle like a cloth-wrapped banjo and rested a hand on the shoulder of the woman in front.

"*Goze*," Pierre said. "Itinerant shamisen players in northern Japan. All blind. A four-hundred year tradition and that's the last group. They're gone now. Somebody tipped me off just before they disappeared. Spent a week with them. *National Geographic* almost wet themselves. Then I got a show at Bunkamura. Print run of fifty k for the catalog. Paid off my place on Bainbridge from that shoot."

"Lucky." Doubly anguishing that Pierre's finances flourished while his own had taken such a dizzying plunge into the red. *He's always been smarter with money. Don't whine.*

"Luck is what I live on," Pierre said. "My good, other people's bad.

Like the guy said, never let a good crisis go to waste. Sometimes you can feel it in the air. Other times you don't know it was there until you see what you've taken. Know what my editor at Orbis said? 'Photographers have always had an almost superstitious confidence in the lucky accident.' I want that on my tombstone. Actually, I got a call from Denny just after I got yours. He's coming, too, in a few days. Wants to do another book."

"What sort of book?"

"Vanishing Shanghai, before it all gets concreted over and turned into condos. Which is happening faster than you'd ever think possible."

Daniel turned. "You mean old houses? Tenements? Because that ties in with *The Riding Instructor*. Which is why I came to Shanghai. To find a backer."

"How much?"

"Ten million. To begin with, anyway."

"And where do you plan to start looking?"

"Your address book."

Pierre raised an eyebrow. "*Pas de problème*. Everybody who's asked me what to do with a spare ten million is already underlined. For the clapped-out shooters retirement fund."

"This isn't charity. It's an investment. The chance to get in on the biggest change in movies since the introduction of sound. I know the Chinese want a way into the global entertainment business. And this is something about Shanghai. I'll show you." He reached for his computer bag, whose padded compartments held a laptop and an iPad. Then stopped. "That's the third time you've looked at your watch since I got here. Do you have an appointment? A shoot?"

Pierre moved over to the window and stared out over the park, rich with the gold of autumn. After a long moment he appeared to reach a decision. "Not a shoot. Something else." He turned. "Lucky you came. You can help."

"Help?"

"Sure. Mutual cooperation. One hand washes the other." He looked at his watch again and Daniel thought of a kid outside the dentist's, trying to stop time by sheer willpower. He'd sensed a tension in Pierre he hadn't felt before, and assumed it was because of Hong Kong. But apparently not. Another woman? He thought of Sophie in some up-market Kowloon condo, discarded clothes strewn across the floor. *Don't get involved in more of his philandering. This wasn't what you came for. Just find the money.*

"I don't think I'd be much use. Can't speak Chinese."

"Don't need to. Just have to be there. Two stand out less than one. Basic rule of composition."

"Where are you going, anyway?"

"Just to meet someone." He went to the door and stood waiting, eyebrow cocked.

One hand washes the other. Was this some sort of challenge? You help me, I help you. *Or maybe not.* A jolt of anxiety. Pierre really was the only hope. Couldn't risk alienating him. Especially not when he seemed so edgy. Better just go and get it over with--whatever it was. Then press him.

BEING IN SHANGHAI brought him closer to the world of Nikolai, the Riding Instructor. Nikolai, too, would have seen the October light at this angle, heard the hubbub of strident voices, sensed the Huangpu river coiling around the city like a snake. In the subway an ad heralded a new perfume named after the city: *"Shanghai--A heady blend of vanilla, balsam and ambergris, with undertones of bergamot."* The subway didn't smell like that. But neither did it have the roachy fetor of New York, or the half-digested miso soup of Tokyo, or the hundred and fifty years of bad air that gusted through the London tube. It smelled new. With heady overtones of money. Lots of it. He sniffed it like a dog.

They passed the football stadium and its loitering ticket scalpers and came to the entrance to a park, where a sign said, "Ethic and moral codes should be duly honored; visitors are expected not to urinate or shit."

"Good to see English flourishing as the language of international communication," Daniel said, and noticed the tautness of his friend's smile.

At a hut on the path to the lake Pierre laid a twenty-*yuan* note on the zinc counter and said something in Chinese. Before the ageing, gap-toothed attendant could respond an old-fashioned telephone jangled. The man picked it up, listened, looked at them without expression, and put it down again. He grunted and snapped nicotine-kippered fingers.

Pierre stiffened. "Wants some ID."

Daniel's passport was a year old. The photograph had been taken just after Sophie found a piece of software that showed how people would look with their heads shaved. "Beautiful shape," she'd said. "Man, those cheekbones. That jaw. Go on. Do it. I'll make it worth your while." So he did. And she had, knuckles white as she gripped the bed frame. But he missed the wind in his hair with the Saab's top down, and let it grow back. The attendant stared at the photo, at Daniel's curls, back at the picture. He grunted again.

"Hold the hair back from your face."

Daniel obliged. "I'll send him an autographed glossy if he wants."

The attendant squinted from the person in front of him to the picture and back, evidently reluctant to trust his eyes. After what seemed an age he put down Daniel's passport and picked up Pierre's. Once more he compared the face across the counter to the picture. The long nose and lank *café noir* hair were the same. But Pierre was also suspect. His passport was testimony to four years' perpetual motion as a photojournalist. No one who traveled that much could be trusted. The old man pored over it, muttering to himself as he flipped backward and forward through the entry and exit stamps. From time to time he would turn to the cover, keeping his place with a grimy thumb while he studied the great seal of the United States as if it held some hidden message.

At last he took Pierre's money and, after searching through a wooden box, unearthed a cracked plastic disk and tossed it on the counter. It was stamped with the number 37 in Roman numerals. With a dismissive gesture he resumed his perusal of *People's Daily*.

When they were out of sight he took a stub of pencil, licked it, and jotted something in a notebook.

A group of *tai chi* practitioners in training kit stretched and dipped with majestic poise. As Daniel and Pierre made their way to the lake they heard footsteps behind them. They glanced around--Pierre first--and stepped aside as three elderly women in shapeless brown pants suits overtook them. The women were all trotting backward. For the briefest of moments a pair of sloe-black eyes met Daniel's, veined and bloodshot and squinting from a web of wrinkles.

The boats were tied up at a jetty, plastic cockleshells of red and blue and green. They could carry two people, and of the seven craft on the water five had been taken by couples. Another contained a single man who was trailing a fishing line. This was in flagrant violation of a further moral code posted at the entrance: "Visitors are not supposed to tease, scare or capture bird, cricket, fish and shrimp." That left one. The occupant was a woman, face hidden in a muffler and dark glasses.

A boy with spiky orange hair and a nose stud took the token. Boat number 37 was in the middle of a tier of six. The boy hopped on and started to untie it. Again, Daniel sensed Pierre's unease. Why had the attendant had given them that particular number instead of the first that came to hand?

There was one boat moored by itself. Pierre barked something authoritative, then unhitched it and stepped aboard. He swung himself behind the wheel and floored the accelerator. Daniel, balance shaky after the thirteen-hour flight, half-fell into the seat beside him. The boat puttered away, barely making a bow wave. Behind them the boy froze in a crouch, mooring rope dangling from his hands.

They made their way toward the far side of the lake, about two hundred yards away. Beyond the park the football stadium loomed against the skyline like a stack of giant pancakes. The woman had disappeared. On a stone bench by the edge of the water two men were immersed in a game of chess, one lighting a cigarette while a third looked on with folded arms. Pierre stopped and raised his Nikon. Then they continued their unhurried exploration.

At the narrowest part of the lake was a bridge, a low arch that hid the water beyond. The woman waited in its shadow. When she saw Daniel he could feel her go tense. Pierre put a finger to his lips and reached over to pull the boats together. He leaned close and murmured, "I think they tried to give us a boat that was bugged."

She looked around. The fisherman shook something off his line. "We're alright here," she said. "If they have a shotgun mic the bridge will protect us. Can't hear through stone."

Even in English her voice had a musicality as if it was an instrument she had mastered. Was this the Suzhou accent he'd read about, a way of speaking prized almost as a national treasure?

"Did you hear about Shaowen Gen? They said he was a terrorist. So they killed him. That good, gentle man. He just wanted to stop people being bullied." She looked around again. The fisherman cast his line. She turned back, and Daniel knew that behind the dark glasses she was looking at him.

"Friend," Pierre said in a low voice. "Old friend."

She took a thumb-sized flash drive from her pocket. "This is video of the execution. Please send it to Ben Beidermeyer at the Lefkovitch Foundation."

Pierre slipped it into his leather jacket. "How did you get it?" he asked in a thick murmur. "Phone camera?"

"No. They killed him by lethal injection. In a van with a wireless link so the local officials could see. A woman in the city hall hacked into the link. Very brave."

She wasn't the only one, Daniel thought. Pierre was a journalist. It was his job to get information. All he risked was deportation. Chinese nationals courted death.

A boat came toward them, with two men. She pushed herself away. Pressing the accelerator, she swung out and was gone, hidden from view by the bridge. Pierre lifted his camera and took more shots of the skyline that gleamed beyond the trees. When Daniel glanced back he was sure the men were looking at them. Then the one in the Yankees baseball cap took a swig from a bottle of *baiju*, wiped his lips with the back of his hand, and passed it to his companion. Just a couple of drunks drifting through the last of the autumn afternoon in an alcoholic haze.

Pierre made another circuit of the shoreline. He stopped to photograph the ducks and the carp and the leaves that floated on the green water. Then they headed back toward the jetty.

FOUR

CORRUPTION ON STEROIDS

BACK AT THE APARTMENT Pierre connected his iPod to a couple of speakers and a subwoofer. They were facing away from the center of the room and Miles Davis's *Birth of the Cool* drifted out toward the park and the skyscrapers beyond, blanketing sound in sound.

"You really think someone's listening?" Daniel had never seen him like this. Nervous, yes, before he left for Afghanistan. Shaken when he got back by what he'd seen. But never paranoid. Maybe not the best time to ask for help finding a backer. Yet he had no choice.

"Windows, too, have ears." Pierre turned the volume up. "Know what the State Department said before the Beijing Olympics? There's no privacy anywhere. Not in hotels. Not in offices. Not even in private homes. And things have gotten tighter since then. First Egypt and the jasmine revolution. That really spooked the Chinese. Now with this big carbon reduction conference coming up in Shanghai they're freaking out. Terrified the rest of the world will see how much unrest there really is. They're watching activists and human rights lawyers like cats at a mousehole."

"That who she was? A lawyer?"

"No. She's an ethnomusicologist. Master's at Fudan university, then a doctorate at Chicago. Dr. Shuying Chen. Beidermeyer was her adviser. Two years' fieldwork in Tibet and now she's back at Fudan."

"So she's an activist."

"You could say that." Daniel sensed him weighing up how much to reveal. He'd never been this guarded before. Pierre went to his MacBook, which was open on the table, and moved it around so Daniel could see.

"Lots of dirty secrets in this city. You get that everywhere. Everybody has them."

Yes, and I know one of yours. Should he bring it up now, to clear the air? He hesitated. The moment passed.

"Shanghai's the same but more so. Corruption on steroids. Just because of the sheer scale of what's happening. And the speed." The screen displayed a slideshow, panoramas of the views from the tops of some of the world's tallest buildings. In all directions except the ocean towers of steel and glass stretched to the horizon. "Can you imagine how much money is being made out of all this? It's beyond belief. And you know what's driving it? A million squalid acts of brutality."

Pierre tapped the keys and a second slideshow began. The photos had been shot in rapid succession so they unfolded like a jerky movie. They had all been taken from the same place and Daniel sensed the photographer had been hiding. They showed a backstreet of low tenements, blackened with age and dwarfed by the highrises pressing in from behind. Three men with heavy chains slung over their shoulders came out of a door, dragging a hunched and bloodstained figure which they beat and kicked. They hit the victim with the chains. Then they got back in the van and left. The last image, a zoom shot, showed the license plate.

"Property developer's thugs," Pierre said. "Happens all the time. Drive out the residents, take over the property, knock it down and make a fortune. Welcome to Shanghai."

Daniel rubbed his eyes, which were dry and itchy from the flight. "Who took the pictures? I can see they're not yours." He'd always admired Pierre's ability to photograph a seemingly unexceptional scene and bring out something new in it. Although they never spoke of it, admiration of each other's gifts was the heart of their friendship.

"Somebody gave them to me. To send out of the country."

"Why didn't they go to the cops?" Dumb question. Must be jetlagged.

"Deng Xiaoping said to get rich is glorious. Don't expect the cops to miss out when they can make a little extra by looking the other way. Shaowen Gen had proof of that. Among other things." He plugged the flash drive into the computer. "I'll send this, then we'll go and eat and you can rifle my address book. Only fair to warn you, the video won't be pleasant. You don't have to watch."

Daniel had read about Chinese executions, how the victim was made to kneel and open his mouth so the bullet that entered the back of his head could be retrieved and sent to his family, with a bill. And shooting was quick compared to chemical choking.

"No. But I should see it. Isn't that what they want, people to see it? Shuying Chen and the woman in city hall?" He shrugged. "I have to watch. For them. They're the ones risking their lives."

Pierre looked at him. "Show me a romantic and I'll show you a train wreck waiting to happen."

"So what about you? Maybe you're the romantic. Remember what you told me once? About keeping everything on the other side of the viewfinder? Like a glass wall, you said. Because once you get involved with what you're shooting you really get screwed. Personally and professionally. People use you."

"I didn't shoot it. Somebody else did." He tapped the keys of the laptop.

Why he was reluctant to talk about what he was doing? It wasn't like Pierre. For someone whose work kept him quiet and unobtrusive so much of the time he was downright gabby, an urge to unburden himself that Daniel put down to his Catholic upbringing. He'd never shown any interest in social action. Was it something to do with Shuying Chen?

"Okay," Pierre said. "Showtime."

The video started with a tingling silence. Daniel felt he was eavesdropping on ghosts. The People's Armed Police officer looked over his shoulder, posing like a tourist. Then pressed the plunger.

Shaowen Gen stared up at the camera. When his muscles stopped working he went limp, no longer able to struggle against the straps that cut into his arms and legs. Nor could he breathe. Mucus bubbled from his nose as his lungs collapsed. His eyes, locked in panic and agony, showed nothing more of his drawn-out passage from life to death--until, at the very end, they widened, as if seeing something visible only at the moment of transition.

The police officer looked into the camera and smirked.

"Jesus." Something inside him shut down, numbing him to what he'd seen. It wasn't like watching a video on YouTube. It hadn't appeared out of nowhere and vanished again in the endless torrent of information. It had passed from hand to hand, secretly, and come from a real woman.

"Do a lot of them like that," Pierre said. "Seventeen hundred last year. At least. They think it's more modern."

He went into his bedroom and came back holding a satellite transmitter the size of a cereal packet. Beyond the park skyscrapers glittered like waterfalls of diamonds in the dusk and when he opened the French doors the roar of the city rushed in. A sheet hung on a line that stretched across the balcony and he set the transmitter behind it, tilted to face south. He went back to the laptop, selected the flash drive folder and dragged it onto the icon of a satellite on the desktop. The satellite spun around, then stopped. Seconds later, *Transmission sent* appeared on the screen.

"*Voilà!* Completely untraceable. No footprint. When it's gone, it's really gone. Like a blown-out photo. Irretrievable."

"Except from the computer."

"Right. Still have to get it off the drive. Not trash it. Overwrite it.

And get rid of this." He gripped the flash drive between fingers and thumbs and, with some effort because it was so short, snapped the plastic casing. He pried the circuit board off with the tip of a knife from the wooden block on the counter and took the pieces to the bathroom. Daniel heard the toilet flush.

"I made a piece of software for hiding messages," he said. "SkyeSlip. Hides them in photographs. But it's a bit limited. Both sides need a password."

"Not for this baby." Pierre cradled the transmitter in the crook of his arm. "Just a shot at the southern sky and an ip address. That's why the Chinese are so spooked. Goes right over the Great Firewall. Can't see it, can't stop it, can't control it. When they found a Reuters guy using one to send video about Falung Gong all they could do was foam at the mouth and accidentally stomp it into the ground."

THE APARTMENT WAS ON A LANE that led to Hengshan Road, an elegant avenue lined with maple trees. Most of the leaves had fallen and been swept away, but the night still smelled of autumn. Lamps on elaborate iron posts, each dangling five glass bowls like a bunch of cherries, cast pools of light on the brickwork of low buildings.

Crowds thronged the boulevard. Three giggling Australian flight attendants brushed past, frog-marching a man with improbably blond hair who was saying loudly, "So Mother said, if you put other men's penises in your mouth don't you ever *dare* complain about my cooking again."

Pierre looked around, as he did all the time. "Interesting. No day laborers."

"Should there be?"

"Most places we'd be falling over them. Literally. They're flooding into Shanghai. Pouring out of the station like a human tide. Sleep anywhere. In doorways, under bridges. Top choice is construction sites--that way they're front of the hiring line at daybreak. But with this big carbon conference coming up they're being hustled away from places with a lot of foreigners. Bad for the city's image."

Above a doorway flanked by terra cotta pots of ferns a sign said La Boheme in red neon letters. In front of a bamboo screen inside the door a bowl of irises stood on a black lacquer table. A waiter in a long green apron escorted them to a table in the corner, away from a gaggle of Credit-Suisse currency traders and their companions who had just ordered a third magnum of Dom Perignon.

Daniel studied the handwritten menu. "How's the *porc aux pruneaux*?"

"Not as good as my mother's. Though she'd only cook it for lunch. The French don't eat pork at night. Think it gives you bad dreams."

"I have enough of those already." Dreams of failure. Dreams of losing Sophie, which were increasingly close to reality. *How can I stay with someone I can't trust? Who won't take responsibility? Just think, Daniel.* He returned to the menu. "I'll stick with the *moules meuniere*. And beef and walnut salad." He handed the menu to the waiter.

"Salmon for me. And a good Vouvray." The waiter inclined his head and slipped away.

A pop and a gust of laughter signaled the arrival of the champagne. Daniel looked around, a moment after Pierre. An exquisite Chinese girl in a black dress with spaghetti straps raised the bottle to her lips, spluttered, and put a pale hand to her mouth. More laughter.

"Like Tokyo before the bubble burst," Daniel said. "The same smell of money. Intoxicating. Not that I got to smell much of it. I was just a kid."

"Born there, right?"

"Just outside. Urayama airbase. But we left when I was two. Always leaving somewhere. By the time I was fourteen I'd lived in five different countries. My father was very ambitious. Youngest two-star general in the air force. The flier's high flier, my mother called him. Then we went back to Urayama."

The second stay was four years, enough to make him think of Japan as home, or the nearest he'd ever had to one. Fascinated by Japanese cartoons, he set out to master the language. His mother, Elizabeth--Elizabeth Skye, author of *Moonshadow* and *Otherwhere* and *Grigorss the Woolgatherer*--would find him with eyes closed and lips moving silently as he traced *kanji* with a fingertip on the palm of his hand, or drew them in the air, as if conducting a phantom orchestra.

The *sommelier* sensed Pierre was the host and poured a little wine for him to taste. Pierre motioned for him to do the same for Daniel, who sniffed it, sipped judiciously, rolled it around in his mouth, then nodded his assent.

"*Moelleux*, they call it. That undertone of honey means it was grown on clay. If the soil was flinty it would have more lemon." He sniffed again. What would the creditors would do with his own case of Veuve Cliquot, bought in happier times?

"*Salud*. To paternity." Pierre raised his glass. "You'll make a great father. Think Orson Welles with a diaper bag."

"Thanks. Sophie's idea of a surprise birthday present. She was right about the surprise."

Yet he knew he should have seen it coming. One sultry June day, just before she graduated from Bauxite High School--her seventh in four years--her mother had come back from work, smelling of setting lotion and in a state of high excitement over a story she'd seen in the *Jonesboro Sun*. It was about a scout from an agency in Japan, coming to Little Rock to look for models. "Soph, the Lord has sent you a ticket out of here," she said. "Always said your face would be your fortune. Spitting image of that actress in *Bonnie and Clyde*. Faye whatshername."

She was right. But after ten years Sophie had had enough. "Perfect place to have kids, this house," she'd said as she gazed at the waves breaking on the shore. "We can play on the beach every day." Daniel, in the first throes of obsession--*item 97: check White Russian involvement in the opium trade*--agreed without thinking.

Over the last few days, as the news sank in, it had begun to fill him with a secret delight. That a new life should be starting amid the wreckage of the old helped keep him from despair.

"Where is she?"

Is he studying the wine label so intently to avoid eye contact? Say it. Say you know what happened in Hong Kong. And then? How would he react? Embarrassed? No, not the great gonzo photographer. Never apologize, never explain. Sorry, maybe. But not deeply sorry. Because it just wouldn't be that big a deal for him.

"Florida. She said she couldn't stay in the house knowing we were going to lose it. Too painful. She bought her parents a condo in Boca Raton, near the ocean. I don't know how long she'll stay. Her dad was in Vietnam. He's pretty screwed up." Each time they visited, Wayne sat wordless in a corner. Whenever a car stopped or somebody shouted in the street his eyes darted to the door and his fingers curled around the arms of the chair.

Typical of Sophie to be so generous. For a decade she'd lived in agency-rented apartments in Tokyo or Paris or London or Milan. Home meant some other transient's eyeshadow in the bathroom cabinet, forgotten vodka in the freezer, dog-eared copy of Linda Goodman's *Sun Signs* beside the bed. If designers gave her clothes she'd wear them until she left town, then pass them on or simply leave them behind. Once, in the grime of west London, he saw her startle a bewhiskered old lady in a Salvation Army bonnet by pulling up in a cab and handing her a pair of lacy black culottes and matching top by Patrick Chow. "Won't keep anybody warm, but you can always sell them," she said, and sped away toward Heathrow.

Sophie, too, was one of his creditors. He'd been forced to ask her for a thousand dollars to get to Shanghai. Of all his debts, that was the one that made him burn with shame.

The mussels arrived, black and steaming in their golden pools. He broke off a piece of sourdough roll and dipped it in the melted butter. He took a small bite, and chewed. Pierre watched.

"Eating slowly's a good habit." Daniel dabbed his lips with a damask napkin. "Didn't I tell you that the first time we met? "

"I remember you said you were going to be successful. And thinking you were probably right. Shooters have a nose for success."

"Yes. I always knew that. I just never thought I'd lose it all."

The currency traders called for their bill. "Last one to the Silk Cat's a wanker!" bellowed a burly Englishman, the Windsor knot of his tie loosened beneath his chins. Girls squealed, and there was a rush for the door. The restaurant grew quieter.

Pierre refilled Daniel's glass. "I've seen people go through mountains of cash. Hoovered it up their noses, mostly. But you didn't do that."

Daniel was silent for a moment.

"It all went into *The Riding Instructor*. Took me over. Completely. Like some mythical monster. It just kept growing. Sophie thinks I'm mad."

"What do you think?"

"On bad days it feels like it."

"What about good days?"

"Good days I feel like a god." He sipped the Vouvray.

"Cool title. I did a shoot of that guy who got the Pulitzer for *Hungry Ghost*. He said the title came first. Like something sticking out of the ground. Just had to uncover the rest."

Daniel's eyes gleamed. "Exactly. And you know what? The more I uncovered, the more I realized I could do something amazing with it. Something really amazing. I could invent a new medium. I could set off the biggest change in entertainment since the talkies."

"Pretty ambitious for a mere ten million. Hollywood talks millions in the hundreds these days."

"That's what I need for a proof of concept. I was promised it. And before the credit crunch I thought I'd got it. But when money got tight nobody wanted to take a chance. Not with something so new. But that's so short-sighted. Advertisers are desperate now the TV audience has imploded. *The Riding Instructor* would sweep the world if it was marketed right. I know it. That's why I tried to fund it myself."

"So what is it, exactly?"

Daniel put his iPad on the table and opened a file. "It starts with a map. A ghost map, with all the detail faded out. See what you make of it."

From upper right to close to the bottom left a much-deformed letter *S* filled the screen. Pierre frowned. "The Huangpu?"

"Right. Hear anything?"

Pierre turned up the volume. The sound was indistinct, woven from a number of strands. "Some kind of audio collage. Ship's sirens. The customs house clock striking. Chinese voices. People speaking English. Can't hear clearly. Like it's all happening in the next room."

Daniel said nothing, just watched.

Pierre trailed a finger across the screen. A magnifying glass in the top corner of the screen pulsated. He tapped it. The map appeared in more detail, with a sprawl of streets and their names printed in a neat hand, Nanking Road, Moulmein Road, Avenue Joffre, Route des Soeurs. He tapped again. This time the map changed completely. From a hand-drawn diagram it turned into a full-color representation, a view of the old racecourse with all the detail of a photograph. He trailed his finger across it and saw the stables, the paddock, the clubhouse. Only it wasn't a photo; it was a three-dimensional model.

"Jerry Hsieh made that in SketchUp. He put old photos through a PhotoShop filter so they looked like drawings. Then put the models into Google Earth."

Pierre followed the sound of hoofbeats and came to an animation of a man and a woman on horseback. The magnifying glass pulsated. And when he tapped it the animation blossomed into video footage of the couple.

"*Bones.*"

"*I'm sorry?*"

"*The racecourse used to be a graveyard. We are riding on the bones of the dead.*"

"*Oh. I didn't know that. Who is buried here?*"

"*The poor. The rich would never tolerate foreign devils galloping over their ancestors. The poor had no choice.*"

Daniel took another sip of Vouvrary. "Try the Cutting Room."

An icon of a pair of scissors opened a new screen. In a panel on the right were all the takes for the scene. Pierre tapped on the clip that showed the close-up of the man's face. It started to play in a second panel at the bottom.

"When the woman says, 'I'm sorry?' tap on the close-up of her face."

That clip also appeared in the bottom panel.

"If this was the end of the scene you could fade out or dissolve. But what you need here is a jump cut. Just touch the icon of the razor blade."

After a moment the footage played with the edit in place. Pierre grinned and shook his head in admiration.

"Amazing. Never seen anything like it."

"It's revolutionary. I knew that right away. It's such a rich experience. The user doesn't just go along with Nikolai as he looks for his brother. He makes choices about which clues to follow. He collects video clips. Then he puts them together with the editing software." Daniel chopped the air into blocks. "He doesn't just become involved with the story. He makes a movie out of it. His own movie. Which is unique."

"So what went wrong?" Pierre dipped a spoon into his pot of *creme brulée*, breaking the skin of caramelized sugar.

"Bad timing. And I just kept getting more ambitious. First I spent a bundle on the rights to archival photographs. The Franco-Chinese Institute has thousands of them. Tough businessmen, the French."

"Like my grandfather. Made piano cases in a little town in Massachusetts. When he died we found eighty grand under the mattress. In fives and tens."

Daniel's own dessert was untouched. "When I decided to use video I realized I needed really good actors. People who can play the same character in different ways. With Hollywood names. For the marquee value. That couple you just saw were stand-ins from the local drama school."

"Anyone interested?

"I haven't got that far yet. Can't do anything without money. Which is why I came. I know you know people."

The bottle was empty. When the *sommelier* approached Pierre raised an eyebrow at Daniel, who shook his head.

"One name comes to mind. Renwen Zhou. A turtle."

"I'd rather have a human being."

"Turtles are returnees." Pierre scrolled through the names on his phone, stopped, touched the screen to dial. "Overseas-educated Chinese. Flocking back in droves. Vultures with MBAs." He turned his attention to the phone.

"Renwen, hi, Pierre. Listen, an old friend's turned up. I think you should meet him ... No, software. Smart guy. Doing a very interesting project about White Russians in Shanghai."

The waiter set down two cups of *espresso con panna*.

"End of next week? Okay ... just a minute." Daniel was shaking his head. He mouthed the word "tomorrow."

"Thing is, he's only here for a few days ... yes, I know ... right ..." Daniel motioned to take the phone. "He's here now, why don't you ... Okay ... Okay. Friday night at the 21. See you there."

He took the phone from his ear. "Mr Quickly. The original one-minute man."

"What does he do?"

"Makes money. As much as possible. Went to grad school at UCLA, started helping American companies set up in China. Then he realized he was on the wrong side of the Pacific. Got U.S. citizenship to cover his ass if things turned bad and caught the next plane back."

"Anybody else?"

"Fiona Schulman's a movie producer. Been here for years." Again he raised the phone, listened, then lowered it. "Berlin film festival, back in a couple of days."

He scrolled through the list again. Daniel sipped his espresso. Caffeine never kept him awake. "Here's someone. Alex Orlovski. Grew up in Shanghai, got out just ahead of the Red Army. He's come back to visit. After sixty years. Made a fortune importing fur coats. How about a Russian backer?"

"Sure. I pitched a couple in Palm Springs. They were in their eighties. Couldn't understand the technology. But if Orlovski's digging up old memories he might be into it."

"Phone's off." Pierre peered at the screen. "Don't see anybody else. But those three are good for starters. Zhou especially. Very well connected."

"No venture capitalists in there? Money people?"

"Only my accountant."

"There's another thing I need to do. Video the old Russian quarter. Second unit stuff to give a feel of the place for the proof of concept." He'd thought he had that covered. But the videographer had got wind of his financial situation and her initial enthusiasm had vanished like morning mist when he was unable to pay an advance.

"Bit late for that. It's all concrete and glass and Starbucks now."

It was like a punch in the stomach. All the strain of the past few days came back, made worse by the horror of the execution video. On his last visit Shanghai had looked like a vast movie studio where a sci-fi blockbuster was going into production while the set for *Les Misérables* was still being torn down. Another stupid mistake. How could he not have realized how fast everything would be washed away?

"But surely there's something left? A few of the kind of old houses Russians would have lived in? Enough for some exteriors?"

"Might still find somewhere in Hongkou. North of Suzhou Creek. Has the same Warsaw ghetto-style tenements. Or used to." Pierre's expression brightened. "Hey, I know someone there you should talk to anyway. Another possible Russian backer. I know she's crazy about the place. And her last husband had a Coke-bottling franchise." He found the number and touched it.

Daniel glanced around the restaurant. It felt more like Paris than China. At the next table an olive-complexioned Westerner in a black sweater reached across the snowy table linen to take the hand of his Chinese companion, who eyed him coquettishly over the top of her champagne flute. What was Sophie doing?

"Tomorrow morning." Pierre lowered the phone. "Olga Derieva. Should have thought of her right away. Another White Russian."

"Been here all the time?"

"No. Another turtle. White turtle. Born here, got out in '49, came back a few months ago."

"How did you meet her?"

Pierre grinned. "A pickup on the Bund. I'd been shooting one of the old art deco buildings. Mahogany panels, stained glass windows throwing colored shadows on the floor. Perfect for a wide angle. The respectable face of the opium business. Up for lease again, at twice what you'd pay in Manhattan. Outside the old Customs House I saw her coming toward me. Bitterly cold day. She was wearing an enormous fur hat, this old Western lady, and walking with a cane. Walking slowly. But haughty. So haughty even the Shanghainese stepped aside for her."

That figured. He'd read about White Russian women and their ways: imperious, desperate, fonder of scent than soap. *You vill buy me please vun glass of vhite vine.*

"I raised the camera. I saw her eyes looking into mine. Violet eyes. Then something weird happened. Instead of pressing the button I paused. And once I'd paused I couldn't go on. I could feel those eyes boring into me. I froze. Just couldn't take the picture. Like she had some kind of psychic judo hold on me. Then all of a sudden she burst out laughing. As if she'd flipped a switch."

"Russian women had a reputation for craziness," Daniel said. "One of them walked into the police barracks, sat on the bed of the guy who'd dumped her and drank a bottle of metal polish. Took two days to die. She wanted him to hear her scream."

The waiter brought the bill in a black leather cover and Pierre reached for his wallet. Daniel's thirty-six hour day was catching up with him. His eyes itched. Sleep waited close at hand, if sleep was the right word for the tormented semi-consciousness which plagued him each night. But the passion that drove him quickened. He was getting closer.

FIVE

PAPER'S MORE REAL

AS A WAY TO INTRODUCE *The Riding Instructor* he showed Olga the map on his iPad. "I'm making a kind of movie you can see on a computer like this." He scrolled across the city and zoomed in and out with a pinch of the fingers, making the Cathay hotel appear and blossom from a drawing to a photograph. "It's set in 1923, in the White Russian community."

"You from Hollywood?" She fingered an amethyst pendant that dangled from a heavy gilded chain.

"Not exactly." He smiled.

"People from Hollywood used Eva Popov's place for a movie. Paid ten grand a day."

"I'm not from Hollywood. It's an independent production. And it so happens there are still opportunities to invest. When Pierre said how interested you were in that world I thought immediately I should give you the chance to get involved."

"Invest?" The violet eyes held his.

"It's a unique opportunity. A chance to be in on something which will revolutionize the world of entertainment. Completely."

"Mister, you're barking up the wrong tree. I've had enough revolution for this lifetime. More than enough." Her lip curled. "Put that goddamn thing away. Paper's more real." She turned back to the original, which was spread out on the table, and peered at it with narrowed eyes. "Avenue Foch. That's where Gergiev's place was. On the north side. Every Friday Papa gave mother money and she'd take us to Gergiev's. Best borscht in Shanghai. Two kinds, hot borscht and cold borscht."

Fyodor Constantin Gergiev had two bullet holes in his head, one going in, one coming out. He'd been put in front of a Bolshevik firing squad in 1919 and by some miracle he survived. Not just being shot, but the night in an open grave, the journey to the Pacific and the siege of Vladivostok, and the headlong flight to Harbin and then south to Shanghai. Unable to speak, he'd opened a borscht restaurant in the heart of Little Moscow. Daniel had read all this. Now, the day after his arrival in Shanghai, here was somebody who had actually met Gergiev and seen his dumbshow and eaten his borscht, hot and cold. Even if she wasn't interested in putting up any money it was a heady omen. He would use the restaurant as one of the locations for *The Riding Instructor*, a shadow on the ghost map that became real when the user followed a clue.

"What happened to him?"

"Red Army." She narrowed her eyes and raised a fist and tilted her head to one side. A hanged man.

On a long-ago afternoon she had visited a Jewish friend of her mother's, bicycling over the Garden bridge and following Suzhou Creek past the Persian silk shops on Broadway until they turned into a maze of alleys. Her mother said Hongkou meant "mouth of the rainbow." Olga repeated the name and said one day she would live there. Now she did, on a lane with purple wisteria hanging from poles. Bicycles rusted against the walls, next to a lilac-colored scooter with a yellow smiley-face on the mudguard. Inside the iron-framed door a short tiled passage led to the living room. If her childhood had been marked by privation she'd made up for it since. The room was crammed with heavy black furniture and every surface covered by a magpie collection of treasures: gilded vases, chunks of crystal, dolls, bowls, jars, an old radio, an ornate brass birdcage.

Daniel's map, too, was a relic from a world that would soon disappear from memory. He'd found it in a used bookstore on the edge of Seattle's University District, just as the project was starting to form in his mind. This, too, he took as an omen. The map became the key to the navigational structure. Produced in 1921 by the Oriental Publishing House of Shanghai, it used the old street names, which were written in a very small, careful script.

Olga scrutinized it and saw the shape of her childhood. She ran her finger along Avenue Joffre and tapped with the bejeweled talon of her forefinger. "Rue Marcel Tillot. Mama's shop was here. Hat shop. Made hats out of felt, cotton, feathers, furs. Somebody brought her a tiger skin once and she made hats out of that. Strung the teeth on silk thread and used them as decoration. Very imaginative. Said it was the gypsy blood in her. Never made much money, though."

"But you survived."

"Yeah, we survived. Mama said it was because of this." She went over to one of the cartons and took out a large envelope. Inside, folded in tissue paper, was a delicate lace collar, yellowed with age. "My grandmother's jabot. The only thing Mama managed to bring from the old house. All the way across Lake Baikal on a sled. That and six gold roubles sewn in her underwear." She laid the jabot on the table and smoothed it out. "I guess it worked. By the time I was born things weren't too bad. Not as bad as they had been, anyway. At least we had a house."

"That's what I'm looking for," Daniel said. "Old houses. Tenements. The kind of places Russians lived in. I need to get video of them. Are there any left?"

"You mean the really crummy places." She fingered the amethyst again. "Might still find a few over by the old railway station. But you gotta be real quick. Probably knocking them down right now. If they haven't already."

She picked up the map and squinted at the minuscule script. The talon tapped Rue Wagner. "Here. This is where we lived. Tiny little house. Papa let out the attic to a bunch of girls from the French Club. Five of them. And a kid."

Daniel peered over her shoulder and recognized the area. "Near the racecourse. Ever go there?"

"Sure did. Every autumn. All Shanghai went to the races in autumn. Offices closed for a three-day break." She fell silent. Daniel, too, could almost hear ghostly hoofbeats.

"Foreign businessmen collected horses. Lots of horses. One of the Jews had a thousand. Very wealthy. From Baghdad. Came on a camel, left in a Rolls Royce. He liked Mongolian ponies. Paid Russians to race them. Papa said the only thing Russians were good at was riding. A Russian rode all the way from Shanghai to Nanking and back in sixteen days. On the same pony. Seven hundred miles."

"Subarov." He'd read the story on a microfiche of the *North China Daily News.*

She glared at him with narrowed eyes. "Yeah. Subarov. For a bet. He won a thousand dollars and went to the Great World to play *fan-tan. Fan-tan* pays four times the stake if you win. At first he was lucky. Four thousand dollars. He'd told his mistress if he had four thousand dollars he'd get them passports. He'd take her to Paris. But he couldn't stop. No Russian walks away from a winning streak. In *fan-tan* you put your stake on a slip of red paper. The Chinese call it the dog's tongue. Subarov put four thousand dollars on the dog's tongue. When he lost he asked one of the guards for his gun. Then he went up to the top of the building and stood by the railing." Olga raised two fingers to her temple. "Goodbye, Subarov."

The dog's tongue. There must be a way to work that in. Maybe as a clue to Petya's disappearance. *Don't get distracted. Don't come up with more smartass ideas. Just get the money. Okay?*

"The Great World's still there. Looks like a tall, skinny wedding

41

cake." Pierre took another shot of the room through the bars of the birdcage and joined them at the map. But Olga beat him to it.

"Here." She pointed. "Between Avenue Edouard VII and Tibet Road."

"Anything left of the inside?" The Great World, too, was a hot spot, a place to find clues.

"Probably not. Heard they'd turned it into a playground." She was still transfixed. "Rue Kraetzer. That's where Papa's office was."

"What did he do?"

She pointed to the wall behind him. He turned, and saw three framed pictures. "In St Petersburg he was an art student. I don't know what he did when he arrived in Shanghai. He never talked about that. First thing I remember he was an illustrator for a magazine."

The images were woodblock prints. One, in blue and orange, showed a man with his chin in one hand and fountain pen in the other and three smiling women behind him: a writer and his muses. Another was of a woman sprawled *en deshabille* in an art nouveau armchair, slip hiked up to mid-thigh to show a gartered stocking-top, a discarded polka-dot blouse, one shoe and an open powder compact on the floor. The third picture showed a yellow-haired Westerner in baggy blue pajamas slumped against the wall of an alley. His head was bandaged and blood dripped from his ashen face. Another Westerner, a fat man in black uniform and a black cap, stood over him and pointed a warning finger.

"You could kick a Russian until you were blue in the face." Olga scowled. "No passports, no country, no status. Nobody gave a damn."

Daniel gazed at the pictures with fascination. "I can use these in *The Riding Instructor.*"

Olga stiffened. "How much you gonna pay?" She fixed him with a violet stare.

"We're still working on the budget. I can't name a figure. But I am interested. Your father was a talented man."

"He sure was. And talent comes at a price, right? You wanna play you gotta pay." She turned to the map again. "Moulmein Road. That's where the Casanova cabaret was. Had a negro pianist at the Casanova. Wore spats."

Half an hour later, having turned down repeated invitations to have a drink, they made their way back down the lane toward Suzhou Creek.

"Too bad she wasn't interested," Daniel said. "But those prints are perfect for *The Riding Instructor*. That Russian bleeding in the alley. One of the people Nikolai talks to is a broken-down opium addict. That guy has exactly the right look. Must have carved a different block for each color, like the Japanese. An artist called Bilibin did that. He came from Petersburg. Maybe they knew each other."

But Pierre wasn't listening, at least not to Daniel. He had his phone to one ear. And when he said, *"Da cuo le,"* and put it back in his pocket his face was as pale as the Russian's in the picture.

"SHUYING CHEN AGAIN?" Daniel couldn't forget that musical voice. Maybe she'd do some narrations for *The Riding Instructor*. Tell a story. Play a singsong girl.

"Won't know until I get there. Art gallery on Moganshan Road."

"So you won't need me as cover."

Pierre shot him a glance. "I guess not."

They turned toward the station. "With so many people having camera phones they must be producing all kinds of stuff," Daniel said.

"Right. Dispossessed tenants. Civil rights people. Officials pissed off at not getting their share of graft. And one day it's going to reach critical mass. The government will have to open up. Or be swept away. But that's still in the future."

"Sounds like you'll be pretty busy."

"Jesus, I hope not. Scares the shit out of me." Pierre's face was drawn, brow creased with tension.

"But you're a journalist collecting information. The authorities can't touch you."

"It's not the authorities that worry me." They reached the subway station. "Please God this is just a flurry before the conference. Getting stuff to foreign reporters in the hope they'll be interested. Which they might, since it's a ready-made story."

"You could always say no."

"Can't do that."

"Why not? It's not your problem."

"Just can't."

Shuying Chen. Must be. Was she married, too? Daniel pushed the thought aside. Back at the apartment he googled Fiona Schulman's website. Vibrant in black and Chinese red, it held a long list of titles launched and prizes won. He looked her up in the *Hollywood Reporter* and found her described as "one of the ballsiest of the ballsy" by a Danish director he'd never heard of. Then he turned to the business section. He was still poring over the latest deals in search of a possible source of funding when Pierre came back two hours later and flung himself on the couch.

"Fuck. Now they want me to go to Xian."

"Xian? That's halfway to Mongolia."

"Going in that direction. Two-and-a-half-hour flight."

"What for?"

Pierre reached for the whiskey. He proffered it to Daniel, who shook his head.

"Moganshan Road's like SoHo in the old days. I went to a gallery called the Bau Xi. The show looked like a ripoff of Georgia O'Keeffe, all petals and pistils and engorged stamens. And big. Hardly anybody there. Then this kid came in. Looked like a student, hooked nose, thin speckle of stubble on his chin. I was looking at a picture of an opium poppy and he came up and stood behind me. Close. I glanced round. He didn't meet my eye. Just tapped his lips with a rolled-up brochure.

After he'd gone round the pictures he sat down for a couple of minutes. Then he got up and walked out. Leaving this."

He tossed a National Tourist Office pamphlet on the low table. It was in English and Japanese as well as Chinese and extolled the attractions of the ancient city of Xian. There were pictures of the terra cotta warriors entombed nearby, and of the city's massive walls, and of the present-day populace going about its business. In the bulleted text that pointed out things not to be missed was a note about the Music of the Silk Road festival. It said, "Come celebrate us musical intertwinings of the millennia."

The entry had been underlined, and at the side, in careful, elegant handwriting he knew immediately to be Shuying Chen's, were penciled the words *bring the instrument.*

"AREN'T I THE POPULAR ONE," Olga said that evening. "More visitors than Rikers Island."

A small, frail-looking man with thinning hair and caramel-colored skin laughed uneasily. "I just wanted to see if you were alright," he said in Russian, and glanced around the cluttered room. His eyes were hazel beneath Asian double lids. "Finding everything you need. Not lonely."

"That's good of you, Dimitri. Didn't expect to see you again so soon. Very ..." She tried to remember the word, and couldn't. Like Dimitri, she spoke hesitantly. They both picked their way through the half-forgotten language as if it was a fog, hiding chasms. "You're the third person I've seen today. Two guys already stopped by for a chat. *Dvah.*" She held up two fingers in a V.

"Americans." A statement, not a question. She fixed him with her violet stare. Of course he knew. He was Chinese now. They used to call it the bamboo telegraph. He looked away.

"Yeah. Wanted to know about the old days. The tenements." She slipped back into English. "Remember our house, Dimi? On Rue Wagner? Remember how there was something wrong with the chimney and the goddamn place filled with smoke every time we lit a fire? If the girls were at work papa would make me bring you downstairs. Can't let the little chap get smoked in his crib like a mackerel, he'd say. Except you didn't have a crib. Just a busted-up tea chest."

"Why they want to know about tenements?"

She shrugged. "To make video of them. Something to do with a computer. Putting different things on a computer. Lots of things. Very small computer, size of a book. Had a map thing on it. Some damnfool way of making things appear and disappear. Wanted me to let them have some of papa's pictures."

"Did you?"

"Me? Hell, no. I never give nobody nothing."

"What else they want?"

"To know where they could find some of the old places before they get knocked down. Dimi, you leaving so soon? Stay a bit longer. Have another drink. Never known a Russian say no to a drink." She gestured at the Stolichnaya on the sideboard. But he was already at the door.

Near the end of the lane two men were sharing a bottle of *baiju*. Dimi approached them with reluctance. One downed a last swig and pocketed the bottle. "Hurry up, Liu Pinyi," he said. "They're waiting." They escorted him around the corner to the road and a black-windowed SUV. Not quite like guards. But even less like friends.

SIX

GIRL ON A ROLLERSKATE

HIS SEARCH FOR OLD TENEMENTS to video took him along the route Olga had taken with her mother, across the Garden bridge. This spanned Suzhou Creek as it joined the Huangpu river. To his right the Russian consulate still stood beside the river. How would they have felt when they saw the hammer and sickle flutter in the Huangpu breeze? To the Riding Instructor it was a place of loathing, headquarters of the Comintern and the forces that had destroyed his life.

Nikolai and Petya are sitting under a bridge with half a dozen other White Russians, huddled around a fire. They are joined by an old man who is trying to wrap himself more tightly in a soldier's tattered greatcoat.

"You're from Feliksovo?" the old man says. "It was bad there. The Reds machine-gunned everybody they found. One family got away, a father and mother and a girl."

Petya whispers, "Katya." He grips Nikolai's arm.

"They hid in a house by the river. But somebody gave them away. Or sold them. The Bolsheviks put them on a raft and towed it out to midstream. With a keg of gunpowder."

The consulate was not an intimidating structure. A low, white building, its red roof and chimneys and curved balconies made it seem almost homely, especially now it was dwarfed by forty, fifty, sixty-story behemoths on all sides. The silk shops had gone long ago. He turned and followed the creek westward, his back to the Oriental Pearl TV tower, which pierced the overcast sky like a syringe.

Making his way inland, he overtook a line of barges, loaded with sand and low in the water, making their way upstream so slowly they hardly seemed to move. A hundred years ago opium was unloaded here. Foreigners brought it from their colonies and supplied the gangsters who distributed it. Working through his to-do list, he'd tracked down a sepia image of a warehouse, a barn-like structure stacked with chests of raw opium pressed into balls. Jerry Hsieh had turned the photo into one of the hot spots hidden on the ghost map. If the warehouse was still there he could shoot video of the exterior and combine it with the scene in which Nikolai finds Chatwin's men taking delivery of a shipment.

A note on the back said it stood on the north bank of the creek, near where it fed into the river. But there was no sign of it. The creek had been redeveloped. Footpaths along the banks had been planted with trees, and behind them new office buildings gleamed dully like brushed steel. At intervals tubs of roses sweetened the air, splashes of red against the turbid brown water.

When he followed a street inland he saw that Shanghai was not one world but two. The glass towers were all straight lines and right-angles and flat planes. But the tenements in the lanes had grown organically, mended, modified, extended and adapted to meet the needs of the occupants. Rooflines sprouted shacks. Chimneys had been haphazardly patched with concrete. Tiles had been replaced with others of a different color.

The character of the place was still evident: dirty, crowded, uncomfortable. The Russians must have despaired at finding themselves here, trapped in numbing cold or sweltering heat, water limited to a single stand pipe. Olga's father rented out the attic to dancing girls. What would it have been like to live in one of these tiny, malodorous houses? With a dozen other people? People who had lost everything, literally, and were hanging onto life by their fingernails?

He couldn't shoot as much video as he wanted. Everywhere he looked he saw air conditioners, fixed to walls or hung below window frames or resting on a shelf laid across the rusty iron railings of a balcony. Every doorway seemed to house a drinks cooler, every few feet an advertising sign hung from the eaves or a motor scooter rested against the wall. He would have to look further.

A THIN DRIZZLE began. He passed a crumbling brick arch and found himself in a lane of a dozen houses, all blackened masonry and flaking maroon paintwork. Bicycles rusted and a broad-faced ginger cat eyed him from a rotting couch whose stuffing spilled from splits in the chintz cover. Even by the standards of the lanes the houses were in bad shape. One of the doors had been kicked in and it sagged on its hinges, which were coming away from the frame. Windows had been smashed, and broken glass glittered on the ground. It wasn't just the structural damage that made him assume the place had been abandoned. It was the smell. The stench of sewage hung over it like a noxious cloud. Nobody could live with that.

A rat appeared, sniffed, then scurried the length of the wall and vanished around the corner. The Russians ate rats. They roasted them over smoky coal fires and made the skins into pocketbooks. Daniel half-expected to see an unkempt figure with a Nagant in his belt as a bodyguard came looking for his next meal.

Instead, he saw a girl, skating toward him through the rain. She only had one skate: several sizes too big, it had a wheel at each corner and was laced with twine. The girl was about sixteen years old and bespectacled, with a grubby white dress like a wedding dress and a plastic flower in her hair. She jolted over the cobbles and juddered to a halt a few feet away, eyes fixed on the camcorder half-hidden under his jacket. She pushed open the door of one of the houses and called to someone inside. A crop-headed old man in an undershirt peered out. He, too, stared at the camera. Then he opened the door wider and motioned Daniel to come in.

Go in? There? The stink of shit was overpowering and rolled past in billows. The man seemed to be explaining something.

"Please enter." The formality of the girl's English startled him. One of the lenses of her spectacles was cracked.

"Well ... thank you."

The room was low and dark. A mildewed calendar nailed to the wall showed a boy and a pig-tailed girl skipping while their smiling mother held up a packet of baby formula. The calendar was five years old. The man gestured toward the back of the house. A crude dam, little more than ankle height, blocked a narrow passage. It was made of stones and bits of broken brick and was not quite holding back what lay on the other side: a pool of raw sewage, glinting darkly in the light from a filth-encrusted window.

The man pointed to the camera.

"Please take video," the girl said.

Daniel took video. Too dark to be useable. But who'd want to watch it anyway?

As if at some signal, the room began to fill with people, six, eight, a dozen of them, jostling and pushing their way in. They were shouting and sobbing and thrusting pieces of paper at Daniel. A bald-headed man in a shirt that might once have been white dropped to his knees and held out two creased photographs. One showed a digger demolishing a house, the other a bloodstained figure sprawled in the lane, skull smashed like an eggshell.

The man kept repeating the same word.

"His son," the girl said.

A woman with spectacles that hung round her neck on a gilt chain mended with fuse wire snatched back the piece of paper she'd just shoved into Daniel's hand. Face screwed up in concentration, she took a stub of pencil no longer than the joint of her finger and scrawled the word JUSTICE in jerky, impassioned upper-case.

"Who are these people?" He had to shout to make himself heard above the hubbub.

"Neighbors," the girl said. "The developer wants to drive them away. So he can knock down the houses and take the land." She gestured toward the back of the house. "Put concrete in the sewer."

"But what's that got to do with me?"

A dumpy woman in a nylon jacket was yelling in his face and brandishing a letter he thought was in red ink. The woman held up her thumb. It was bound with a dirty bandage. She'd written in her own blood.

The man who'd invited him into the house pointed at the camcorder again and began his own impassioned plea.

"You are journalist," the girl said. "Tell people."

Before Daniel could reply a new element entered the hubbub, the clatter of running footsteps. Four men appeared at the door. Pushing into the already packed room, they kicked and punched indiscriminately and started dragging people out. The man who had lost his son was still on his knees. Daniel saw him cover his head with his hands while two men with baseball bats, unable to swing downward because of the low ceiling, took turns hitting him with vicious sideways swipes, as if beating a carpet.

The dumpy woman pointed to a man in a polo shirt and Raybans and started screaming at Daniel. She was pulled outside, where her screams turned to strangled gasps.

He stuffed the papers in his bag and raised the camera. One of the thugs dragged a sobbing woman across the floor, a fist in her thinning grey hair. Daniel panned across the room, shooting a jerky sequence of fists and elbows and faces contorted in fury, convulsed in anguish. The men hacked their way through the crowd as if chopping down weeds. Making for Daniel.

The man in the polo shirt sprang forward and knocked the camera from his grasp. It hit the stone floor with a tinkle of glass as the lens shattered. He pushed the Raybans up and stared hard at Daniel. Then he kicked the camera toward the back of the room, where it gouged a scar in the rotten plaster and splashed into the sewage. At the same time one of the others snatched Daniel's camera bag and pulled out the papers. He ripped open the side pocked and rummaged, then turned it upside down and shook it. The papers fluttered to the floor, following the battery charger and its cable. He ran his hands over the bag and twisted it. When he was sure it was empty he grunted something at Raybans and shook his head.

The room emptied as quickly as it had filled. The shouting died away and a wave of fury rushed through Daniel as the adrenaline kicked in with its lust for violence. His fists clenched. He wanted to lash out, to smash the face of the man in Raybans with a bottle, a bat, anything, to feel the crunch of breaking bone, to smell blood.

As his breath slowed he became aware that the stink was making him nauseated. He had to get out, to gulp clean air. The camera would never work again. But the card held his footage of the lanes. He looked for something to fish it out with, a broom or a pole or a coat hanger, and realized how bare the room was.

The girl slipped off her roller skate and removed a purple sock. Then she hoisted the wedding dress and stepped over the dam. She bent and picked up the shit-smeared camera, which she held out to Daniel.

"Thank you," he said. "Thank you. Not many people would do that. What's your name?"

"Lilly." She eyed him soberly. A pretty name for a not-so-pretty girl. The man began to speak again. His lips puckered as if he'd been sucking a lemon.

"My grandfather says please show the video in your country. His name is Jin Fengqui."

A small plastic flap hung open at the side of the camera. The card had gone.

"Jesus."

The adrenaline ebbed away. An old, half-forgotten sensation came to the back of his jaw and he threw up. The vomit floated on the dark pool.

The card was the size of a postage stamp and no thicker than a dime. Beside the hole in the wall gouged by the camera he put a hand down and ran his fingertips over the stone floor. Jin and Lilly looked on in silent incomprehension.

His fingers brushed against clumps of shapeless matter, fibrous, disintegrating, cold. Once he touched something metallic, like a knife. Please God, don't let me cut myself. Then he felt the card. With a pincer-like motion he took it between the nails of his thumb and forefinger and lifted it from the sewage, which trickled down his arm. Too dark to see what state it was in. At least it wasn't broken.

He looked around for a way to clean up. "Water?" He mimed washing his hands.

Lilly took a blue plastic bucket from under a table and slipped out of the door.

Jin started talking again. Daniel cut him off.

"Listen, I'm not a journalist, okay? You made a mistake."

In the lane, Lilly screamed. A moment later she was shoved back inside by the man in the polo shirt.

He kept a grip on her arm and with the other hand pushed the Raybans up over his forehead to see what Daniel was holding. He moved closer and peered at the rectangle of plastic. Nostrils flaring in disgust, he threw some remark over his shoulder. Three men in the doorway laughed.

He said something else, and with a muttered curse a pockmarked man in a leather jacket walked over to Daniel and held out his hand.

Fight? There were four of them. The adrenaline rush had gone. And there was nothing to use as a weapon.

"You don't want this." But even as he spoke he remembered the kicks, the beatings, the woman dragged away by her hair.

The man in the leather jacket stepped forward and shouted in his face, a halitotic gust whose threat was unmistakable. He jerked a hand in peremptory command.

Daniel gave him the card. He fingered his watch.

Raybans snapped an order. The pockmarked man dropped the card on the stone floor and stamped on it, cracking the plastic. He ground it under his heel, which he twisted from side to side as if crushing a scorpion. He stamped on it again. Raybans started haranguing the man and the girl, who listened with heads bowed. After a final threat, he turned and walked out, ignoring Daniel. The pockmarked man spat in the pool of sewage and followed. Silence returned.

So this is what it's like to be intimidated. And not be able to do anything about it. A feeling of shame. And disgust.

Jin had withdrawn to somewhere inside himself as if there was safety in not moving, not making a sound. He must have behaved that way before. More than once.

"I'm not a reporter," Daniel said. "I just wanted video of the old houses." He gestured at the smashed card.

Lilly translated this, and the old man's reply.

"He will give you video of the lane. Come tomorrow." She bent, gathered the papers, and held them out. "Take these."

Daniel felt the sensation behind his jaw again. He managed to say, "Okay." Then he stumbled to the door, desperate for fresh air.

Seven

THE GREAT WORLD

"I WAS RIGHT about Pierre knowing people. I've talked to someone already. A Russian." Must stay positive.

"What did he say?" She was on the bed with the laptop on her knees; he could see the headboard. A book lay face down on the bedspread, with a picture on the cover of a couple bent over a newborn baby.

"She. Old lady with a three-pack-a-day voice. Definitely interested. Of course, these things take time." Lying was easier over a video link; subtleties of body language and expression got lost in the shift from three dimensions to two. But he'd been shaken by what had happened at Lilly's house. Could she tell? Change the subject. "What about the baby?"

"Went for a check-up as soon as I got here. Doctor says we're both fine."

"Yes. I was sure you would be."

"You always take things for granted, Daniel. That's the difference between us."

"Confidence. You have to believe things will work out."

"Things will work out? That's why we're losing the house, because you thought things would work out."

"Sophie, they will. Believe me." Don't get dragged down that road. Change the subject again. "How's your mom?"

"Older. Sadder. What you get from living with Wayne. You know what that's like. Just bad days and worse days."

Three weeks after he turned nineteen Sophie's father had shuffled down the tail ramp of a Hercules transport outside Saigon. He was ignored by the men on the ground, who had *Hell Sucks* or *One Mean Motherfucker* or *Just You and Me God--Right?* written on their helmet covers. Everybody knew the first few weeks in-country were the most dangerous, and who wanted another dead friend?

Wayne Wolf didn't die. Nor was he wounded, at least not physically. But forty years later he would still wake screaming and shaking with terror. Daniel could imagine the nightmares that haunted him. The cold sweats. The guilt at having survived and the secret wish that he hadn't. The memories. The gusts of blind, all-consuming rage. Driven by his demons, he and Sharon and their long-legged daughter moved from one rented apartment to the next, never staying more than a few months. Sophie grew to hate the frequent upheavals that marked her childhood. While Daniel viewed the prospect of moving to a new place with excitement, she looked on it with dread.

"Still the same as ever." She picked a speck of lint off the bedspread with long pianist's fingers. "The second day I went into the living room. And there he was with his ear pressed to the wall. He thought he'd heard something. He looked terrified. Like a rabbit. And he's been doing the same thing in here."

The image on Daniel's screen veered as she swung off the bed and turned the laptop's camera to the wall. He could just make out a mark on the white paint.

"Here. And here. And here."

Each time the camera jerked over the room it gave a vertiginous glimpse of the ceiling or part of the window frame or a magazine on the floor, then settled on another faint smear of human grease.

"Oh, Jesus. I've got to get you out of there." He hated the way not having money made him powerless to look after her. It was a kind of disloyalty. And they both agreed disloyalty and betrayal were the greatest sins.

"I grew up with it, remember? I just thought it was all behind me, having to move from place after place."

"Sophie, I swear, it's all going to work out. Believe me. I know how you feel. I really do."

"If y'all know how I felt you'd bring some money. Go and work for Rob Sheldrake. He asked you. For that museum project."

"That's hack work. I can't give up *The Riding Instructor*. Not now. It's what I was born to do. It's going to be something great. And the timing is perfect."

"So why don't other people see it that way?"

"Sophie, I'm trying. I'm going to see someone else. Another Russian. Something will come out of it. I just know it. Trust me."

IN THE HOPE that a rush of memories would kick-start Alex Orlovski's interest in backing *The Riding Instructor* he arranged to meet at the Great World. A six-storied L-shaped structure, it stretched around a corner just southeast of People's Square. The part that looked like a wedding cake still rose from the middle. But now the building was overshadowed by an elevated highway. It was under renovation, and clad in green nets and scaffolding. The heavy wooden door was closed.

Orlovski rapped on it with an ebony cane, waited, rapped again. When there was no response he tucked the cane under his arm, groped in the fleecy innards of his Astrakhan coat and took out a pack of Camels. He thumbed the wheel of a tarnished brass lighter, and after a fit of coughing hawked up something red onto the sidewalk.

"Old days it never shut." He hawked again. "Whores. Magicians. Story-tellers. Never stopped."

The Great World was built by an entrepreneur who'd made a fortune in health tonic. As well as *fan-tan* in the basement, it offered six floors of gambling machines, magicians, singsong girls, pimps, barbers, earwax extractors, a dozen different groups of actors, writers of love letters, a mirror maze, balloons, shooting galleries, peepshows, massage benches, firecrackers, and a stuffed whale.

"You came here?" Again, Daniel was amazed to meet someone who had frequented the places he'd read about with such fascination.

More coughing. "Every Saturday. Me and Suslov. With money from the bottles."

"Bottles?"

"Suslov knew a farmer. Out past the racecourse." He waved the cane in the direction of the highway and the square beyond. Where foreigners once galloped horses over the bones of the dead, Shanghainese now drove cars. "Hundred eggs for one gin bottle. Sold the eggs, came to the Great World."

"Why did he want bottles?"

"To trap devils. Chinese think devils only go in straight lines. Catch them in a bottle, they can't turn back."

Daniel, in full pitching mode, was attuned to every opportunity. "Interesting idea. You know, Alex, there could well be a way to work that into *The Riding Instructor*. Because it's not just a movie. It's part-game as well. A hybrid. Something completely new." He looked up at the mildewed structure above them. "Think of it as a very rich cake. With lots of different layers."

The door opened and two workmen appeared, manhandling what looked like an old steamer trunk. As they came out, Orlovski pushed past and went in. Daniel followed. When one of the workmen said something Orlovski responded in Chinese. Daniel had the impression it was more natural than his English.

They stood in the gloom and gazed around what had once been the entrance lobby. It had been stripped bare and wires sprouted from holes in the tin-paneled walls like nests of serpents. "Slot machines here. Like Coney Island." Orlovski tapped the floor with his cane. "Old Latvian woman over there sold crickets. Bamboo cage was extra ten cents in small money. Chinese money."

He shuffled toward a broad staircase, leaning on the cane. "Movie theater upstairs cost twenty cents. Saw Chaplin. The Chinese loved him. Almost caused a riot." He climbed with painful determination and stopped halfway up to rest. The stairs came out on a landing that overlooked an open-air stage. He wheezed and rested his hands on the railing, whose white paint was cracked and blackened with mold.

"Acrobats here. Best in the world. Ten years' training for two minutes on the stage. Like rubber. Bend over, go through a barrel. Bend backward, go through bent backward."

Daniel remembered the shoot-out at the end of Welles's The Lady From Shanghai. "Where was the mirror maze?"

"Upstairs. Next to the whale."

"Think you can make it up there?"

"Not dead yet."

They set off, one step at a time, Orlovski with a tight hold on Daniel's arm. As they reached the next floor a workman came down with a length of rusty pipe balanced on his shoulder. He said something and hefted the pipe to a more comfortable position.

"Can't go up. Construction."

"Can you ask him if the mirror maze is still there?"

The workman laughed.

"Nothing up there. Just concrete."

"Like most of the city." Daniel kept a firm grip on the old man's elbow as he picked his way back down the stairs, step by step. "That's another benefit of The Riding Instructor. It helps preserve something that would be forgotten. It's educational. It shows what the lives of the White Russians were like. People like you."

Orlovski said nothing.

"Why did you come back?"

He fished out another Camel. "Getting old. Wanted to see it again." He fixed Daniel with a rheumy eye. "Old men get like that."

"Where are you going next?"

"The house."

"Okay if I come? I want to see how the Russians lived. *The Riding Instructor* has to be as authentic as possible. In every detail."

"It's a free country." Orlovski's laugh, deep and chesty, threatened to turn into another bout of hacking. He managed to suppress it.

He moved down the street in a dot-and-carry shuffle. At each step he planted the cane on the sidewalk and hauled his right foot toward it with a rasp of breath. When they reached an intersection he stopped and gazed across at a fluorescent-lit convenience store. His eyes were the blue of cornflowers.

"Mother's shop was there. She made dresses. Beautiful dresses. Rooshyan women know about dresses. Kept a samovar in the room behind the curtain. Business bad, drink tea. She drank a lot of tea."

They were halfway across the road when the lights changed and drivers surged forward, horns blaring. Orlovski ignored them, forcing Daniel to do the same. When they reached the store he stopped again. Bemused by the stream of traffic, he looked around and tried to get his bearings. He pointed up the road with his cane.

"We lived this way. Other side of the park." He tried to go faster and Daniel heard his breathing grow more labored. He sensed the old man's fear that the last traces of his boyhood would disappear before he could see them again. He must know his breath would not last much longer.

The road was stacked with high-rise apartment blocks. When they came to the park he stopped, the wheeze of his chest like gravel churning. Daniel put a hand under his arm again and led him to a bench. Ducks dabbled in a stream that purled beneath the willows.

"Sunday afternoon, snake man came here. Snake went up his nose, came out of his mouth." His attempt to mime this was cut short by coughing. Daniel wondered if he could video somebody doing that. Another of the Great World's attractions.

The air was full of ghosts. "One night there was a big fire. Fifty, maybe sixty places burned." Again he pointed, although Daniel couldn't see what at. "Chinese tried to put the fire out with drums, boom boom boom."

He gripped the cane and got to his feet. "House this way."

But it wasn't. After a hundred yards he turned and looked back at the park, then at the apartment block in front of them. He jabbed the asphalt. "Our lane went here. Oblomov lived on the corner. Had rabbits in a tea chest. Made gloves. Made stew."

He gazed at the glass towers. "Bodyguards lived there. Five in a room. Guarded Li Wenshu. Li was king of the beggars, had a lot of money. Robbers come ... *poof.*" Like Olga, he made a pistol with two fingers and a thumb. "Nagant. Joke was, get a Nagant, you'd never starve to death."

The Nagant was a seven-shot revolver. Former lawyers and teachers and engineers all begged, borrowed or stole Nagants and tried to hire themselves out as bodyguards.

"Was there a lot of work?"

"Rich businessmen scared their kids would be snatched, held for ransom. Didn't pay, kid's ear arrived in a box. Beautifully wrapped. Sometimes both ears. Sometimes nose." He paused, overwhelmed by memories. "No work, you went to Yu Yuan garden. Like my uncle. Played the game."

"Game?"

"Put one bullet in, spin the cylinder, make a bet." Again, he held two fingers to his temple. "Chinese love to gamble. Uncle Sergei raised the odds, put another bullet in. Then another. Big crowd gathered, all waving money, all telling him to put another one in. So he did. And another. All around people waving wads of cash. Thick wads, greasy from *xiaolongbao* dumplings. In the end he had six bullets loaded. One chance in seven of getting lucky. If he did he would walk away a rich man. Very rich man."

There was no need to ask what happened.

For a long time the only sound was Orlovski's breathing, waves prostrating on a pebbled shore. Daniel was about to point out that family loyalty was a key theme in *The Riding Instructor* when the old man spoke again.

"Always dog eat dog in Shanghai. Always some people were shit. Used to be Rooshyans were shit. No money, no friends, no status. Kill a Rooshyan, nobody give a fuck."

He looked at the apartments, at the BMWs and Audis parked outside, at what had happened to the world of his boyhood. He fixed Daniel with a watery blue glare.

"Forget about them. You hear? Rooshyans in Shanghai are an old story. Finished. Leave them in the graveyard. Let them rot in peace."

Another kick in the gut.

HE LEFT ALEX TO BROOD and set off back across the park in the direction of the subway station. Ringed by skyscrapers, it was once the site of the old racecourse. But any ghostly hoofbeats were drowned out by the din, a cacophony of children's voices and traffic noise, of ice-cream sellers' jingles and the over-loud splashing of fountains. He found himself on a broad stone path lined with trees. They didn't block out the looming skyline, but at least they softened it, a green curtain that hid the lower floors of the towers of concrete and glass. Benches stood at intervals in front of a low wall and he sat to collect his thoughts.

Olga and Alex had been long shots. He hadn't seriously expected them to give him ten million dollars, no matter how positive he tried to keep his thinking. But then, who would? Again, as it had done ever since Pierre made the call, the name of Renwen Zhou came to mind. Ambitious. Pushy. Hungry to make a mark. Not afraid of big money. Definitely the front runner. Albeit in a pretty thin field. And he'd been to grad school at UCLA. He'd have taken business, an MBA. What had been the subject of his dissertation? He took the iPad from his computer bag and went to the UCLA website. But there was no list of theses.

He was looking to see if there was any reference to Zhou in the alumni yearbook when a woman sat down on the bench, close enough to make him glance up. She smiled. Crooked teeth, squinty eyes, cheap leather jacket, distressed jeans condom-tight. He smiled back, faintly, and returned to the doings of the alumni. Matt Finkelstein had set up a micro-loan program in Namibia. Hollis Matsunaga had become the first ...

"iPad very good. You American?"

"Yes."

She moved closer. "What you looking at?"

"Just checking something."

"You looking at video of girls."

"Not at the moment."

"Show me." She leaned over and pressed her leg against his. She smelled of stale tobacco. He moved away.

"You gay?"

"Yes."

"Show me what you looking at."

"Nothing that would interest you."

She reached forward and touched the picture of the university president smiling up at her. "Who this man? He gay too?"

What happened next happened very fast. Part of him sensed two men approach. As he turned one of them lunged forward and grabbed the computer case from the bench. The laptop was recharging on Pierre's counter and the man must have expected the bag to be heavier because he overbalanced and almost fell. The woman snatched the iPad and sprang up. Following what Daniel knew instantly was a pre-arranged plan, she sprinted away to his left while the two men with the empty laptop case ran back the way they'd come, to his right.

He chased the woman. He was taller and fitter and unencumbered by tight jeans and within a few paces he got hold of the collar of her leather jacket. She screamed and jerked her head around and tried to bite his hand. He came to a halt. She swung the iPad to smash him in the face. He caught her wrist and twisted it. She screamed again and he twisted harder. The iPad fell to the ground. All the rage he'd felt at Lilly's house coursed through him, the hurt and humiliation of his failure rising up like a red cloud.

When his mind cleared she was sobbing. He let go. She stumbled away clutching her hand and disappeared into the crowd of stollers thronging the path as quickly as a stone thrown into a pond.

There was no sign of the two men.

EIGHT

DISTANT THUNDER

HE COULDN'T JUST WAIT for the meeting with Zhou. He had to find other possibilities. How about movie companies? The government-run Shanghai Film Studio churned out propaganda and was widely considered a joke. But the independent sector must be growing. He googled Shanghai movie producers and looked with Yahoo and Bing and Duck Duck Go and came up with a few names. But information in English was almost non-existent. Fiona Schulman might be able to help but she was still out of town. Banks? Get real. The only way he'd get ten million dollars out of a Shanghai bank was to rob it.

Part of the reason he'd come to grief with *The Riding Instructor* was that new ideas just kept bubbling up and feeding his obsession. They still did. He cursed himself for letting it happen, for allowing the project to take him over so completely. He needed it the way an addict needed crack, no matter what the collateral damage. He hated what he had done to Sophie because of it. But he couldn't leave it alone. When the task of hustling for money oppressed him he still found himself taking refuge in the production itself. That, too, had its problems, a seemingly endless stream of them. But they were the kind of problems he relished, and knew how to solve.

He had a gift for making unexpected connections. Back at the start of the year he'd come across a piece in the *Seattle Times* about a researcher who studied the languages of whale pods by using undersea microphones. A few weeks later, on the plane back from an interactive media expo in Paris, he sat next to Peter Laverne, the entertainment director of an Alaska cruise line. They gazed down at the icebergs that rose so impossibly white from the conifer waters off Greenland. Laverne said, "Nine-tenths of them are below the surface. Finding a way to interact with that world would be a big thing in my business."

"Whale songs," Daniel said, without giving it a moment's thought. "Pipe them up to computers on the ships. Put musical keyboards on the computers so passengers can join in and jam with the whales." He outlined the concept with his hands. "Then post the whole performance on the web. People can send links to it instead of postcards." Laverne hurried off the plane at Sea-Tac jabbing numbers on his phone. He set up three meetings before he'd collected his bags. No wonder *Wired* called Daniel "a digital Renaissance man and one of the most creative minds of a particularly creative time. Think Orson Welles with a laptop."

Now, feeling he'd run up against a brick wall in the hunt for funding and unable for the moment to see what to do next, he let himself slip back and luxuriate in the boundless realm of his imagination. The Great World had set his thoughts racing. He wanted *The Riding Instructor* to be complex and multi-leveled, just as the Great World itself was. One level would hold annotated graphics of things found in the course of the quest: a race card from the autumn meet, or a page from one of the city's Russian newspapers, or a plan of an opium fumerie. Then he'd thought of using pictures of objects. *Papaver somniferum*, the opium poppy. A Nagant and its mechanism. The dog's tongue might be another possibility.

He decided to add another level. A Week in the Life of a Russian: Could You Survive? would be a simple text-based game and track decisions and their consequences. The goal would be to make enough to live on for seven days. A wrong decision cost money, and without money you died of starvation. *Teeth. Money could be made pulling gold teeth from the mouths of the dead found on the street each morning. No, bad idea; people who died on the street wouldn't have gold teeth. At least, not by the time they died.*

He was puzzling over the best way to cause a diversion in order to steal empty bottles from the Casanova nightclub when Pierre came back from Xian and immediately plugged in his iPod.

"Good trip?"

"Could have been worse. At least I didn't get arrested. Which is what happened to Mayling Yu. The woman who made the execution video."

"Jesus. How did they find her?"

"Searched all the computers in city hall. She must have trashed the file. But it seems she didn't overwrite it." He opened the Johnnie Walker.

Daniel became aware that forces he'd never given any thought to could affect his life. He sensed a threat, like distant thunder, and fingered the strap of his watch. The authorities would put the chain together link by link and find it led to Pierre. And to him. "So that means they're after Shuying."

"Can't assume that. Unless she's already under suspicion. Mayling would just have left it somewhere for pickup. A dead letter drop. Wouldn't know what happened next. They protect themselves by ignorance. At least, that's what Beidermeyer said."

"He was in Xian?"

"With Shuying."

Pierre opened his MacBook. A man's face filled the screen. Past middle age, it was wreathed in white curls and beamed at the world from behind gold-rimmed bifocals.

Daniel studied it. "Avuncular."

"Very. He twinkles. Good at putting people at ease. Very affable. That's one side of him, anyway. Always seems to be smiling. But in fact he never stops scanning the room, the street, the people coming toward him. The camera catches that. Freezes things the eye doesn't register." The next picture had been taken from further away, with a zoom. "See how different he looks when he thinks nobody's watching."

"He's an ethnomusicologist?"

"That's his day job. But it's pretty obvious he's a spook. Or a former spook. He spent the early sixties in Vietnam. Became the world's top authority on the daughter-in-law songs of the Hmong."

"What's the Lefkovitch Foundation? Doesn't have a website."

"No. I asked Shuying. All she said was it's a nonprofit body with interests in human rights."

"And they want your satellite gizmo."

"A loan." Pierre drained his whiskey and held the bottle toward Daniel, who shook his head again. "Just for the carbon conference. Beidermeyer said the execution video's had nine thousand views on YouTube. People are talking about it on Twitter. Even discounting the snuff film ghouls, that's a lot of interest. He wants reporters covering the conference to write about Mayling Yu. Make a fuss. That way the Chinese might just spare her life. A concession. So they come out looking like good guys."

He scrolled through other pictures. "Xian's very different from Shanghai. The Moslem part, anyway. A lot of low, mud-built houses. Smells of wool and dried-up leather. Desert smells." He paused at a shot of shoes lined up outside a mosque. "Women in headscarves cooking persimmon buns on old oil drums. Very smoky."

Fire. A blaze in the Casanova's kitchen would distract everyone long enough to steal the empty bottles.

"Of course, it's still China. Surveillance cameras everywhere." Pierre pulled up an image of a line of metal boxes bracketed to the city wall. "Courtesy of Uncle Sam to begin with. Some outfit from Akron, Ohio got them started. Sold them tracking zooms. Laser microphones for listening through windows."

"So they might have seen you handing over the transmitter."

"But they didn't. Smart guy, Beidermeyer. Thinks on his feet."

He opened a photo of a dusty Volkswagen bus. Its original blue had been covered with brightly-colored symbols. Along one side was a creature that could be a crocodile, although its body was short and stubby. A fish with bones showing started on the door and wrapped around to the front. There were chevrons like a sergeant's stripes turned upside-down and a pattern of spirals against an ochre background. At the back drops of scarlet dripped from the beak of a black bird and turned into the figure of a dancer.

"Aussie family. Drove up through Thailand and Burma. Kelly's a one-man band."

A tanned, stocky man with short blonde hair and a square chin appeared on the screen, instruments all around him: a twelve-string guitar, a battered leather suitcase that was scuffed at the corners and had a roughened mark in the middle, a high-hat cymbal and chrome stand, a harmonica rack with a kazoo. Propped against the van was a length of hollow tree trunk, bleached by wind and sun and thick as a man's thigh.

"A didgeridoo." Pierre grinned. "He called it his weapon of mass distraction."

The next shot showed a girl, also stocky and blonde and with Kelly's pugnacious chin. She looked about eight years old. "Petunia. Smart as a whip. Never set foot in a school. Speaks Chinese better than me. And sells the CDs." The next shot showed her seated behind a shoe box of disks, almost full, and a branch which she'd tied to the leg of a small collapsible table. The branch was forked and from each fork CD cases dangled like presents on a Christmas tree. Pierre fished three out of his bag.

"So you bought the collected works."

"We all did. Petunia said she'd cut us a deal. Hundred *yuan* for three if we all bought them." He turned off the iPod and slipped one of the disks into the MacBook. A shimmering wall of rhythm pounded from the speakers as Kelly pumped out a fast beat on the suitcase, accenting it with the high hat and embellishing it with percussive guitar and bursts of bluesy mouth harp. The didgeridoo produced a single booming note that writhed and twisted like a giant serpent.

"Beidermeyer knew the symbols on the van were based on some ancient Aboriginal rock paintings. So Kelly warmed to him immediately. And when Beidermeyer gave him fifty bucks he took us for a ride around the city walls so I could hand over the gizmo away from the eyes and ears."

The CD case showed a photograph of Petunia leaning out of the van and waving as it cut across a desert landscape. Daniel put it back on the table. "But a transmitter can only send. It can't receive."

"Doesn't need to. Shuying just wants to send Beidermeyer a list of people who'll talk to the reporters. Easier if she does everything herself. She's still trying to find people. They'd be taking a big risk. They'll have heard about Mayling Yu."

"Good news for you. No more wrong numbers."

"Not for the time being." Pierre grinned. "And in the long term we're all dead anyway."

"How did you get involved to begin with?"

The grin vanished. "An obligation." He turned away and began to log the photos.

Shuying. But why didn't he want to talk about it? In time the effects of his Catholic childhood would surface again and he'd confess everything. Everything? No. Not that he'd tried to seduce Sophie. It was hard to imagine he even thought about that, let alone wrestled with his conscience over it. It just wasn't important.

Daniel's fists clenched. Think about the game again. How else could a hungry Russian get money? Make something? Steal something? Sell something? Women sold their bodies, in various ways. Of course, so did men, at Mme. Litvinoff's Salon of Love.

"You are asked by Mme. Litvinoff to entertain the wife of the head of

a Western trading company. Her husband is known to keep a careful eye on her and the last two lovers have disappeared. Do you:

a) Decline, which means you won't be asked again?

b) Agree to one assignation, after which, if you are still alive, you will say you are temporarily indisposed because of a twisted back?

c) Agree, and gamble on being able to make the woman fall in love with you, whereupon you will kill the husband, marry her for the passport, and escape from Shanghai with a lot of money?

NINE

A THING FOR MOON ROCK

A LITTLE AFTER TWO in the morning, when Catalina Jones had finished her set, blown kisses to the audience--"Vantayun, thank you! Thank you very much! See you again soon!"--and taken her lanky black frame backstage for the post-performance coke and champagne, Daniel looked around again.

"He'll come." Pierre spent of lot of his life hanging around, usually in much less salubrious surroundings. "Making people wait is Renwen Zhou's way of showing who's boss. One of them, anyway."

The buzz of conversation picked up around the lacquered tables of the 21 Club--Le 21, to give it its proper name, or Catalina's Vantayun. Screens on the linen walls glowed with ads for Remy Martin cognac, rich with the colors of autumnal France. When a waitress in a grey silk shirt and black jeans ushered in three newcomers, Daniel recognized the thin man with a pony tail and collarless shirt as an up-and-coming Seattle architect who had been profiled in the *New York Times*. He'd devised a way to build environmentally-friendly houses out of old tires.

He sipped the last of his whiskey. The ice had melted long ago. "Thanks for setting this up. Always easier to make the first move through a friend."

Pierre reached up and touched the arm of a waitress as she passed and indicated their empty glasses. She nodded curtly. As she turned away they saw she had a tattooed serpent curling across her bare back.

"I wouldn't describe Zhou as a friend. But he's useful to know. Works for Wenming Nan."

"And what does Wenming Nan do?"

"Concrete. Cornered the market in it. Completely. And just about everything to do do with it. Can you imagine what that means? Shanghai finishes a new seventy-story building every week. Using Nan's materials. He also supplied concrete for the last round of subway stations. All one hundred and sixty of them. The guy is stratospherically rich. Zhou's busy making himself his main man in the next generation. The people who know about the rest of the world. Who'll take over when the communist party implodes. In a good position, too, if he doesn't overreach, try to get too far ahead before he can destroy his enemies. Nan needs new blood if his empire's going to last."

"Ever met him?"

"No. But I've worked for him. Zhou saw some nudes I'd shot. He asked me to do something similar for the boss. A private edition. Of his underage girlfriends."

Every afternoon for a week a black Mercedes SUV had waited outside Pierre's apartment, motor running, while he loaded lights, stands, a Manfroto tripod. The drive was always the same, along Hengshan Road past the twin spires of the resurrected St. Ignatius cathedral. Then west, cutting through streets where old men in vests shared balconies with caged linnets to leafy suburbia and a Tudor-style house with beams and a steeply pitched roof.

Each day the same hard-faced woman in a cheongsam led him up the stairs to a room presided over by an enormous toy panda that perched on a Louis XV chaise longue. And there reclined the girl of the day, dressed in whatever attire she--or her mother--thought likely to please the patron. French maid, waif, and Barbie doll loomed large in Nan's erotic landscape. The woman in the cheongsam took up a position beside the door, folded her hands, and waited while the girls, flat-chested and hairless, put on pantomimes of sexual excitement.

"Been trained what to do," Pierre said. "Like dogs performing tricks. Human dogs. More depressing than erotic."

"Must have paid well, though." Daniel had never given much thought to money. Now he had none it never left his mind. Money for *The Riding Instructor*. Money for Sophie, to save his marriage. Money to keep the house. Even when he wasn't consciously thinking about it the need didn't go away, ineluctable as the diagnosis of some fatal disease. It stamped his brow with a permanent furrow.

"Sure. When Zhou asked how much I wanted, I remembered what someone said about working for the very rich. Set a price, multiply by three. That way they don't despise you for being cheap. He didn't even comment."

The serpent girl brought their whiskies, stony-faced.

"There's a billion people in this country," Daniel said. "All scrabbling to get rich. How did Nan get to the top of the heap?"

"Army. I heard Nan's not his original name. Took it from Nanking. He was five years old during the massacre. Hid in a water jar while the Japanese raped his mother, then killed her. Tossed his baby sister in the air and used her for bayonet practice. Nan ended up in Mao's red army. Built roads. Made connections."

"Any interests apart from jailbait?"

"He does have a thing for moon rock. There's a pile of it in some NASA storehouse. Ambassadors present chunks to the leaders of nations amenable to U.S. influence. Especially African nations with copper. Nan's people take off in hot pursuit, swap it for something with a bit more bling. Then it goes to a stone carver in Japan who's a living national treasure. And the carver whittles it into the sexual parts of Nan's girlfriends."

"Working from your photographs?"

"This was before I came on the scene. Nan said they'd get a present if they posed for the carver. A Mazda Miata. He got twelve hundred of them in one of his takeovers."

A Westerner with moussed hair came in, trailing a very thin Chinese man in black, and looked at them inquiringly. When he got no response he pouted and marched over to a table on the other side of the room.

"Anyone refuse?"

"You don't refuse Wenming Nan. Enough stories going round to make sure of that." Pierre toyed with his whiskey. "One girl got a flask of acid smashed in her face. And workers who wanted more money ended up head-first in concrete. With their feet sticking out. I've seen a photo."

"Must be a hard man to buy a Christmas gift for. What do you give someone who's got twelve hundred Miatas to spare? A small country?"

"Could do worse. Right now he's buying up half of Laos. Wants to turn it into a gambling resort. Already one of the world's two hundred richest people."

"One hundred richest."

Neither of them had noticed Renwen Zhou approach. Prada sunglasses pushed up on his head held his hair back and emphasized the curve of his nose. His lips were thin, yet his mouth had a kind of sensitivity. He was still in his early thirties, but heaviness was starting to soften his features, the result of too many *xiaoyang* dumplings, too many hours at his cherrywood desk. Daniel tried not to dislike him immediately.

"That's what *Forbes* says. Of course, *Forbes* doesn't include criminals."

Zhou shook hands and seated himself at the table. Without looking around he grunted, "Remy." The waitress who'd been hovering behind him, a girl with fishnet stockings and the words Just Do It on her t-shirt, slipped away. He turned to Daniel.

"Tell me about this Russian idea."

Again, as he made his pitch he felt all his passion for *The Riding Instructor* reawaken. Something about the rootlessness of the White Russians struck a chord in him.

As the project took shape in his mind he went to visit Peter Malin, an anthropologist who'd studied the old Shanghai community and interviewed as many members as he could track down. His life's work lined the walls of his office in files and binders and battered boxes of reel-to-reel tape. When he saw Daniel's interest he started pulling down folders and blowing the dust off them.

"He had tapes of interviews, transcripts, photographs, newspapers, menus, concert programs." Daniel opened a photo of the racecourse on the iPad. Zhou glanced at it with indifference. "Original hand-written sheet music. And the more I found out, the more it fascinated me. The White Russians had no money, no possessions, no passports. And here they were, stranded in the world's capital of ostentatious wealth. Most of it came from the sale of opium. But they had nothing to sell."

The stories in Malin's files told of desperation, fear, and starvation, of syphilis and assassinations. Through them ranged gangsters, beggars, bodyguards, and, glimpsed occasionally through gilded doorways, people who lived in sprawling mansions and collected racehorses by the thousand.

"It was a kind of hell," Daniel said as the girl bobbed down with Zhou's Remy Martin. "And it had all the elements of *film noir*. Distrust. Desperation. Cruelty. Orson Welles would have loved it."

"And presumably did," Pierre said. "Wasn't *Lady From Shanghai* one of his?"

"Yes. But that has nothing to do with the place. Except that Rita Hayworth says she worked there. And she has that enigmatic line when Welles asks if she was lucky there. She says, 'You need more than luck in Shanghai'."

"Of course you do." Zhou swirled his cognac and inhaled the bouquet. "You need *guanxi*." He left the translation to Pierre.

"Connections."

"Right." Daniel plunged ahead. "Shanghai had strangeness and alienation, extremes of wealth and poverty. And ruthlessness. That's the tone of *The Riding Instructor*. That overwhelming sense of ever-present menace."

Zhou waved a hand in dismissal.

"All that finished long time ago. People not interested in that. Interested in what's happening now. What's happening tomorrow." He looked around the 21 and its patrons. Catalina Jones had emerged from the dressing room and joined a boisterous party of public relations hacks who fussed over her at the biggest table in the club. "Shampoo for the lady!" shouted a florid man in a striped shirt, waving an empty Moet bottle at the bar.

"Don't underestimate the attraction of old Shanghai," Pierre said. "People who come with foreign companies get offered fancy new apartments in Pudong. A lot of times they turn them down. They want to live in the French Concession. For the history."

Zhou frowned. "That's just foreigners. We Chinese used to have a saying, better a bed in Puxi than a house in Pudong. Not anymore. Pudong more important than Wall Street now."

"Shanghai is just the setting," Daniel said. "The story is timeless. It's mythic. It's a quest that takes the seeker into the depths of hell. Like Orpheus and Eurydice. Only instead of Orpheus looking for a lover, Nikolai is looking for his brother."

The disinterest on Zhou's face showed that classical references were not the way to go. He changed tack. "Letting the viewer make his own movie is the biggest change in entertainment since the talkies. And games are already selling more than recorded music. This is where the big money is going to come from."

Again, Zhou waved a hand in dismissal. "Can't make money selling games. Too easy to copy."

"*The Riding Instructor* can't be copied. And the money won't come from selling it. At least, not in the way you'd sell a DVD."

He leaned forward, eyes locked on Zhou's.

"It can't be copied because it won't exist, except on remote servers. Users will log onto it. Through the cloud. And that's where one stream of money will come from. They won't buy it. They'll subscribe to it. Could be month by month. Could be hour by hour. Could be by pre-paid card."

Zhou said nothing.

"That's just the users. There are other possibilities." He ticked them off on his fingers. "Advertising. If it's limited to one ad at the start of the session people will accept it. Sponsorship. International licensing to companies that want to set up their own servers and run versions in another language. Japanese and Korean are the most obvious. But I can see the French being interested."

Zhou was gazing around the club. "Chinese star," he said. "Chinese investors put money in, they want a Chinese star."

"The story is about a Russian. That's the whole point. But maybe he could have a Chinese girlfriend."

Zhou looked contemptuous.

"Or a Chinese friend. A wise man. Someone who helps him at a critical moment. Saves him through some ability or know-how that Westerners don't have. That might work."

"Who would be the users?" Pierre asked.

"People who want to explore their creativity. As well as making their own movie they can write the score. Or arrange the music I found in Malin's files. And record it with Garage Band."

Zhou swirled the last of the cognac in the bottom of his balloon glass.

"New kinds of entertainment are going to drive the global economy," Daniel said. "Look at the Japanese. Pouring billions into cartoon books and animations for export. Entertainment is environmentally clean. It doesn't use natural resources. It doesn't leave a carbon footprint. *The Riding Instructor*'s a chance to beat them at their own game."

Zhou lifted a wrist and studied his Cartier watch long enough to let them see how the gold and titanium bracelet hung, supple as a snake.

"There may be some possibility. Maybe I'll get back to you. *Ciao*."

And with a perfunctory wave of farewell, or perhaps dismissal, he was gone, ruffling the air ahead in a bow wave of power and making three fishnet-stockinged waitresses race to open the studded oak door before he reached it.

"Not a man who broods over his own shortcomings," Daniel said.

"*Tong* is the Chinese word for it," Pierre said. "That arrogance. It's a Shanghai thing. Shanghai and the Shanghainese are hip and everyone else is a hayseed."

The tattooed girl brought the bill, tucked in a black leather folder, and waited.

"Smart move, playing the Japan card." Pierre reached for his wallet. "That's who they really want to thrash, the Japanese. Americans are just a bunch of spoiled brats as far as the Chinese are concerned."

TEN

SAXON BLOND

FIONA SCHULMAN was old enough for her hair to be turning silver, although it was such a pale, Saxon blond and cut so short the change made little difference. The creases each side of her nose had probably been there since early adulthood. Her handshake was firm, and she sat as upright in her rattan chair as if she was riding a horse.

"Pierre's very talented," she said in a warm contralto. "Great sense of form. Where did you meet?"

"In Tokyo." He laughed. "Salacious story."

"The best kind. I'm all ears."

Pierre had gone fresh out of college to document the ways in which the Japanese were using video. His first stop was the Open Eye video gallery, where Daniel, ever precocious, had a just won top prize in a competition.

"What for?" Her gaze was unwavering, eyes the color of robin's eggs holding his.

"Kid thing, really. I was still in high school, living on base. Bunch of marines turned up. I crawled out and hid under a half-track to video their drill and chanting. *I don't know but I been told, Eskimo pussy is mighty cold.* I played it to some friends. Backward. I got them to imitate what they saw and heard, and taped that. Then I played that tape backward, too."

Her laugh was a deep chuckle. "I can imagine. Everything would be slowed down. Otherworldly. Like it was happening underwater. Definitely smart-ass."

"That's what Pierre said. And when I suggested he should shoot a porn shoot he agreed right away."

"I'm sure he did. Never one to turn down a chance, Pierre." Something in her voice made him think she spoke from personal experience. "How did a foreign high-school kid come to have an in with the Japanese porn business?"

"I knew someone from the gallery. Susumu Arakawa. Had very bushy eyebrows and a black leather cap. He took us to the apartment where he was shooting. There was a microphone above the bed, hanging from a hook screwed into the plaster. Guy called Deguchi was the sound man. He wore this enormous pair of headphones." Daniel's fists went to his ears. "Made him look like a giant bug. Taeko, the girl, was very noisy. The bed creaked, rocked faster. The windows started to rattle. The microphone began to sway. Then things fell over in the cupboards. All the while Deguchi hunched over the tape recorder trying to keep the needle out of the red."

"Don't tell me." Schulman played with the string of amber beads around her neck. "The earth moved for her."

"Exactly. Richter four point two. The floor juddered. Something heavy crashed to the floor in the apartment above. Taeko screamed louder. Deguchi's mouth hung open. Then the microphone dropped from the ceiling in a shower of plaster and hit the metal bed frame. He jerked as if he'd been shot. And bit off the tip of his tongue."

"To be caught by Pierre's camera."

"Actually, no. He missed that. What he got was even better. The aftermath."

Arakawa had dabbed at his assistant's mouth with a wad of tissues and made soothing noises. Deguchi looked imploring and frightened. He tried to speak, but the words were lost in bubbles of blood. The girl wound herself modestly in a sheet, went to the kitchen, and came back with a pair of chopsticks in a wrapper.

"That's the picture. In the background, beneath the splintered laths, Taeko's wrapped in the sheet. She's picked up Arakawa's leather cap and she's pushing it back from her forehead like a cop on a hot day. She's looking down at the three men at her feet. Closest to the camera there's Arakawa, in profile. To his left, still clamped in the headphones, is Deguchi, all gore and anguished eyes. And in the middle, naked and grinning, squats Uno, the male lead. He's raising the chopsticks. And holding the tip of Deguchi's tongue, in a batter of blood and plaster."

"The Keystone Cops meet the Marquis de Sade."

"Exactly. Grotesque. Inexplicable. Pierre said when he saw it in the developing tray he couldn't believe he'd done anything so good. And when Orbis picked it up for *Japan in the Blink of an Eye* and for the press release when it was published that image kick-started his career."

He studied her business card. The edges had a design like sprocket holes on a strip of film. "He said you were well established here. Well connected."

"A fixer has to be connected. To know which buttons to push."

"What do you fix?"

"Broken promises. Broken hearts." She laughed. "Broken budgets. I'm a movie producer. At least, that's what I tell people I want to impress. Really I'm just a gofer with pretensions."

Daniel gazed around. The office was on the second floor of a renovated row house near Hengshan Road subway station. A plant with glossy leaves stood in a brass pot by the window, through which he could see the bare limbs of a plane tree. Above the marble fireplace a sketch by Egon Schiele showed a reclining girl propped on her elbows. "Business must be good."

"It keeps me in lemongrass martinis."

"Ever done anything mobile?"

She looked at him. "I've been known to."

"Because that's where the money's going to be. It's there already.

82

iPhone games made over five hundred million dollars last year. Half a billion. In an economy like this. And that's just phones. The really big market will be content for this baby." He put the iPad on the table.

"For which you've got something suitable."

"For which I've got something perfect. It's called *The Riding Instructor.*"

As he launched into his pitch his passion for the project surged again. There was something inherently powerful about the idea of *The Riding Instructor*, something that stirred deep emotions.

"It's the story of a quest. An obsession. Nikolai's been devastated by the Russian revolution. His only link with the past is his brother. Petya is blessed. He has their mother's sweetness of heart. This is all that keeps Nikolai from despair. Then one day Petya vanishes. Nikolai goes looking for him. And finds himself plunging ever deeper into the darkness."

"Does he find him?"

"Yes and no. There are different endings. Which one the user arrives at depends on which clues he's followed. It's a garden of forking paths. Users have different experiences, different outcomes. Which they make into a movie." He leaned forward. "Their own movie. Unique to them."

Schulman was listening to the soundscape. She trailed a finger to the western side of the city and homed in on a fragment of conversation between two women.

"Darling, it's on Bubbling Well Road. Isn't that just too perfect? She employs two sorts."

"Russians?"

As soon as the clip began to repeat Schulman tapped on the magnifying glass. The map showed the area around Jessfield Road. When she clicked again another of Jerry Hsieh's reconstructions filled the screen, a leafy thoroughfare of large, Western-style houses and manicured lawns. This time the voices came from a conservatory at the back of one of the houses. The women sat either side of an elegant art deco table, on which were orchids in a Lalique vase and a half-empty bottle of Beefeater gin.

Schulman tapped a third time and the women came to life. One is Helen Chatwin, Nikolai's student and lover. The other, voice throaty with cigarettes and drink, is her friend Mary.

"Of course. The ones she calls the Blues just talk to you and twiddle their mustaches."

"And the others? What do the others do?"

"The others, the Reds ... well. One of them did it with Henrietta Churchill on his horse. Galloping across the countryside, skirt up around her waist. And screaming. Can you imagine?"

"Yes."

Again, the Rushes folder held different takes, shot from different camera positions and with differences in delivery. Schulman compared the different iterations of the word "yes," then selected the breathiest and spliced it into the end of the sequence.

"How does that tie in with the disappearance?"

"They're talking about Madame Litvinoff's Salon of Love. Nikolai goes there when he hears one of the gigolos was at the club the night Petya vanished."

She roamed around the screen and followed another scrap of conversation to the cocktail lounge at the Cathay Hotel.

"I ran into a Russian woman on the Bund the other evening, Mr Chatwin. Literally, ha ha. We sort of bumped into each other. She was awfully pretty. She said she was a princess."

"They all do. Stay away from Russian women, Knowles. Because all they want is a passport so they can get out of here. And if they think you're the muggins who can get it for them, God help you."

"That's Helen's husband. He's head of a trading company. One of the main opium importers."

Schulman found more sounds, which led to other places appearing on the map: the customs house, the office of *World*, a Russian newspaper, the Jesuit weather station at Ziccawei. When she homed in on the Russian consulate she overheard plans to kill members of the White Russian community. To see who was making them she had to outwit the guards, dodging between empty rooms as they made their rounds. She laughed when she won.

"That's just a small part of what's going to be in the finished production. It's extensive." Daniel spread his arms as if he'd been crucified. "Users will be able to find at least two hundred hot spots."

"And all the time they're putting together video clips. That's amazing." Then she shook her head. "But I don't think it's going to work."

"Why not?"

"Limitations of the iPad, for one thing. You need a lot of room to hold a movie. And all the rushes. And the software to edit them. Not to mention raw computing muscle."

"But that's the whole beauty of it." Daniel leaned forward again. "The timing's perfect. Because now everything can be kept in the cloud. You just visit it. Piece by piece. And because the server is so powerful everything gets done immediately. There's no sitting around waiting for clips to render."

She toyed with two bracelets, one of bone and one of beaten silver, that encircled her tanned arm.

"How did you get the idea?"

"I saw a photo, Russians at the Shanghai racetrack." He reached over and tapped an icon on the iPad. "They all look pretty beat up. Pretty desperate. And this one guy, off to the side, looks if he doesn't belong anywhere. Not even with the other outsiders." A slight, disheveled figure stood ramrod-straight and stared at the camera with burning eyes.

"There's something about his face. So haggard. So anguished. I scanned the image into the computer. And when I zoomed in I felt I was looking into his soul. Not only that. I had the strangest sensation. I wasn't just looking at him. He was looking back at me. Into my soul. And next day I got the idea. Not the technical details, but the outline. And the title."

He'd thought of showing the photograph to Olga Derieva, just in case she recognized him. Yet he knew instinctively that she would not. The picture must have been taken at least ten years before she was born. And something told him the man had died long before that.

Schulman filled their cups with pale tea from a studded iron pot and said, "Why didn't investors back home go for it?"

"They did. I had enough promised to make a proof of concept. Then Lehman collapsed and they pulled the rug out."

She sipped her tea thoughtfully.

"It's a very good idea. Maybe even a great idea, and I don't use that term lightly. But I don't think I can help. All my funding sources are in the States and Europe. I don't raise money in China. I just spend it here."

"What about Chinese movie producers?"

"Extremely unlikely. To the point where I'd say out of the question."

She picked up her BlackBerry. "Local people can be hard to connect with. But there's one guy you should try. Close to big money. And he's picked my brains a couple of times so you can use my name. Renwen Zhou."

Again. He felt a tingle of excitement, like a blackjack player who realizes the odds have swung in his favor.

"Pierre knows him. We met last night."

"What did he say?"

"Non-committal. I did get the feeling he was interested, though."

"Hard to tell what Zhou's thinking. Except that it's going to about what's best for him. Let's see who else I've got." She turned to the Blackberry again and scrolled down. "Here you are. Here's a hot one. Little Miss Fixit." When she laughed dimples scored her cheeks like parentheses. "The other Miss Fixit. Monica Trebone. Definitely worth meeting. Brings together foreign products and Chinese money. A rainmaker." She studied the screen again. "Zhang Jo's a TV producer. Won't have money but she'd be worth talking to."

The tea had a delicate scent, some flower he couldn't name. Jonquil, perhaps. A Japanese poet wrote of the juices of his lover as having the perfume of jonquil pressed in seawater. An image of Sophie came to mind, head thrown back, lips parted. He pushed it away.

"Know any venture capitalists? Any angels?"

She smiled, a private smile. "Angels, yes, I've met a few of those." She scrolled down the screen. "Nobody in China. But you could try Jeremy Blick at Fischer Dreyfuss. In San Francisco." The name was new to Daniel. He made a mental note.

"One other thing. Ever use any location scouts around the city?"

"A few years back. But these days productions with historical settings go straight into the studio. The wrecker's ball shows no mercy."

Daniel finished the tea. He stood up. "Thanks, Fiona. I know someone's going to take the bait. It's just a matter of finding them."

She extended a slender hand, the one with bracelets. "Good luck. If anybody else comes to mind I'll let you know."

"I'd appreciate that." He moved toward the door.

"Where are you going now?" The deliberation in her speech made him sense an invitation. Better pretend he hadn't.

"To shoot some video."

ELEVEN

SOMEBODY TURNED HER IN

"THE OLD WAYS of surveillance still have their uses," Beidermeyer said. "One spiteful neighbor is worth half a dozen video cameras."

Outside the apartment night was falling, a purplish dusk shot through with Shanghai's never-ending churn of traffic as twenty million people prepared for darkness. Pierre closed the blinds before turning on the lights. As he did so Beidermeyer plugged his iPod into the sound system. A Uyghur ensemble filled the room, the singer's voice rising and falling above a beat like the drumming of horses' hooves.

"That what happened?" Daniel's voice was thick. "Somebody turned her in?"

Beidermeyer's arrival with the news that Shuying had been arrested was like word of a sudden death. It was only two days since the Xian festival.

Beidermeyer shrugged. "Can't tell. Shuying's too smart to make enemies. But one is all it takes. And they didn't just stumble across her. They came looking. As soon as she got back to Shanghai."

From the other side of the park sirens approached. Beidermeyer fell silent. The tension in the room remained after the vehicles sped past and the sound died away. Again, Daniel sensed that forces he had never imagined were coming closer and affecting his life, forces of immense power. And this time there was a link. The attendant in the park had tried to give them a bugged boat. What did they know about Pierre? Who had called on that clunky old phone?

He voiced the unspoken question.

"What if she's tortured?"

The ghosts of all that Beidermeyer had seen and done rose up from wherever he had buried them and passed across his face. He adjusted his glasses.

"Please God, that won't happen. Two reasons. One is her reputation in the States. She's done projects at the Smithsonian. And given talks at Julliard. People know her. People who can exert pressure. As soon as I get back I'll make some calls." He glanced at the Gladstone bag by the door.

"What's the second reason?"

"The carbon conference. Just as it can help Mayling Yu. China can't afford to antagonize Washington by torturing a well-connected American-educated academic. Not with the whole world watching. Even if she is Chinese." For a few moments he seemed lost in thought, toying with the heavy gold signet ring on his left hand. Then he looked up.

"What do you want to do, Pierre? She'll say you lent her the transmitter. To send music from the festival. She's got files on her laptop to back that up. But I doubt if they'll believe her."

Pierre gazed around the apartment. Among the photographs on the walls were images of the Shanghai that was vanishing. Three grinning boys on a demolition site held up a snake. In a lane festooned with washing a barber cropped hair while waiting customers smoked and squatted against a brick wall. An old man, naked except for baggy drawers and a newspaper draped across his middle, dozed on a plastic chair beside the road. Bicycles rusted. And always, in the background, skyscrapers pressed forward like an army of giants. The photos would go in the new book. But he still needed more.

"Staying won't help," he said. Tension deepened the lines on his lean French face. Again, Daniel saw the old man he would become. "But running would make things worse. They'd think I really was involved. Better stay and bluff it out."

In the quiet between tracks a door slammed and the voices of a man and a woman, raised in argument, came up the stairs, then faded away. The Uyghurs began another mournful, impassioned dirge.

"A month ago they'd have thrown you out of the country," Beidermeyer said. "They still could. But I don't think they will. Not now. Not without hard evidence of something illegal. Ideally, they'd like to seize all satellite transmitters at the point of entry. But half the world's media will be here in a few days. That's five thousand journalists they need to impress. And they won't do that if they impound the tools of their trade."

Daniel went over to the water cooler on the kitchen counter. It bubbled obligingly as he poured a glass for himself and another for Pierre, who nodded his thanks.

"The press will be a shield," Beidermeyer said. "I have connections. Big names. On-camera people from the networks. I'll tell them what's happened."

"No." Now Pierre's voice was husky. "If word gets out she helped send the video she's as good as dead. And if you tell a journalist it will get out. No matter what they promise. It's too good a story to sit on."

Beidermeyer raised a pacifying hand.

"It's your decision. But don't underestimate the power of the media. You can use it to your advantage. It's your ace in the hole." He steepled his fingertips as if in prayer. "Doesn't solve the communications problem, though. Somebody else will put the contacts list together. The challenge is getting it out of the country. Too late to just mail it."

"Use a virtual private network," Daniel said. "That's what foreign companies do. Their own internet. One of them would help you."

Beidermeyer shook his head.

"VPNs get hacked. And nobody wants to risk their foothold in China. The market's just too juicy. Look at the search engines. Handing over information that gets people thrown in jail so they can stay in business." His eyes rested on Daniel. "Pierre said you have a new wrinkle on steganography. The black art of hiding messages."

"I did do something," Daniel said after a moment. "SkyeSlip."

"Herodotus talks about tattooing them on the shaved heads of slaves. Then waiting for the hair to grow back."

"My way's faster. It hides them in photographs." He pulled his MacBook closer. After a flurry of keystrokes he looked up at Pierre. "What's on your camera?"

The first picture was of a wind-burnt worker from the countryside asleep beneath a huge billboard, possessions spilling out of two plastic shopping bags. The ad was for China Airlines and showed a plane high above the clouds and the English words, *Our world is your world*.

Daniel made a copy of it. The Uyghurs' swirling rhythm drowned the patter of the keyboard. At one point he stopped and frowned, unsure of the right sequence of keystrokes. Only when he was certain he remembered correctly did he start typing again. Then he put the original photo and the copy side by side on the screen and turned the computer to face Beidermeyer.

"Notice any difference?"

Beidermeyer leaned forward. He peered over the top of his bifocals, then tipped his head back to look though the lower part.

"Not that I can see. But these eyes are past their prime."

Pierre bent closer. "Maybe I'm imagining it. Is the original just a hair sharper?"

Beidermeyer took a handkerchief from the pocket of his linen jacket and polished his glasses. He rested his elbows on his knees to look again. Then he shook his head. "Too subtle for me."

"Too subtle for most people. They're virtually identical."

Daniel made the copy fill the screen. Then he opened SkyeSlip and from a menu selected Show Least Significant Bits. The photograph turned black. Another flurry of keystrokes. And there, in place of the picture, was his proposal for *The Riding Instructor*--synopsis, budget, resources needed and resources in hand, potential market.

"Other people have put things in the empty space in eight-bit digitization," he said. "SkyeSlip does more. It's invisible until you enter a password. Nobody searching the computer will know it's there. And it has a poison pill. Use the wrong password and it overwrites itself. Same if you try to open a photo that doesn't have a message. Disappears without trace."

"Why did you make it?" Beidermeyer's tone had the studied neutrality of a doctor inquiring when the symptoms had begun.

"Just fooling around. I liked the idea of concealing things in plain view. But it wasn't what I needed. The poison pill function was an old coding exercise."

"Have you shown it to anyone else?"

"No. It was really just practice. Like a pianist's scales." He remembered Sophie at the Steinway. And the gulls jeering as the helicopter whisked it away.

Beidermeyer probed further. "How much can you hide?"

"A six-forty by four-eighty pixel picture can hold four hundred thousand letters. About the length of a novel."

"Doesn't that make a suspiciously big file?"

"Not if you use a big one to start with."

"We don't need to hide *War and Peace*." Beidermeyer was peering at the proposal through the bottom of his glasses. "Just some names. Plus a few details."

He fixed Daniel with a penetrating gaze.

"This can do some good in the world. It can help people fight the thugs who are making their lives a misery."

Daniel thought of the woman being dragged across the room by her hair. He felt again the humiliation of having his bag searched and camera smashed and the card destroyed, of being pushed around and not fighting back. Helping the protesters would ease the shame. Or some of it.

"Okay." He moved next to Beidermeyer on the leather couch. "It's easy. Like setting up a database, with a couple more steps." He bent over the keyboard. "The first thing is to pick a password."

Ten minutes later Beidermeyer had a hastily written to-do list hidden in a photograph of a girl on a tricycle cart using a cellphone. And he'd opened the proposal for *The Riding Instructor* which Daniel had concealed again in an image of a man with two red tai chi fans.

"Shuying's friends need to send me the list of people who want to talk," he said as Daniel copied SkyeSlip onto a flash drive. "With enough meat on the bone to get the reporters' attention. About the links Shaowen Gen found between property developers and corrupt officials."

"How will they meet?" Pierre poured another glass of water.

"The contacts will arrange that. They use the classic tricks of the trade. Probably a pickup in a cab."

Daniel went to the closet where he'd hung his jacket. "You should take these." He gave Beidermeyer the sheaf of letters and said how he'd got them.

Beidermeyer skimmed through the crumpled pages. "Petitions. They're being forced out of their homes without compensation. The developer's using *chengguan*."

"*Chengguan?*"

"Thugs with badges. Officially their job is to keep workers from the countryside in order. Kick them out when they're not needed and make sure they don't riot. In reality, they do anything that's too dirty for the People's Armed Police. Which is not a lot. So they make ends meet with side jobs. The guys who frisked you must be moonlighting for the developer as well as working for the cops."

"But what were they looking for? Like those people in the park.

They weren't run-of-the-mill muggers. They didn't want just any iPad. They wanted mine. And the only thing different about mine is that it holds *The Riding Instructor*. Why would the cops be interested in that?"

Beidermeyer shrugged. "Anything new is suspect. And word always gets out. Someone will have told someone who will have told someone else. Then somebody in authority will have said they want to have a look at it. Matter of routine. They'll try again. Just make sure you have a backup."

He turned back to the letters. "It's not against the law to write petitions. The government can't take them to court. So they've made special jails for petitioners. Black jails. Like black holes. People go in and don't come out again. They're not part of the judicial process. There's no record of them. They just disappear. But the Chinese are getting hip to the outside world. They know about the carbon conference. And they know their own government doesn't want to look bad. They think if the foreign media ask questions the authorities will be forced to come up with some answers. Getting them to admit that black jails exist would be a big win for the protesters."

The Uyghurs launched into another slow, impassioned lament.

"Then I guess I have to help." Again Daniel remembered the man with his murdered son and the thud of blows as he was beaten. And his own shame.

"Good." Beidermeyer's gaze did not move. "Because someone will have to code the message. Would you show somebody else what you just showed me?"

No. No way. Far too risky. Especially if they know about Pierre. "Sorry. That isn't why I came to Shanghai. I have to find funding for *The Riding Instructor*. I can't get involved in this. It's just too distracting."

Again Beidermeyer raised a pacifying hand. "I appreciate that. I'll quite understand if you refuse. But I thought coming from a background like yours you'd welcome the chance to fight back. I know your father would have."

Daniel stared at Pierre, who was suddenly busy with the water cooler.

"I don't speak Chinese."

"Everything will be in English. We'll use a woman, so it looks like you're on a date. Go to a karaoke place. A lot of couples do that if they don't have anywhere else to go. There's one in Xintiandi called the Blue Moon. It has private rooms where you won't be disturbed."

It's all been set up. Already. Before he even asked me. He just assumed I'd agree. But surely that wasn't possible. Was he getting paranoid? He gazed around the room, at the photos on the walls, at Pierre pretending to fiddle with the ice maker, at the irises in a flask on the table. And felt his eyes drawn inexorably back to Beidermeyer's.

Your father would have.

Every time he faced a difficult decision he asked himself what the flier's high flier would do. Some men would think this a weakness. Daniel thought it a strength. Why was he unwilling to do what Beidermeyer asked? Because it would take time. Because it would be a distraction. Because he was afraid.

And what had his father taught him about fear? That lesson he prized above all others?

"Alright. I'll do it. But nothing else. How will I know when to go?"

If Beidermeyer was relieved he showed no sign of it. "They'll tell you when they're ready."

"How?" Pierre turned back to face them. "Even if they don't arrest me they'll be listening to the phone. And watching." He glanced toward the window.

"E-mail," Beidermeyer said.

"E-mail is monitored."

"Only when it's sent." Beidermeyer's eyes gleamed, the professor

95

enthralled with the beauty of an idea. "If it never goes anywhere it can't be followed. But others can still read it. If they know the writer's password." He turned to Daniel's laptop and logged onto a web mail site. He typed an address at Shuying's university and entered the letters dZonJze in the Password box. Then he opened the Drafts folder and selected a document. It contained a number of entries arranged like a blog. He scrolled down and came to one in English:

"Three musicians want to perform. They are very good. They have a lot of experience. Others will audition soon."

"That's for me," he said. "She must have posted it just before she was arrested. The drafts folder was her idea. But she won't be able to use it again. They'll infect her computer. Malware. So they can see every keystroke she makes. That's what the government's Golden Shield policy is all about. Tighter control through closer surveillance. You see why SkyeSlip looks like a gift from the gods."

He turned to Daniel. "They'll put a message in the drafts folder saying the ensemble is complete. You post the time of the next rehearsal. Then go to the Blue Moon three hours before that time."

"Sounds simple." Pierre poured himself another glass of water.

"It is. Simple means safe. It's complicated things that go wrong."

"And you'll be watching the drafts folder." Daniel memorized the password, *drunken Zak once nudged Jane zanily earless*.

"Unfortunately not. It's behind a firewall. Can't get to it from outside the country. The Chinese version of the classic technological imperative. If the means exist to control something, control becomes inevitable."

He disconnected the iPod and put it in his pocket, along with a flash drive with a copy of SkyeSlip. The clamor of Shanghai came back. In the street a horn blared, followed by the thud of a collision and the tinkle of glass. Voices cursed and hurled accusations and counter-accusations.

"Don't forget," he said, pointing to the window and cupping a hand behind his ear. He put the petitions in the Gladstone bag and unlocked the door.

"Good luck," he said, and bathed them in his most avuncular beam. Then he was gone.

TWELVE

OUTSIDE THE VORTEX

HE HAD TO TALK to Sophie. To hear her voice. To connect with somebody outside the vortex of brutality that was sucking him in. Not that Sophie was much comfort any more. At first he hadn't realized how deeply he'd hurt her, how badly he'd damaged what held them together. But each time he made a video call she seemed further and further away. She was becoming a stranger. And he'd thought he knew her better than he'd ever known anyone.

She was not naturally cold or distant. Far from it. People turned to her instinctively when they needed help. He'd seen that the night they met, at Tom and Yoshi's party. Tokyo sweltered in the clammy heat of the rainy season. Shortly after midnight a thin, tear-stained girl locked herself in the bathroom. Problem. Not because nobody could use the bathroom--that was just another source of hilarity, like the helium-inflated condoms which rose from the balcony and sped into the clotted Shinjuku sky, dangling discarded thongs. But in it was a little silver box, whose contents were much in demand.

"She still in there?" Tom tapped on the door. No reply. Yoshi appeared at his side, tubby for a Japanese, his head a halo of curls. He put an ear to the door. Tom pushed his way through the room to a slender blonde girl in a black cashmere turtleneck. Daniel had found his gaze drawn to her several times during the evening.

"Sophie, can you talk to her? She's hysterical."

The hubbub quietened. All eyes turned to the bathroom door. Behind it the girl screamed something about heartless motherfuckers.

A Citibank futures analyst with a rolled-up banknote between his fingers said, "Fuck, she's OD'd."

"Call an ambulance," a woman said.

"And say she's coked up to the eyebrows?" Citibank looked around for his coat. "This is Japan, man. They'll lock us up and throw away the key."

There was a murmur of agreement. People moved toward the door. The girl Daniel had come with took his arm. He didn't budge. He wanted to see what Sophie would do.

She put one hand on the door and bowed her head, listening.

"Marcie, it's me, Sophie. Y'all okay in there? Open the door. We just want to help you. Let me in, honey. Please."

That accent.

Marcie sobbed.

"Open it, Marcie. It's alright. You're gonna be okay."

Daniel's companion, about whom he remembered nothing except that she worked for a Japanese PR firm, tugged his arm. "Daniel, come on. If I get caught in a bust they'll fire me." He jerked free. "You go, then."

The girl, startled, stepped back. "Well, screw you! Asshole!" She turned and hurried out of the apartment, out of his life.

Tom said, "It's my place. I'll call the ambulance." But he made no move.

"*Sho ga nai*," Yoshi said in a muffled voice. "It can't be helped."

Sophie tapped on the door again. "Marcie. Please. Open up." She turned, and saw Daniel looking at her. "Scumballs. They got her drunk and took her somewhere to party. One of them made a video. Presto! A star is born."

"You Tube?"

"Porn Hub." She leaned close to the door again. "It's alright, honey. Come out. I'll take care of you. Okay?" More sobbing.

"She's scared shitless the agency will see it and tear up her contract." Tom, tall, gaunt and bottle-blonde, had his arms around Yoshi, whose face was buried in his shoulder. "Japanese clients want their models virginal."

"Marcie, listen to me. Who was it? What were their names?" She frowned and pressed her ear closer to the door. "Kirk? Is that what you're saying? Kirk?"

"Curt. Curtis Blacker." Tom buried his fingers in Yoshi's curls and cradled his head. "Blacker the banker."

"Got his number?" It wasn't just the southern drawl. Her voice seemed to come from deep inside.

Tom disengaged himself and padded over to a bamboo writing desk. From a drawer he took a folder of business cards, riffled through it, then slipped wo out. "Currency trader, Holmbeck Dessages, head office in Geneva."

"Never heard of it." She spoke to the door again. "Marcie, it's going to be okay. Don't worry. Don't be frightened. I'll get him to take it down. Nobody will see."

Daniel went to the desk and tapped on a laptop. "Mid-sized private bank, founded 1896, still run by the same two families."

"Who's top cat?"

"The president is Julius Dessages. Great-grandson of one of the founders."

"E-mail address?"

Daniel shook his head. Sophie studied the card again.

"Tom, let me use your phone." That voice.

She tapped the number with long, pianist's fingers.

"Curtis, hi, this is Sophie Wolf. Friend of Marcie's. You do remember Marcie? Right. That Marcie. Thing is, Curt--you don't mind if I call you Curt? No, I didn't think you would--Marcie has a problem. A predicament. For reasons personal and professional she'd like you to take the video off Porn Hub. Right. That video. Me? No, I don't think I'd be interested in hooking up. For one thing you don't sound like my type. Physically. In German Curt means short. Pretty appropriate, from what Marcie says. And we don't have time if you're leaving. No, I know you don't have any plans. But that's going to change. Why? Because of an e-mail I have in front of me. To j-underscore-dessages-at-holmbeck-underscore-dessages-dot-ch. Just a note. Saying one of his employees has been acting in a way far from befitting such a respectable institution. And a link. Exactly. Got it in one. You will? Thought you might. Right now, okay? Okay. Y'all have yourself sweet dreams, Big Boy. And fuck you too."

She spoke to the door again. "He's taking it down, Marcie. Come out. Please. For me."

There was a click. Sophie turned the handle. Marcie sat slumped against the bathtub, shaking. Her breath came in gasps. Vomit stained her tanktop, which bore a glittery silhouette of Elvis, legs splayed. Sophie pushed back a bracelet of plaited elephant hair and placed two fingers on a wrist no thicker than a broomhandle.

"Fast. About a hundred and twenty." She laid the back of her hand on Marcie's brow. "And she's burning. Got any Tylenol?"

"In the cabinet." Reaching up, Tom brushed against the little silver box and knocked it into the washbasin. It was empty anyway.

Marcie hunched over the toilet, threw up, and sank back against the tub. Sophie stroked her head. "A shower would cool her down." She put her hands on the girl's shoulders. "Marcie. Marcie! You're going to be alright." She shook her gently. Marcie's head lolled. Bubbles of foam appeared at the corners of her mouth. Daniel helped lift her into the tub, startled how little she weighed.

He watched Sophie cross her arms and pull her own sweater over her head. Then she slipped her jeans off and raised each leg to step out of her panties.

She played the water over Marcie's head and face, lifting the wet hair away, letting the spray caress the lobes of her ears, the back of her neck, her shoulders. As she did so, she began to hum, then to sing in a low, tender voice that struck him as infinitely sweet:

Hush little baby don't say a word

Mama's gonna buy you a mocking bird

By the time she got to the dog named Rover Daniel was in love.

He still was.

This time when he called she looked paler. He thought it might just be the video. But it wasn't.

"How are you feeling, Sophie?"

"Well, my husband's gone bust, I'm pregnant, and pretty soon I'm going to be homeless. Other than that I'm on top of the world."

The outburst caught him off balance. A wave of self-loathing surged through him. He was the one who'd done this, shattered her life. Soured her. Looking at his own image in the little square at the bottom of the screen he saw something contemptible. He had no right to expect her to feel sorry for him. Get a grip.

"Don't be bitter, Sophie. It's going to be alright. It'll take a bit of time. But I'll do it. I've got another contact. In San Francisco." Something in him shied away from mentioning Zhou; he felt an instinctive resistance to counting that particular chicken before it hatched.

"What happened with the last one?"

He hesitated. "The chemistry wasn't right."

"Call Sheldrake."

"Sophie, please. I'm doing all I can. I'm going to call San Francisco right after this."

She brought her face closer to the camera. For a moment her expression seemed to soften, as if her old feelings had come to the surface again. Then the anger and the anguish returned.

"So call," she said, and cut the connection.

SHE KNEW SHE WAS hurting him to try and lessen her own pain. Rub his nose in it. Make him feel it too. If they'd been in the same room she would slapped him, punched him, kicked him. But a video link did not allow that visceral satisfaction. Part of what she felt was simple shock. How could she have been with him for five years and never realized he was capable of such stupidity? Such selfishness?

Of course, she'd known from the start there was something poetic about him, something unworldly. If ever she'd met anyone who heard a different drummer it was Daniel. After their third impassioned night in her Ebisu apartment he'd said, "Come on. Get dressed. There's something I want to show you." She thought he meant somewhere nearby: her guess was the metropolitan photography museum. Instead, they took a bullet train to Kyoto and a cab from the station to a garden. They sat on a low wooden platform and gazed at fifteen rocks, set in raked gravel and bounded on three sides by a brindled ochre wall. There was something serene about it that she couldn't put her finger on, much less put into words.

"Not so much a garden as an abstract sculpture," he murmured. "Only it's not abstract. It's representational. Of infinity. And not even a representation. It is infinity. Invisible. Ungraspable. Can you feel it?" And to her surprise—she thought the inventiveness of their love-making must have awakened new parts of her mind as well as her body—she could.

Now, staring at the dead screen, she was sickened. She, too, must have been mad. Blinded by love. How could she have wanted a child with a man so unsuited to being a parent? Daniel was the way he was because of his mother. No doubt about that. His father, the flier's high flier, must have kept at least one foot on the ground or they would never have made him a general. Elizabeth was the one with her head in the clouds, Elizabeth who took off on flights of fancy without a compass and lured little Danny along for the ride.

She wondered if the child inside her would be like that.

Thirteen

YOU'RE NOT THE FIRST

LIKE A ZEN GARDEN, a website is finished when there's nothing left to take away. He'd been repeating that idea ever since he'd heard it, to reporters angling for a quote, at SkyeWare's Monday meetings (back in the palmy days when he still had a company to meet), to people who wanted to work for him.

Whoever designed the Fischer Dreyfuss site thought the same way. It was a minimalist-inflected masterpiece of Times New Roman on a cream background, the upper-case headings pastel-coded by section. Subtle and understated, and all the more effective for it. As well as accounts of past success, it carried a video pitch by Hugo Fischer about the current situation, "a time when the need is greater than ever for bold, innovative ideas that will serve as the springboard for the economic recovery. The kind of ideas that Fischer Dreyfuss continuously seeks out, and turns into gilt-edged opportunities."

The message, like Hugo's tailoring, exuded confidence, competence, class. The offices would be in some heritage gem in the Financial District, a walnut-paneled link to the power and reassurance of old money. Money which would not vanish when a tidal wave of foolish investments went bad. Jeremy Blick handled the media portfolio.

"That's funny," he said. "I was just reading about you. In *Wired*."

Daniel imagined him sipping esspresso with a slice of lemon while he skimmed through past issues in search of possibilities.

"Must have been a pretty old story. The last piece was by Bella Burns. December, if I remember rightly." Which he did.

"No, this was new. In the print edition." Paper shuffled on a desk six thousand miles away. "Here we are. In Random Access. So you haven't seen it?"

"No. I haven't."

"Ah. Well, sorry to cast a pall over your day. It's just a short little thing. Looks like they cobbled it together because the editor wanted to run the photo."

"Photo?"

"Quite striking. Black and white. A piano hanging in the sky, chased by birds."

"What does it say?"

Blick delivered bad news with the aplomb of a pro.

"It's headlined, Golden Boy Hits Bum Note. It says you went bust because of some fantastically ambitious project. Is that true?"

Another humiliation. "You could say that." Jerry Hsieh would see it and realize why he hadn't been paid for six weeks.

"You're not the first. Not the end of the world. Francis Ford Coppola went bankrupt for ninety-eight million dollars after *One From the Heart* and look at him now."

"Exactly. That's why I want to talk to Fischer Dreyfuss."

"Alright. Give me your elevator pitch."

"Entertainment. That's the future. Not hardware. Stories. Making them up and passing them on. Over the web. I have devised software to let people do exactly that. Using the iPad and the cloud. To direct their own movies and distribute them. With Hollywood actors. Selecting scenes to carry the story, cutting them together. Even composing the score. There are multiple revenue streams involved, coming out of the global subculture this medium will lead to. Advertising. Sponsorships. Subscriptions. I have a proof of concept production underway."

"And you are looking for...?"

"First, ten million to finish the proof of concept. It's for a thriller called *The Riding Instructor*. Set among Shanghai's White Russian community in the twenties. I'm here at the moment, working on it."

Blick didn't even pause. "Definitely ambitious. But not for us, I'm afraid. We're not looking high-risk at the moment. Not in this climate. Try again when things get back on an even keel. Unless you find someone before then. Good luck. Goodbye."

HE'D HOPE TO MAKE his return to the scene of his humiliation unobtrusive. He didn't want to be mobbed by petitioners again, still less to attract the attention of the *chengguan*. Given the choice, he'd rather not have gone at all. But he had to get some usable video, and at least the search for it made him feel he wasn't completely wasting his time. He glanced back as he made his way to the lane, expecting to meet eyes that looked quickly away. He didn't. To all appearances, he might as well not have existed. Yet he knew that was not the case. He could feel he was the object of attention. And he knew who was watching. Everyone.

The door of Jin's house was closed. He rapped on the cracked wood. He sensed people nearby, afraid, keeping deathly quiet. It was sinister, this lack of sound. He was aware of two worlds, barely a stone's throw apart but as separate as earth and sky: the world of the apartment dwellers, with their European cars and espresso makers, and the world of Jin and his neighbors, crouched in the gloom as if expecting an air raid.

The stink was worse than ever. He knocked again, harder, and rattled the handle.

"Lilly! Jin! Open the door! Please!"

He peered through the grime-encrusted window. Aware of someone behind him he turned and came face to face with the petitioner who'd written in her own blood. She was nursing the thumb in her clenched fist.

He pointed at the door.

"I need to get in. To see something. Lilly said I should come."

The woman started what he took to be an impassioned harangue, or complaint, or denunciation, waving her bandaged thumb for emphasis. What the hell for? She must know he couldn't understand, yet she wouldn't stop shouting. Tears started to course down the begrimed furrows of her cheeks. Immediately he was ashamed. Afraid of losing her home. He knew what that was like. He put his hands on her shoulders, gently, and turned her toward the door. She didn't resist. Nor did she stop shouting; she just addressed the flaking paintwork instead of Daniel.

The impasse was broken by the arrival of Lilly, bumping over the blackened cobbles on her roller skate. Her grandfather followed on a rusty Flying Pigeon, wicker basket on the front coming apart where it rubbed against the mudguard. In it was a battered, box-like camcorder that looked as old as the bicycle.

Jin ushered him into the reeking murk and closed the door, leaving the woman with the bandaged thumb to sob in the lane. The dam was leaking and the shit and sewage had seeped into the room and formed a tear-shaped puddle. How could they watch anything without a monitor? There wasn't even electricity. They evidently cooked over an open fire: charred sticks lay in a semicircle of bricks, on top of which was a jagged square of wire mesh. Rice congealed in a tin bowl. Could they really be living like this?

"Grandfather has brought you the video." Lilly proffered the camera. It wasn't a make he recognized and he wasn't sure how to work it. Jin grabbed it, pressed a couple of buttons and thrust the display close to his face.

Whoever shot it had been up on the roof, looking down as an orange digger jolted over smashed bricks, beams, bits of broken pipe. The debris was all that remained of whatever had once stood on the other side of the lane. The digger stopped and the videographer jerked around to show a battle in progress. Figures in blue with the English word Police on their backs and men in military fatigues were dragging protesters out of the house below. A man in a jacket with the sleeve half-ripped off was shoved into the lane and thrown onto the rubble. He rolled over, then didn't move. There was another flurry of activity and a cluster of police officers appeared, dragging out a screaming man in a white shirt. The shirt was stained red with the blood dripping from his face. Just as an old woman came stumbling toward him the video ended.

He wanted to help. The events of last time had created a bond. But what he could do? Even if such an old tape could be digitized SkyeSlip wasn't powerful enough to hide it.

"I'm sorry. This isn't what I want. I need video of how the lanes used to look. Not this."

Lilly conferred with her grandfather. The old man started shouting. Of course. He'd do the same, stuck in a rotting house with a pool of shit, waiting for the thugs to come back with their baseball bats. But when Jin took the tape from the camera and tried to thrust it into his hand he pushed it away.

"No! I don't want it. It's no use to me." He turned to leave. Jin beat him to it, placing himself in front of the door.

"Take it." For a young girl there was something very insistent in Lilly's voice. Was she going straight from adolescence to becoming an embittered old woman? Perhaps it was just the Shanghai way of speech, always aggressive, always demanding. "People have to know what is happening. So we get money for a new place."

He could walk away. She and Jin could not. They had to cook on a fire and live with the stink of shit and the constant threat of the *chengguan* and the man in Raybans kicking down the door. He had to do something.

"Look. I can't help you myself. But I can put you in touch with people who can. Give me your address. I'll see it gets passed to the foreign reporters. Someone will contact you."

She said something to Jin. The old man's lemon face froze in a rictus of despair. She turned to Daniel. "Give me paper."

There was none in the house. Nor did he have any himself. The only thing to write on was the Notes app on his iPhone. He opened a new note and called up the tiny keyboard. Lilly put the phone on her palm and squinted in concentration as she touched each letter with a grubby thumb. Jin looked on with distrust and incomprehension.

She hesitated to give the phone back. How she must long to leave this decaying, lightless tenement with its cooking fire and take her place in the shiny new world of clever devices she kept glimpsing through the cracked lens of her spectacles.

The stench and the gloom and the low ceiling made him claustrophobic. He moved to the door. "I have to go," he said. "A reporter will come in a few days. Good luck."

The watched in silence as he fumbled with the bolt and stepped outside. The woman with the bandaged thumb had disappeared. Without looking back he hurried to the archway and made his escape.

SINCE JIN'S MATERIAL was useless he still had to replace the footage destroyed by the *chengguan*. Pierre had lent him a point-and-shoot camera that took high-definition video and he set out to retrace his steps. He remembered the street from last time: on the corner a store sold boxes and crates and old wooden trunks bound with rope. They were piled around a chipped mahogany desk that might once have graced a lawyer's office on the Bund. The duck seller still had plucked birds hanging from hooks on a pole and his nose buried in a book. And he recognized the market made out of polystyrene boxes: sheltered by brightly-colored umbrellas. they lined the street and held yams, snow-pea shoots, taro potatoes, *bok choy*, *mo qua*, other vegetables he'd never seen.

Behind the bitter melons and jumbles of malodorous cartons were the kind of places he wanted to shoot. Again he was struck by how different they were from the gleaming towers. The houses, too, must have been planned. But the original order had been overwhelmed by decades of poverty and decay and the improvisations those things led to. Sheets of rusting corrugated iron patched leaky tiled roofs. Bamboo poles bound with twine braced sagging balconies. And from every horizontal projection--from rods, ropes strung between drainpipes, pegged to railings and spread over chairs--hung washing.

Posters had been left for time and weather to imprint on the walls so their messages lingered on, faint as whispers from the grave. This had once been an area of brothels and opium dens. He needed clips that users of *The Riding Instructor* could put together as they followed Nikolai through these streets and alleys in the search for his missing brother. He shot roofs and balconies and half-open doors, avoiding anything that would not have been found in the 1920s. Men in plastic chairs pored over newspapers while a fat woman in shorts scrubbed the back of a shrieking child in a tub. Nobody looked up as he passed. But he felt them watching.

At the end of a lane whose gateway had been half-demolished the new city encroached in the form of a construction site, a crater the size of a football field and twenty feet deep. Workers manhandled T-bars that dangled from cranes as delicate as dragonflies. Acetylene torches threw out bursts of golden sparks and the air was full of hammering as carpenters knocked together forms for the concrete.

On a pillar of earth in the far corner stood a solitary house. There was something surreal in the way it perched on its muddy stalagmite above the din and bustle. He switched the camera to still mode and zoomed out to give a sense of its surroundings. The image he captured was not very dramatic. But he knew enough about photography to see its potential, this lone dwelling that rose so obstinately out of its flattened surroundings. Pierre had the skill and the gear to do it justice. He could make an eloquent picture, perhaps even eloquent enough for the cover of the new book. Lonely and precarious, the house spoke of stubborn perseverance, of the occupant's insistence on going his own way, of following his own dream regardless of the consequences. He hadn't expected to see that in China. Someone after his own heart.

As HE TURNED AWAY he came face to face with a woman who stood watching him. The fancy wrap-around Italian sunglasses struck an oddly discordant note with her office-worker's nondescript skirt and jacket.

"I am friend of Lilly." She proffered a hand with scarlet-painted nails but didn't give her name. "She told me. I show you where to get video."

He looked around for the male companions who would jump him at the first opportunity. Nobody obvious. But that didn't mean much. How would he tell?

"Video?"

"Lilly told me. You want video of old houses. I help you."

"I see. Where?"

"Over there." She gestured vaguely at the other side of the construction site. "You come." She tugged at his arm. He let her lead him toward the road.

"Did Lilly say why I wanted it?"

"To put on small computer. iPad."

He frowned. "Is that right. To put on small computer." He thought for a moment. "Would you like to see it?"

She nodded and darted a glance over her shoulder.

"Well, I wish I could show you. But you know what happened? Some people tried to steal it. In the park. A woman grabbed it. Can you believe that?"

He felt her stare at him from behind the sunglasses.

"I managed to catch her. But there was a struggle and she dropped it. On the pathway. Know what that means?" He drew a finger across his throat. "One dead iPad. Right now it's on its way to the Foxconn plant in Chengdu, courtesy of the China Post courier service."

She stopped. "Dead?"

"Screen's cracked. And the power button doesn't work. Doesn't look good. Probably have to get another one." He smiled the most insincere smile he could manage.

For a long moment she looked at him from behind the Bulgari knock-offs, processing the information, wondering what to do. Then she cursed, span on her heel, and hurried away back toward the mud and din of the construction site and the unseen figures he had no doubt had been following them.

Fourteen

EGG SOUP WITH SPEARMINT

MONICA TREBONE was still out of town. He hesitated about leaving a third message. Desperation had a smell, like fear, and people reacted accordingly. He'd already said everything he had to say. Yet he couldn't just cut the line. He had to feel he was doing something.

"Monica, Daniel Skye again, Fiona's friend. Looking forward to meeting you when you get back. *Ciao*."

Scalding milk screamed in the espresso machine as Pierre fixed *café latté*.

"If Zhou really is interested how long is he likely to take getting back to me?"

"Things move fast in Shanghai." Pierre handed him a bowl, specks of nutmeg dotting the froth. "Faster than Tokyo. Don't have all those endless meetings. It's more openly autocratic. People like to be seen making far-reaching decisions."

The wail of sirens cut through the morning air. Coming along Hengshan Road. He could feel Pierre follow them in his mind's eye, past La Boheme and the tea shop with racks of comic books and the store packed with fake Disney memorabilia. If they were coming to the apartment they would turn when they reached the park, where mothers pushed baby carriages through the fallen leaves, and the racket of the sirens would bounce off the walls as they pulled into the narrow lane. But they sped on in the direction of the cathedral, and the sound faded into the city's non-stop growl.

"Jesus," Pierre said. There had been no word from Beidermeyer and no new message in the drafts folder to say the list was ready. "I'll go mad if I just hang around."

Daniel cupped a hand around his ear and pointed toward the window. Pierre nodded. He tore off a piece of croissant, buttered it, and dipped a spoon in the apricot jam.

Daniel spread a modern street map next to his old one. "Dongdaming Lu used to be called Broadway. Ran along the north bank of the river. Had a bunch of whorehouses for the sailors." He traced another road northward with his fingertip, then stopped. "The house I saw is somewhere around here. Liyang Lu. Which used to be Dixwell Road."

"That one of the hot spots?" Pierre brushed croissant crumbs from his lips.

"Opium den. Nikolai goes there to find a sax player who was at the Green Falcon the night Petya disappeared."

"Too bad there's nothing left."

"Nothing material. But maybe the owner has some old photos. Want to come and translate?"

THE NAIL had been hammered in from under the chin, passing through the windpipe and coming out at the top of the head. Blood from the mouth, sprayed across the door by the last tortured pumping of the heart, was congealing on the warped panels of the door in three scarlet streams. The front paws were curled and the tongue lolled out. The cat's body stiffened in the autumn sun. All that remained was to take it down and throw it on a garbage dump.

"Oh, God." Daniel peered over Pierre's shoulder at the blown-up image on the camera's LCD screen. "They don't play around, do they?" Again, he felt a surge of admiration for the occupant.

They could see a ladder propped against the house, long enough to reach the ground. Others were scattered around the rim of the crater, descending from the street into the claggy red mud.

"Let's take it nice and easy." Pierre meandered over toward the nearest ladder. "Situations like this, don't hide it, flaunt it. Don't get in a pissing match with a skunk. Just play dumb and grin and keep shooting. Make a show of it. Nine times out of ten they'll think you're an idiot and leave you alone."

"What about the tenth time?"

But Pierre had already disappeared below the lip of the crater. By the time Daniel reached the bottom a man in mud-spattered jeans and a grubby singlet was waving his arms and shouting. Pierre strode forward, took one of his calloused hands in both of his own and shook it enthusiastically. "I'm gonna to pretend I can't understand a word you say," he said in English, grinning broadly and clapping an arm around the man's shoulders. "Won't that be fun?" He gave him a squeeze and burst into peals of laughter. The man looked confused. Pierre said something in French and nudged him slyly in the ribs, as if he'd just told a dirty joke.

Two other workmen come over, one with a rivet gun, one with a pickaxe. Pierre grinned and bounded forward. "Delighted to meet you! You must be my new best friends! And I'm a famous photographer!" He waved the Nikon in their faces, as if by some chance they hadn't noticed it. He grew serious. Stepping back, he scrutinized them first from one side, then the other. He adjusted the grip of the pickaxe wielder so he appeared to be brandishing it like a rifle. "*Parfait! Ne bougez pas! Non, non, non!*" He wagged a finger in mock disapproval, and grinned again, letting him in on the joke. The rivet gunner he gripped by the shoulders and moved back and forward like a tailor's dummy. When he was satisfied by the pose, two worker-heroes striving to build a glorious tomorrow, he dropped into a crouch. He shot from below, from the left and from the right. Then he sprang up and shot from above, holding the camera over his head.

Stepping close, he played the images back. The man with the rivet gun stared at the screen in slack-jawed wonder. Pierre clapped him on the back. "Thank you! It's been a pleasure! *Au revoir!*" And with a cheery wave he was gone, loping across the mud in the direction of the house. The pickaxe wielder, whose knobby cheekbones stuck out from his haggard face, hawked and spat.

Daniel remembered how the *chengguan* had appeared in Jin's place and expected to be attacked at any moment. This time he would fight back. Bottle? Piece of pipe? Length of two by four? He looked around All he could see was a large bolt, orange with rust. He picked it up and took grim pleasure in its weight.

It wasn't just the property developer the owner was defying; it was also gravity. The sides had been cut with surgical precision, and there was no extra width at the base to add support. What kept the column of earth from just crumbling away?

"Nail house," Pierre said, and Daniel remembered the Japanese saying: the nail that sticks up gets hammered down.

Pierre cupped his hands and called out. The door swung open and a dumpy figure peered down through black-rimmed glasses. He took hold of the ladder, went to the edge of the column of earth, and let it down. It was made of two bamboo poles, rungs lashed between them with baler twine. When Daniel and Pierre reached the top Fugen Pan extended a hand, then pulled the ladder back up. He stood stiffly beside the door, the sun glowing on his face, and spoke in a strained voice. Pierre translated. "Mimi. His daughter's cat. This morning. The *chengguan* got a ladder and climbed up and caught her. He didn't dare go out when he heard them."

Pan pulled the nail out with pliers and Pierre got close-ups of his hands, smeared with blood as he laid the cat in a hole he'd dug in what was left of the ground and covered it with dirt.

"They are stealing his land." Pan smiled as Pierre translated, and Daniel thought if he were a photographer he would do a series about the way Asians smile in times of trouble. "Of course, they denied it. But a friend of his is a surveyor. He made measurements with a theodolite."

Pan led them inside to a dark room that smelled of kerosene. He reached into a lopsided set of drawers and drew out a roll of paper, bound with red ribbon. He spread it on the table and Daniel held down one end. "He says the lot is ten-point-two meters by seven-point-five meters." Pan pointed to the figures with a grime-encrusted finger. "His friend found the area at the bottom measures only ten meters by seven-point-one meters. They have stolen five and a half square meters."

Pan went on in the same quiet voice. At one point he turned and gestured toward the west. "Everybody else took the offer of a new home, way out in the boonies. But he wants money. If the developer pays up others will want money too. So he's using intimidation. The first thing he did was cut off the electricity."

Pan's mother shuffled over from her seat by the stove, a sawn-off oil drum in which a few sticks crackled fitfully. Her hair was like cotton wool and her eyes little more than slits in the wrinkles of a forgotten apple. She held out a palsied hand, silvery and dry as the discarded skin of a snake, and mumbled a welcome. When she greeted Daniel she squinted up at his face.

"She says the dark patches under your eyes mean something's out of balance. Maybe your liver. Do you have headaches?"

"Yes. A big one."

She peered closer, then turned and disappeared through a door in the corner.

Pan was a retired math teacher. His wife had died in a train crash thirteen years ago. The other member of the household, their daughter Jinglu, was also a teacher. But Jinglu was on the point of leaving. "She's scared to go to work. As soon as she climbs down the ladder they start shouting she's a trespasser. Every morning. And when she goes to the store they jostle her and make her drop things."

By the light of a candle Pierre shot Pan sitting on a plastic chair holding a photograph in a black frame. It showed him as a young man in a short-sleeved white shirt, and his wife, and Jinglu, solemn and pig-tailed. The three of them were in front of the house. Other houses stood on either side, where now there was only a crater of red mud.

"Does he have any other old photos? Of how the neighborhood used to look?"

"A few. His grandfather bought this place when it was built, in the 1920s. Dixwell Road was lined with houses for Westerners. Big houses. Right behind them were the lanes, where the Chinese lived, along a creek. Foreigners and Chinese didn't usually live so close."

"Any Russians?"

Pan shook his head.

"Not living here. But when he was a kid a Russian water seller used to come around. One *fen* a cup. He carried it in pigs' bladders on a pole across his shoulders."

Selling water. That could be part of the Week in the Life game. All it needed was physical strength and some customers. Everybody had to drink. Its very simplicity would make it a competitive business. And competition was always cutthroat.

Pan reached into the bottom drawer and rummaged through the contents. One by one he unearthed half a dozen dog-eared black and white prints. Most were family snapshots. They gave little sense of place beyond a white-painted wall, some brickwork and an archway. But one was unlike anything Daniel had seen before. It could almost be a backstreet in Venice. Two buildings faced each other across a narrow body of water. They were connected by small bridges. But the water looked more like an open drain than a canal. And it wasn't straight. The buildings followed its curve, sprouting galleries and passageways and staircases along the way. The photo seemed to confound the viewer's expectations, like an Escher drawing. Jerry Hsieh would love it.

"Can I borrow this? To scan into the computer?"

There was a hiss as Pan sucked in a breath, and Daniel knew what the answer would be before Pierre spoke.

"That's his grandmother, looking down from the balcony. This is the only picture he has."

The old woman came back, carrying a fragrantly steaming bowl.

"Egg soup with spearmint. For your headache."

He blew softly on the soup to cool it. When he took a cautious sip he found it watery but not unpleasant.

Pan was gazing at the photograph. His mother said something, Pan replied, she said something else.

"She's telling him to remember all the people who help them. They bring food, make videos. She says people should always help each other."

Pan gave Daniel the picture.

"Thank you. I appreciate it very much. I'll bring it back in a couple of days."

As they climbed down the ladder he could smell the earth, a pungent, primeval odor with something metallic about it. He wondered how long the cat would lie undisturbed before diggers brought down the column.

"He's not in a good position," Pierre said as they walked to the subway. "He'd be safer if the court ordered him to leave. At least he'd get some compensation. That's what happened to Shuying's father. Eventually."

"Her father? Have you met him?"

"You could say that." He fell silent.

Don't press him.

After a minute Pierre said, "Lived in a lane off Nanking Road. Lots of money to be made redeveloping that area. He didn't want to move. I happened to be walking past when they were trying to change his mind. I knew it went on, of course. But this was the first time I'd seen it. Usual thing. *Chengguan.* Five of them. They used baseball bats. And they had towels wrapped round their faces. Which I guess was why they didn't stop me taking pictures while they smashed his legs. *Pour décourager les autres.*"

They passed a straggle of people reading a newspaper that had been posted along a wall.

"When the party ended somebody must have followed me home. Because the next day Shuying turned up at my door. She wanted to know what I was going to do with the pictures. I said I'd sent them to the States. She asked how, and I showed her the satellite gizmo. The rest is history."

They reached the subway station. Pierre halted.

"Her father's in a wheelchair now. She's never asked why I didn't try to stop them. Never mentioned it. That's the elephant in the room. I don't know whether she thinks I'm a coward or just inhuman. Actually, I don't know whether I'm a coward or just inhuman. It makes me more ashamed each time I think about it." His eyes met Daniel's. "That's why I didn't want to tell you. Guilt."

"Journalistic dispassion."

"You could say that. But I still have nightmares about it."

Daniel moved to the entrance. Pierre, as was his habit, glanced around to see if there was a decisive moment in the making. "Jesus."

Daniel looked back and saw a man in a Yankees cap. He was lighting the cigarette of his crop-headed companion. But he was looking at Pierre.

"The park." Daniel remembered the *baiju*, passing from hand to hand. "He was in one of the boats."

"Fuck. He was in the gallery, too. Came in after me."

"Cops?"

"Can't tell. Shanghai's finest come in all shapes and sizes. But they look more like thugs to me."

The man slipped the lighter back in his pocket. He raised both hands and began to mimic a man nailing something in place with a hammer. Then he let his eyes roll and his mouth fall open and his tongue loll out. "*Nyao ... nyao ... nyaooo ... nyaoAOOOaoo.*"

His companion stopped grinning when Pierre raised the camera and kept his finger on the button, breaking the flow of events into shards. Yankees fan closing his mouth. Lifting his head. Scowling. Shaking a fist. Turning. Looking back over his shoulder. Shouting an obscenity. Vanishing into the crowd.

"Thought so." Pierre studied the display, flicking through the images. "Cops don't back off."

"So why are they interested in you?"

"They know I shot Shuying's father getting beaten up. I guess they want to see what I do next. And stop me if necessary. But who knows? It's Chinatown, Daniel. It really is."

FIFTEEN

MEETING TOMORROW

"SWEETHEART, I'M SENDING YOU THIS so you don't forget me and start chasing Chinese girls. Every morning when I wake up I look at the ocean and think of you, on the other side of it. Don't stay away too long. Your loving wife, S."

Beidermeyer had sent the e-mail and its attached picture of Sophie from an address in her name. Pierre must have mentioned her, probably when he mentioned SkyeSlip. And his father. Gabby, gabby, gabby. And Beidermeyer would have beamed and nodded and filed the information away in his memory for possible future use. When had he last written a love note, this elderly professor masquerading as Sophie? For all the twinkling and the joviality, Daniel sensed a loneliness in Beidermeyer, an old spook haunted by memories too terrible to share. Another ethnomusicologist. One hand washes the other. Was he the one who'd told Pierre about the *goze*, the blind leading the blind across that snowy landscape into oblivion?

The photo was his screensaver. He must have left it on the flash drive with SkyeSlip. He'd taken it himself, one blowy April day of high billowing clouds and nodding daffodils. It was in black and white and showed Sophie on the beach, near the house. She was meandering barefoot along the shoreline while the ocean bowled whitecaps that exploded on rocks strewn with bladderwrack and bleached spars, the domain of seals and sea eagles. The wind was tossing her hair around and she held it out of her eyes with one hand. They'd made love earlier, and the picture captured something of her languorous satisfaction. Looking at it, he smelled her scent again, felt how lithe and slender she was, heard her teasing southern drawl grow urgent.

He massaged his temples with his thumbs. The egg soup with spearmint had worn off. When he opened the photograph in SkyeSlip the message appeared immediately.

Testing, testing. Got Lilly's address. These are journalists who are interested in case Pierre changes his mind or you have other need of them. Shuying's people will send the contacts list to me and I'll pass it on. They should act soon. Time is getting short. BB

Then came a list of news organizations and reporters, with phone numbers and e-mail addresses. Some he knew, the result of his own pursuit of media attention. *Esse est percipi*--to be is to be seen. At one time he'd set his computers to flash that message at random as a reminder. That's what he'd told *Wired,* anyway. And to stay in the public eye he'd seized any chance to talk to reporters. Steve Holm, a great bear of a man with a mid-western drone as flat as an Iowa cornfield, had interviewed him for a *Seattle Weekly* piece about storytelling in the digital age. Karla Meikle had written about SkyeWare for the *Baltimore Sun.* And Jeff Ziegler had done a profile for *Zeitgeist* before he joined CBS as a producer.

Which was all well and good. But it didn't bring him a hair closer to finding money for *The Riding Instructor.* If he didn't hear from Zhou by the end of the day he would call.

Pierre came back from a meeting with the editor of a travel magazine and put on *Bitches Brew.* "Anything in the drafts folder?" Daniel checked again. And saw a new message: "Ensemble is ready." His belly tightened.

Pierre looked over his shoulder. "Better do it tonight. The conference starts in a few days."

"Right. Beidermeyer's getting antsy. Night's better anyway. We'll be less conspicuous. Who goes to karaoke in the daytime?"

"Bored housewives." Pierre glanced at his watch. "Three-forty. Set it up for seven o'clock. Which means posting it as ten. Remember how to get there?"

"Cab to the Yuyuan bazaar, shake off any pursuers in the crowd, another cab to Huaihai park, then east two blocks and take the first street on the left." Daniel paused. "Just one problem." He laughed, to cover his shame. "I don't have much money."

"Don't worry about that." Pierre took a sheaf of bills from his wallet, peeled off a few for himself, and handed over the rest. "Consider it an investment in *The Riding Instructor*."

Daniel wrote "Rehearsal at ten this evening" in the drafts folder.

"Don't hit send!" Pierre's warning stopped him just in time. After a moment's horror he smiled. Faintly.

When Miles paused between tracks they heard the Rottweiler in the apartment below scratch at the door and howl. A flight of helicopters clattered overhead, slicing through the afternoon as it headed toward the river. Pierre looked in the refrigerator, then reached for his jacket. "Need anything from the store? Razor blades? Shampoo? Inflatable woman?" Daniel shook his head.

He turned the music off. He was alone with the picture again. Sophie Wolf. The name suited her, with those watchful grey eyes. A loner, for all her willingness to help. Wayne's restlessness meant that as a child in a world prone to sudden change she'd been wary of close friendships. What was the point, when they were always cut short?

He, too, was wondering what their child would be like when the house phone rang. Remembering what Pierre had said, he let it go to the answering machine.

"Message for Daniel Skye," a voice said without identifying itself. "Tomorrow at two. My office."

He bounded across the room and grabbed the phone.

"Hello, Renwen. Good to hear from you. I knew you'd be interested. Tomorrow, then. That's great. Looking forward to it."

Zhou grunted. "Nan Tower 1, seventy-second floor." Then he hung up.

How many times had he pitched *The Riding Instructor*? Despite the rejections he knew it was the best idea he'd ever had. Now the passion flared up again. He would convince Zhou and Zhou would convince Wenming Nan. He'd would make *The Riding Instructor*, and *The Riding Instructor* would solve his money problems once and for all. And earn him a place in history.

He was bent over the script, polishing it yet again, when Pierre came back and set a green canvas shopping bag on the counter. He went to his MacBook and opened iTunes again. "They were out of inflatable women so I got sauce instead. Nothing like booze for calming the butterflies." He held up another bottle of Johnnie Walker and offered Daniel a tumbler.

This time he didn't say no, even though Pierre's whiskey had unwelcome connotations. "Whoa! That's enough. Any ice? Zhou called. We're meeting tomorrow."

Pierre grinned and touched his glass against Daniel's.

"Looks like you're on your way."

"I sure hope so."

Pierre put an oval of Caprice des Dieux on a cheese dish. A multigrain loaf went in a wooden bin, eggs, milk and mushrooms into the refrigerator, as did yogurt and half a dozen pears. Then he went back to the computer. "Better see if there's a response. Shooters always think ahead. Have to. Even if it's only to the next moment. Especially to the next moment. Will that cloud cover the sun? Will the president notice that banana skin?" He opened the drafts folder.

"Change of plan." Daniel looked up. "Seems the woman can't make it tonight. No indication why."

"What do they want to do?" But he knew the answer even as he asked.

"Rehearsal postponed until tomorrow. Five o'clock. That's two."

He raised his glass, but stopped when he saw Daniel's face.

"Oh, no."

Daniel nodded.

"*Merde.*"

"I'll have to reschedule."

"Zhou?"

"No. Not Zhou. I said I'd help. But I won't piss off a potential investor. Finding money for *The Riding Instructor* is why I'm here. That's the priority."

"And screw the protesters."

"Yes. Screw the protesters. Don't you realize? My life is at stake here. Sophie is freaking out. And she's pregnant. I don't have any fucking choice."

"Okay. Keep your pants on. I understand." Pierre turned back to the laptop. "Earlier or later?"

"Later's better. Not even bored housewives go to karaoke in the morning."

"But later means less time before the conference. Less wiggle room if things go wrong."

"Twelve o'clock, then. Shouldn't take more than half an hour at the most. That gives me ninety minutes to get to Zhou. He's in Pudong. Is that enough?"

"More than enough. Takes far less than that." Beneath the most recent message Pierre wrote, "Rehearsal at three p.m. tomorrow."

Sketches of Spain shimmered on the air, a heat haze in sound. The smell of garlic filled the apartment as he tossed mushrooms in an iron skillet, then whisked up six eggs and poured them sizzling into the pan. Night had fallen. One of the halogen spots that left the room in pools of shadow shone directly down on the flask of purple irises on the table. He slid the omelettes onto square black plates and they ate without speaking while Miles's trumpet drew *sumi-e* depictions of a parched and dusty landscape.

"Shouldn't take long to respond." Pierre took the dirty tableware to the sink. "They must keep the folder open all the time."

Daniel checked. "Nothing yet."

He opened *The Riding Instructor* again. Every time he thought he'd finished a new idea would come to him, a new fork in the path. He remembered what Olga Derieva had said about her mother arriving in Shanghai with six gold roubles sewn in her underwear. Petya could have been killed because he discovered a plot to steal gold. A White Russian general had smuggled it into the city to fund a new offensive against the Bolsheviks.

"It's on." Pierre pointed to a new message. "Rehearsal confirmed."

Daniel's stomach tightened again.

There was a flash. Pierre lowered the camera. "Candid portrait. Some people touch a crucifix. You touch your watch."

Daniel pulled back his sleeve. The watch was plain, with luminous green hands and numerals on a black face and a webbing strap.

"My father's. He was wearing it when he was shot down. Said it brought him luck. Never took it off. One day it stopped. My mother took it in to get it fixed. That night he was killed in a helicopter crash."

He turned back to the map. The Yu Yuan garden, where Orlovski's uncle had bet his life and lost, was in the oldest part of the city. That's where Nikolai would learn about the theft of the gold. Another juicy project for Jerry Hsieh. If he was still willing to work without pay.

Sixteen

YOU WANT GUCCI?

HE PAID THE DRIVER of the second cab and glanced back, half-expecting to see a Yankees cap. As far as he could tell he wasn't being followed. But that didn't mean much. The sidewalk was as crowded as the road and beside the park the lunchtime traffic was gridlocked. Even the cyclists had come to a halt, unable to find room between the cars. Not that they didn't keep trying. The driver of a glossy black Honda leaned out of his window and hurled abuse at a woman on a Flying Pigeon whose pedal had gouged his paintwork. The offender stared ahead impassively. The driver kept one fist on the horn and continued his tirade, to the indifference of the cyclist and everybody else.

Daniel turned onto the street. Two glossy women stood in the middle of the sidewalk, shouting into cell phones. Why did Shanghainese conversations always sound so violent? A third woman, leg bent, rummaged in the Louis Vuitton bag at her hip. Above her head a neon sign showed a man's face coming out of a crescent moon. Two minutes to twelve. He felt the eyes of the women on him as he went inside.

He found himself in a red-lit cavern with tables around the walls. At one end was a stage with three microphone stands and a large screen on which a mascara'd man with his head shaved in the shape of a lightning bolt snarled and gyrated. The tables were mostly empty, but a scattering of women in twos and threes sipped martinis and bobbed their heads to the pounding beat.

Y-M-C-A, it's fun to stay at the Y-M-C-A...

Above the bar was a blow-up of a woman's face, head thrown back, beneath the word EX-TA-SEA.

"Beer," he said, mouthing the word and pointing to the display beneath the array of spirit bottles. The tank-topped barman, snake-hipped, didn't seem to take any notice. After making Daniel wait almost to the point where he asked again he gyrated over to the case, picked out a bottle of Budweiser and sashayed back.

"You want Gucci?"

"What?"

"Gucci." Without taking his eyes off Daniel's he reached under the counter and pulled out a cardboard carton. He dipped a hand inside and pulled out a watch on a red wristband. He dangled it in front of Daniel as if trying to hypnotize him.

"No thanks."

"You like Rolex."

"I don't want a watch."

"What you looking for? You want Blackberry? Nokia?"

"No."

He made his way to a table in the corner and looked around. A bored-looking girl in a black and white hooped top rested her chin on her hand and jabbed a cocktail stick into her glass not quite in time to the beat. Not her.

Seven minutes past twelve. The women from the street came in. The one who'd been looking in her bag smiled. He shook his head and felt scorn and contempt as she turned her back. He took out his laptop and tried to concentrate on a paper he'd downloaded about structural problems in writing open-ended fiction. By 12.20 he'd finished the beer. When the barman whipped the glass away with polished insolence he felt compelled to order another. Like standing alone on a spotlit stage. The rescheduling must have caused a problem. If nobody came by 12.40 he'd leave.

At 12.37 a woman entered. She was bundled in a nondescript nylon jacket and wore no make-up. Her hair, streaked with grey, could have been cropped by an army barber. Without looking at Daniel she spoke to the barman, who gestured toward the back of the room. She counted out some coins and he gave her a counter with a number on it. She said something else and he took a can of lemon tea from the cooler and slid it contemptuously across the counter. She turned and walked away, disappearing behind the stage. The Louis Vuitton woman watched, then said something that made the other two laugh.

A minute later he picked up the laptop bag and sauntered across the room as if going to the washroom. He felt the barman watch.

She was waiting at the end of a narrow corridor lined with doors. He held out his hand, but didn't introduce himself. Not that she or anyone else would have heard.

Y-M-C-A, you know you'll find it at the ...

The woman's own hand was dry and rough and cold from the can of tea. She held it out awkwardly, not used to shaking hands. Her eyes searched his face for a moment, then looked away.

The corridor was empty except for a chair at the end. Each door had a small window, like the observation slit of a cell. One of the doors swung open and a man and a girl lurched out. The man was singing and the girl, pencil-thin and shoe-horned into skintight jeans, had an arm hooked around his neck. When she saw Daniel and the woman she stared at them with eyes that had trouble focusing. The man threw his head back and yowled, but couldn't reach the note he was straining for. The girl dissolved into giggles and they stumbled toward the exit, trailing *baiju* fumes like vapor from a jet.

Lights above the lintels showed most of the rooms were empty. The woman looked from door to door, then opened number thirteen. The thumping of the music died away. A white leather couch flanked a low table, opposite two matching chairs. On the table was a plastic binder holding song lyrics and a heavy glass ashtray. Beside it lay a microphone, and on the wall was an LCD monitor.

The woman perched on the edge of a chair. Under the nylon jacket she wore a pale green dress with a rose picked out in dark sequins. Some of the sequins were missing, and loops of black thread dangled down. It was a size too small and flattened whatever shape her breasts might have had. She must have borrowed it so she could dress the way she thought women dressed for an afternoon assignation.

A small blind covered the window. But there was no way to lock the door. It opened outward, so there was no point pushing one of the chairs against it. Following his gaze the woman said,

"Nobody will come. We have one hour." He had not expected her to speak so clearly.

He said, "We should play some music anyway, just in case someone blunders in." He picked up the songbook. Most of the titles were Chinese. At the top of the third page, though, was *Hotel California*. He punched in the number and turned down the volume as the screen came to life.

She watched him take out the computer. When he moved closer he sensed her stiffen. Because he was a foreigner or because he was a man? Both, probably. She must know why couples used private rooms. How old was she? Forty? Japanese women looked younger than Westerners. Chinese women might well be the opposite, given their tougher lives. The fact that she spoke English and presumably knew something about computers meant she was educated. But she was not slick or sophisticated. A schoolteacher, perhaps.

He'd put SkyeSlip on a flash drive which he now plugged into the laptop. Then he opened Beidermeyer's message and the photo of Sophie. How strange to see it in these circumstances. He turned the computer around so the woman did not have to lean toward him.

"There's a message hidden in the photo," he said. She nodded and stared at the picture as if she could make it appear simply by an act of single-minded concentration.

"The first thing is to open SkyeSlip. It's on the flash drive. You need to set up a password. Only you will know it."

"English word?"

"Or Chinese. But it has to be in the Roman alphabet."

He looked away while she tapped the keys. "If you use a different word SkyeSlip will destroy itself and vanish. For ever. Same thing if you open a photo which doesn't have a message. So if you ever need to get rid of it ..."

He left the sentence unfinished. The woman said nothing.

He showed her how to uncover a message. "You try. In this picture are the names of some of the journalists who are coming. You won't need them. Just for practice."

As she reached for the keyboard he saw she was wearing a ring, a band of gold that cut into the flesh beneath the swollen joint of her second finger. She typed swiftly, keys pattering as she repeated without hesitation or mistakes what he'd just done. When the list appeared she furrowed her brow and leaned closer. Memorizing it. Not photographically at a glimpse, but methodically, imprinting it onto her memory by act of will.

"Hiding something is just as easy." He opened a photograph Pierre had taken on Moganshan Road, of a young man in jeans and a muffler with a bag slung over his shoulder. He showed her how SkyeSlip found empty spaces in the coding. Then he hid the journalists' names again. "Like pouring water from a kettle."

She leaned forward and watched intently. She was wearing heavy, flesh-colored stockings of the kind he associated with old women. Again, he sensed her committing the keystrokes and menu selections to memory. He knew that learning Chinese characters developed the power of memorization like a muscle and lead to sharper visual awareness. Perhaps that was her secret. Once more, she repeated perfectly what he had just done. He got her to hide another message, starting from scratch with a paragraph about open-source editing software from *Wired* and a picture of the old Shanghai racecourse. She did it without hesitating and without making a mistake.

"You're very good. Do you have any questions?"

"No. Thank you." He handed her the drive, which she slipped into her jacket pocket. She said, "Wait fifteen minutes."

He looked at his watch. Twelve minutes past one.

"I can't do that. I have another appointment. It's important."

"Fifteen minutes. For safety. Please. Yes?"

"Alright." He'd leave after five. She'd never know. And even if she did, what could she do?

"Thank you."

And she was gone. He wondered what password she'd chosen.

He put the computer back in the bag and gazed around. The lyrics binder was open on the table; a bit redundant, since they appeared on the screen. A Chinese girl in a pink t-shirt with a picture of a puppy was crooning into the microphone.

Fourteen minutes past one.

Would Zhou have a projector? Watching the empty spaces on the map blossom into an opium fumerie or the Great World or a gang boss's Bugatti was more impressive when they spread across on a wall. Good audio helped, too. Galloping hoofs morphed into the creak of bedsprings and the orgasmic cries of Helen, Nikolai's lover. That always played well.

Sixteen minutes past. One more minute.

At one sixteen and twenty seconds the door opened and a police officer stuck his head in. He stared at Daniel.

Daniel stared back. His heart went from normal to Olympic sprinter speed, leaping over the intervening stages. *The woman. They must have been waiting. Somebody must have told them about the drafts folder. Shuying.*

The officer turned and called to someone in the corridor. A voice called back, and moments later a second cop appeared at his shoulder, holding a can of Coke. He stared, too.

A radio crackled, not far away.

Run! They're blocking the door.

The cop with the Coke barked something. It seemed to be a question.

Bribe them. How much? More than I've got.

A third cop appeared in the doorway, bareheaded. He said something and they all laughed. The bareheaded cop wandered off and the first one stepped back into the room. He pointed to the screen and said something. Then he laughed again.

A joke. A sadistic one if they think they've just caught an enemy of the state.

The first cop said something. It seemed to be a question, because when Daniel made no reply he repeated it. But slightly differently, trying to make it easier to understand, as if talking to a child. Or an idiot. Or a foreigner.

What am I doing here? I like to sing. I'm waiting for a friend. I'm meeting a woman. Not that woman. What woman?

His bag was on the table. The cop unzipped it and peered at the contents. He grunted. Then he walked out of the room with it, shutting the door.

I'll miss the meeting.

The officer with the Coke put it down and assumed a more formal posture, hands crossed in front of his crotch. He was now a guard.

One of them must speak English. Or they'll send for someone who does. Or take me to headquarters.

"I am an American citizen. If you are going to keep me here I want to see the consul."

No reply. In the corridor a radio crackled, then fell silent.

"Does anybody here speak English? There must be someone."

The guard's eyes passed over him as they might pass over a centipede on the floor.

The radio crackled again. Once or twice there were voices in the corridor.

He looked at his watch. One thirty-seven.

"Am I under arrest? I demand to know." The guard didn't even look at him.

Even if the woman tells them about SkyeSlip, all they'll find will be the names of the journalists. That isn't secret. It isn't anything to do with China. They can't arrest me for that.

"I have to make an important call. Where have you taken my phone?" No response.

They won't let me go until they've questioned the woman. At the earliest. And who knows how long that will take? What will Pierre do when I don't come back? Tell Beidermeyer?

An eternity passed. No phone. No computer. Four walls and a guard. *This is what they say jail is like. It isn't the years that drag. Or even the days. It's the minutes.*

The door opened and the first cop reappeared. He was carrying Daniel's bag over his shoulder and had a cardboard carton balanced on one arm. He put them on the table and opened the carton. In it were a dozen brick-sized boxes. Each box held an iPhone, much like Daniel's own. But when the cop took one out of its styrofoam crib and held it up there was a difference. The bite out of the apple, instead of being on the right, was on the left.

"China iPhone." He rubbed his thumb against his fingertips and said something. It sounded like a question.

He wants me to buy them.

The relief was so intense he almost burst out laughing.

"No, thanks. I already have one."

The cop said something else and shoved the carton toward Daniel's face, just to make sure he realized what was on offer. His colleague, one eye on the door, grunted something encouraging.

"No. I don't want them."

The cop shook the carton, as if it were a comatose drunk.

"No."

Eventually the salesman realized his pitch was doomed. It wasn't just the language barrier: the phone he was demonstrating did not actually seem to work. He tossed it back in the carton and flounced out like a scorned lover, followed by his colleague.

The computer was still in his bag. So was the phone.

The door was open and there was nobody guarding it. As he emerged into the lobby the cops were going through the contents of a pile of boxes by the entrance. They ignored Daniel. The bareheaded one was running the flame of a cigarette lighter over a Gucci wallet to see whether it was leather or plastic. The barman looked on with indifference.

Churning. They seized fakes for the publicity--probably to coincide with the carbon conference--then sold them back to the distributors.

As he hurried into the street he took out his phone. 3.17. He scrolled to Zhou's number. No answer. Nor was the call put through to voice mail. He hung up, tried again. Same thing. He looked around for a cab and saw one approaching.

"Nan Tower 1." The driver seemed to understand and headed eastward toward the river.

Twenty years ago Pudong was marshland. Now it had been so intensively developed and studded with skyscrapers that it was said to be sinking under its own weight. Nan Tower 1 was a decade old, which made it almost a heritage building by Pudong standards. The lobby was vast, marble-floored and galleried up to the eighteenth storey. The lack of a ceiling for two hundred feet made him feel like an ant in a glass box. Guards in blue uniforms, hands folded, watched without expression as he set off for the reception desk.

"I've come to see Renwen Zhou."

The receptionist wore a dazzling white blouse and a smile that was coquettish but perfunctory. Maybe she'd been one of the concubines.

"Name?" She lifted a phone.

"Skye. Daniel Skye."

She repeated this information. Her smile faded. She listened. Then she put the phone down and said something terse in Chinese.

"I have an appointment. I know I'm late. I got held up."

"Not available."

"We had a meeting set. Important meeting. I can explain."

"Not available."

"I'll go on up. If he's busy I can wait."

She must have signaled the guards. As he turned to find the elevator two were at his elbow, others approaching at speed from far-flung corners of the lobby.

"We have something important to discuss. Very important. I have to see him."

She said something brusque. The guards gripped his arms. Then they hustled him across the marble steppe to the door, through it, and out to the street beyond.

SEVENTEEN

BOCA'S NOT GOING TO DROWN

"YES," Daniel said. "I went to his office. He really liked it."

"Say anything definite?" Sophie was propped on the bed again.

"Not in so many words. It's a big decision. But he was definitely hot for it."

He'd never lied to her before. He'd never had to. Which was just as well: she could usually tell when people were being untruthful. "Comes from growing up with Wayne and Sharon," she'd said. "He kept saying he was better, that he wasn't going to freak out anymore. And she kept saying she believed him. They did it for my sake as much as their own. Maybe more. Spun a web of lies to stop me worrying. And I pretended to believe them. To stop them worrying."

At the bottom of the screen he could see what she was seeing, his own face in an inset the size of a matchbook. A liar's face. He'd wanted to tell her the truth, to say he'd screwed things up with Zhou. Yet he knew how much the prospect of losing the house was hurting her. He didn't want to give her more bad news. It seemed to work. She was calmer than last time. More reasonable. Willing to talk.

"How's the baby?"

"I'm going for an ultrasound," she said. "If Leo stays away."

"Leo?"

"Hurricane. I guess it must be hard to keep up with things like that in Shanghai."

"A big one?"

"They're talking category three. Started somewhere off the African coast and keeps getting bigger."

Another horror. One after another. Would they never stop? They'd watched the coverage of Katrina together, seen people stranded on roofs, waving desperately to the TV helicopters while corpses floated in the streets. No evacuation plan, no medical help, no drinking water. The thought of Sophie in a situation like that was unbearable. He felt panic surge.

"You've got to get out of there."

"Boca's not going to drown. New Orleans was black and poor. Boca's white and wealthy. Everybody plays golf and votes Republican."

"Which means they'll have their own exit strategies. The Lord helps those who help themselves. They won't be waiting for the government."

"Oh, we have an exit strategy. Or Wayne does. San Antonio. Dwight's place."

She'd told him about her uncle. When she was thirteen he'd cornered her in a hallway, put one hand up her skirt, the other in his pants. She hadn't said anything to her parents: she'd thought it must be her own fault.

"Jesus. That's too bad. But it'll only be a couple of days ..."

"No it won't. No way am I going there."

"Sophie, you don't have any choice. There's not going to be any evacuation plan and ..."

She sprang up and brought her face to the camera so it filled the screen.

"Do you really think I'd go back? To that fucking pervert leering and jerking off? You are beyond belief, Daniel."

"Look, Sophie, be reasonable. If there was any alternative ..."

"Reasonable? You asking me to be reasonable?' Screaming now. "You've lost the house and everything else because of the fucking voices in your head and you want me to be reasonable?"

"Sophie, you have to calm down ..."

A blur, then Daniel's screen went black as she slammed the laptop shut.

He googled hurricane statistics for Florida. On average Boca Raton was hit every five years. The last time was seven years ago.

"JUNK MAIL CAPITAL of the nation, Boca," Pierre said. "More sharks on the land than in the water." His Miles Davis collection seemed endless. They'd reached the soundtrack for *Lift to the Scaffold*, recorded in 1957, and its haunting, spare anguish crept over the apartment like mist.

"If I get money soon I can use part of it to secure the house," Daniel said. "Then she can go back. Right now she says it's too painful to stay there, thinking we're going to lose it. I've got to get back on track with Zhou. Got to. I don't know why he's so pissed off. He's set his phone not to take my calls. And the e-mail I sent bounced back."

"The Shanghainese can be very quick to take offense. Another aspect of *tong*. Like living in the middle of twenty million Siamese cats."

In the pause between tracks they heard the Rottweiler bark and scratch at the door.

"The Asian way would be to take him a present." Pierre poured more whiskey. "Expensive, though. Look at his taste in watches."

"Or use a go-between."

"Don't think I'd have much influence."

"But Fiona Schulman might." Daniel reached for his phone. "She said he'd picked her brains a couple of times. At least she could find out what's going on. Why he won't even let me explain." Her voice mail said she was out of town. He cursed under his breath and asked her to call back as soon as possible.

The dog downstairs, spending the day as it spent every day, shut in and alone, began to whine. He thought the sound was like the gates of hell, creaking open to welcome in the latest of the damned.

ON HIS ANTIQUE MAP the Yu Yuan garden lay just south of the Boulevard des Deux Républiques, which followed the arc of the old city walls. The walls had long since disappeared and the boulevard been rebuilt and renamed, but he had no difficulty finding the garden. A pedestrian street led toward it between two long buildings with fantastically up-swept roofs. Tasseled red and yellow lanterns dangled from wires strung across the street, which was lined with stores selling Barbie dolls, Disney memorabilia, monograms carved in stone and the mysterious roots and mushrooms so prominent in Chinese retail.

The garden was packed and seemingly jumbled, a collection of halls and pavilions shoehorned between miniature lakes and linked by crooked walkways. It was the dream project of a Ming dynasty scholar who spent twenty years trying to fashion, out of water and rocks and architectural ingenuity, a place fit for the gods. Seeing it, they would descend to Earth and bring with them the secret of immortality. Yu Yuan meant garden of ease, and it was meant to be a source of endless delight.

On the ghost map, the adagio from Mozart's Third Violin Concerto. Petya stands playing at the end of the footbridge that zigzags across the garden's manmade lake. It's a raw winter afternoon, the trees leafless and strollers in the garden bundled up against the cold. The last note shimmers on the air. Nikolai has been holding his cap out to people who have stopped to listen. He has collected nothing.

Petya is aglow with the music.

"Nikolai, listen to me. We are both still alive. Isn't that the most important thing?"

Nikolai buries his face in his hands.

He'd made an interactive guide to Chinese and Japanese gardens for an airline and he knew gardeners made small spaces seem large by breaking them up. By giving only glimpses of a pond or a vista or a miniature mountain they encouraged the mind to imagine what was hidden from the eye. And true masters used limited space to reveal infinity, as they had at the Kyoto garden he'd visited with Sophie.

He joined the crowd that thronged through the gate and past two stone lions baring their teeth at the entrance. Behind him a party of fat-legged Japanese schoolgirls giggled and squealed and snapped each other with their cell phones. In front stood a building with red-lacquered pillars. The latticework of its windows was embellished with carvings of birds and plum blossom. It still looked the way it must have looked in the nineteen-twenties. He raised the camera. Then he noticed. Beyond the white wall and its topping of tiles that undulated, serpent-like, to a dragon's head, a crane swung girders. They were part of an immense, overbearing structure of concrete and glass. It was thirty stories high and V-shaped, like the peace signs the Japanese girls flashed incessantly at each other's cameras.

The ambience was more Disneyland than Ming China. He wanted to shoot video showing Nikolai's path to the Hall of Heralding Spring. But every time he pressed the button a family or a group of old people following a guide with a flag or a gaggle of kids in distressed jeans barged into the frame.

To the left was the lake with a fifty-foot mountain of fissured rock brought from Lake Tai, a hundred miles away. On his right a covered gallery led deeper into the mysteries of the garden. As he entered, one of the Japanese girls gave an ear-piercing shriek. He glanced around. She hunched up and cowered while her friends flapped their bags in the direction of an inquisitive bee.

Two men were watching him.

When he saw them they turned away and looked at the mountain. But their eyes had been on him. He was sure of it. Perhaps the bosses of the woman in sunglasses hadn't believed his story about the iPad being broken. Or it could be the cops. Maybe they'd caught the woman from the Blue Moon after all. She would tell them she'd met a foreigner. Or the barman would. And they'd have seen who he was when they took away his bag. His name and address were in it.

And yet. Maybe it really was just paranoia. The traumatic events of recent days had shaken him more that he would have thought possible. And there was something inherently unsettling about Chinese culture anyway. The garden was full of deceptions that fooled him about its size and shape. It might well leave him prey to other kinds of imaginings as well.

The gallery twisted and turned past glimpses of other passageways, ornately-decorated windows, tiled roofs, huge and luxuriant banana leaves. It led to a second chamber, bisected by a wall. The two halves also doglegged, following the same course, and every few feet windows showed the parallel path and its view. Daniel followed the left-hand corridor, and when it came out beside a small pavilion he slipped around the corner, pressed his back against the wall and waited.

The Japanese girls shuffled through, telling each other about the bee and how dangerous it was and consoling the victim. A woman in a white padded coat and dark glasses went past, arm in arm with a neatly-barbered youth in an expensive-looking leather jacket. A grandmotherly figure holding the hand of a small girl in pink passed by. The girl clutched a doll and when she spotted Daniel she turned and stared until she was tugged away out of sight. A silver-haired man in a brown coat and checkered muffler appeared, murmuring into a cell phone.

But no sign of the two watchers. Had he imagined it? Was it another sign of the unease that had come over him when he heard the dog whine, the growing sense that he was out of his depth in Shanghai, that things were happening around him that he couldn't even see, let alone understand?

The Yu Yuan was small, the illusion of space being a product of the designer-scholar's skill. Anyone following would have to stay close. He turned toward the Hall of Heralding Spring and made his way past ponds of carp, serene white walls and grotesquely pitted rock, latticework and languidly-drooping willows. Again, he found himself swept along in the crowd, as if on a subway platform. Impossible to shoot video. He'd come back early one morning, before the children and the guides with their flags and whistles. Nor could he pick out anyone following him. Half Shanghai was at his heels. Those matronly women in slacks? The couple with cell phones? That heavy-jowled man with the receding hairline? It could be anybody. Or nobody.

Every time he spotted a baseball cap he went tense. But none of them bore the Yankees logo. He let himself be carried along, surging back toward the Bridge of Nine Turnings and the street beyond. As they passed a huge fern whose trunk was wrapped in straw he saw a surveillance camera bolted to the top of the wall.

That dismayed him more than the lions snarling at the entrance.

EIGHTEEN

A MATTER OF PRIORITIES

"I HAVE GOOD NEWS and bad news," Fiona Schulman said. "Unfortunately the bad outweighs the good."

He pictured her in her office, with the Schiele sketch above the fireplace and the bare limbs of the tree at the window. She'd called Zhou on some pretext to do with the next Shanghai film festival. When she steered the conversation around to Daniel and *The Riding Instructor* he exploded.

"He was monumentally pissed. Chewing the carpet. He said he'd set up the meeting and you just never showed. Or even called. What happened, anyway?"

He couldn't say he'd been with a woman in a karaoke parlor. He gazed around Pierre's apartment as if an answer was to be found in the photos on the walls. It wasn't.

"Something personal. My wife's pregnant."

"And you had to congratulate the father."

He laughed. "What's the good news?"

"That was the good news. He was hot for the idea. The bad news is that he was so hot for it he called in his superiors. When you didn't turn up his standing with them went straight down the toilet."

"Oh, God."

"He's either lost face completely or gotten egg all over it, depending on the culture."

"Jesus." Daniel cursed himself for getting involved with the protesters. Again, his own stupidity astonished him.

"Any luck with Monica?"

"Seeing her tomorrow. And I've left a message for the TV producer. But what I really want is to patch things up with Zhou."

"Won't be easy. He's ambitious. Very. He's not going to forgive and forget. Not unless it's to his advantage, anyway. Maybe if you give him time."

But time was something else he didn't have.

LATE THAT AFTERNOON, as Miles launched into *Sanctuary*, a photograph of a maple tree in full autumn splendor arrived in his e-mail. It was attached to a note that said, "Hi, darling. Still missing you. The leaves need sweeping. Hurry home. Sophie."

The real message was longer.

I've stirred up interest in helping Shuying. Two people from the New York Philharmonic flew down to Washington to deliver a letter to the Chinese ambassador personally. That will carry some weight. His daughter is a pianist and the mother has been pushing to get her into Julliard.

But I haven't heard from the woman you gave SkyeSlip to. That's worrying. Time's getting short. The press will start moving over in a day or two. It's vital to arrange meetings before they get to Shanghai. The security people have tightened all kinds of surveillance. We know they have black boxes on internet service providers to monitor e-mails. Cell phones and landlines are always risky. If the authorities learn who's on the list they can cut the head off the protest movement. SkyeSlip really is the only safe way.

I've translated the petitions and sent them to the reporters. The developer who's harassing people is Wenming Nan.

"Fuck."

"Classic conflict of interest," Pierre said. "They'll be having seminars on this in grad school."

"What conflict?" Daniel's shout made him jump. "There is no

conflict. I'm here to get money for *The Riding Instructor*. Okay? That's my interest. Okay? The protesters are your interest."

"Not mine. Everybody's. Everybody who's against violence. Everybody who think's it's wrong that some people are beaten up and killed so others can get obscenely rich."

"Okay. I've no problem with that." He tugged at his watch strap. "It's a matter of timing, right? A matter of priorities."

"A lot of people think not getting kicked out of their homes without compensation is a priority. They've got a lot at stake."

"You know what's at stake for me?" Shouting again. He beat his chest, gesticulated, thrust his chin forward in classic bar-fight foreplay. "Everything. My marriage. My career. My future. And I'm not going to screw it all up because you have a bad conscience."

"My conscience is my own fucking business"

"Fucking business is right. How's your sex life these days, Pierre? Getting much? Shooters don't have to try very hard. And you're not picky, are you?"

Pierre stared at him, face hardening.

"Animal. That's what she called you. Not a human being. Not somebody who gives a shit about what they do. Just an animal."

"Oh, Christ. I never thought ... "

Incredible. Never thought. The sheer fucking arrogance.

"Never thought she'd say anything? Is that what others do? Say nothing? So the guys don't come after you with a machete?" He thrust his face inches from Pierre's. "Because that's what I wanted to do."

Pierre averted his eyes. "Jesus. I'm sorry. I really am sorry. But it's not like anything actually happened. It was a party. You know those models' parties. I was drunk. Sophie was drunk." He looked up again. Gallic shrug, palms upturned, c'est la vie. "Things just got out of hand."

"She was drunk because you--" a jab of the forefinger "--you made her drunk."

"Daniel, nothing happened. She told you, right? Nothing

happened. If we'd had sex she'd have kept quiet."

Know all about it, don't you, how cheating wives cover their tracks.

"What happened was you made Sophie feel like a whore. What happened was you made a fool of me. What happened was you destroyed our friendship."

The Rottweiler began to whine again.

DANIEL STARED OUT over the park. The memory of the bereaved father in Jin's house, clutching the picture of his dead son while the *chengi* beat him, haunted him like a recurring nightmare. Then he thought of Sophie, of the failure to get the money and what that would mean. Of their child. Of the chance that lightning would strike twice and bring him another idea one-half--even one-tenth--as good as *The Riding Instructor.* No. He had no doubt what he had to do.

Pierre busied himself with the pictures to show Denny Marks. Still at Orbis, Marks was Vice-President, Acquisitions, now. "We can sell that," he'd said when Pierre pitched the idea. "A narrative about the tidal wave of change and what it's washing away. Get it to me yesterday, okay?" Pierre moved pictures around on the screen, trying to find the best way to tell the story. He compared shots of a young woman in a deck chair by the side of a narrow street, feeding her baby with a spoon while a crane swung girders across the sky. He dragged a slider to bring out details in the shadows and cracked panels appeared in the doorway behind her shoulder.

As the lights came on in the park he reached for the Johnnie Walker. "I guess that's cleared the air pretty well." He poured two tumblers. "Here's to the full and frank exchange of views."

Does he really think it's something that can just be glossed over? No more important than different opinions about a movie? Apparently so. That must be what happens when you're a photographer, shut off from the world by a wall of glass. Life becomes all shapes and surfaces. In every other way he's a good friend. Generous. Helpful. Which is lucky, in the circumstances. And he did say he was sorry. Don't nurse a grudge. Bite the bullet. Face it, you don't have any choice.

"To peace in our time." They clinked glasses.

Pierre swirled his drink around, making the ice cubes rattle. "Strange they haven't sent the list to Beidermeyer. Shouldn't take long to get the names together. Plenty of people will want to talk, despite what happened to Shuying and Mayling Yu. Or even because of it. You wouldn't believe how ballsy these guys are."

"I don't think the woman would have screwed up. She was smart."

Pierre shrugged. "Sometimes messages just vanish. Nobody knows why. Maybe her e-mail was being watched. Or they saw her with someone suspicious. The Golden Shield policy's all about joining up the dots. Not just cameras and microphones. They have software to analyze the results. And smart cards that register when you walk past a scanner. That's what those white poles on the streets are for. Not just in Shanghai and Shenzen. All over the country."

"Surprised they don't tag everyone with a microchip. At birth. The way they do with endangered species."

"They'll be thinking about it." Pierre raised his glass. "Welcome to the brave new world."

His phone began to vibrate. When he answered his face went rigid. "*Da cuo le.*"

He sat back in his chair. "Can't believe this. They want another meeting. In an hour. Probably to hand over the list if something's happened to the woman."

"Can't they put it in the drafts folder? That's easier."

"Too dangerous. Even before they grabbed Shuying. And God knows what she's told them. Ever heard of the tiger bench?"

He tapped the keyboard. The screen showed a bloodstained woman sitting upright on a bed with her arms tied back. Her legs were bound to the frame with belts and beneath her heels was a pile of bricks. Her legs were stretched so her feet bent toward the knees. A man in uniform held an electric baton to the soles.

"They use a car jack to raise the height. Slowly. Until the legs break."

He knew such things happened. Of course. But they happened to strangers, to nameless people locked away in unknown places. To think they might be happening to Shuying, someone he'd met just a few days ago, was like a kick in the gut.

"Beidermeyer thought her connections would save her."

"Yes. Please God he's right. But look at it from their perspective. They think she sent the execution video. Or gave it to me to send. So she might know what's going to happen next. If they find out who wants to talk they can grab them now and save themselves a lot of trouble when the conference starts."

Miles Davis poured anguish into the ears of the listeners across the park, those unseen figures whose presence seemed beyond doubt. Night was falling and Pierre lowered the blinds. Then he went back to the laptop. He closed the image of the tiger bench and returned to the black-and-white thumbnails that ran in a strip across the top of the screen.

Daniel wanted to tell him to ignore the message. Then he remembered Shuying's father and the men with baseball bats and towels round their faces.

After moving more pictures around and adjusting exposures and changing his mind and adjusting them back again Pierre drained his glass and stood up. "Time to go."

He was about to close the computer when the trill of a skylark announced the arrival of e-mail. The mailbox icon showed a red dot and the numeral 1. The Subject was DANGER! and the From line said, Shuyings friend. Instead of a message there was a snatch of jerky video which started to play automatically.

It had been shot at the festival in Xian. Pierre and Shuying and Beidermeyer were walking through the park, toward the camera. As they passed Pierre could be heard saying, *"... helped me a lot. That's how I got started, that first trip to Japan ..."* Beidermeyer nodded. There was a jump cut to Pierre, photographing Shuying as she ran delicate fingertips over the didgeridoo. Then the screen went blank.

Daniel broke the stunned silence. "Really from Shuying's friends?"

"Can't tell. Don't think they made it. But they might have got hold of a copy. They have access to all kinds of places. Mayling Yu wasn't the only one."

The heating pipes rumbled. Shanghai sounded more than ever like some unimaginably powerful beast, growling in the night.

"Forget the meeting. You've helped them a lot already."

"You know I can't do that." Pierre stared at the frozen image on the screen. "There's a message to abort a rendezvous. They wouldn't do it like this. Must be the cops. Heard the call and guessed it was a signal. So they decided to scare me off."

"But that doesn't make any sense. They don't want you. They want the list. So if there's a chance you might lead them to it they wouldn't try to stop you. They'd encourage you. Stop you from what, anyway? They know you haven't got the satellite gizmo."

Pierre buried his face in his hands. "Alright," he said at last. "Maybe it really is the way it looks. A warning to be extra careful because the list is so critical. But it doesn't make much difference who sent it. The situation's still the same. Beidermeyer needs the names and the protesters want a meeting."

"Suppose it is from the cops. What would they expect you to do?"

"Freeze."

"Right. So if you rush out and look like you're panicking they'll try and stick to you like glue. And while you lead them on a merry dance around the city--keeping in full view all the time--I'll slip out and make the rendezvous."

Pierre looked at him. "Helping the protesters isn't your interest. You were pretty clear about that."

"No. It isn't. But keeping you on the street is. Beidermeyer said they'd leave you alone unless they had hard evidence. That's exactly what they'll have if they see you pick something up." He leaned forward. "And you know what that means? If they take you they'll take me as well. Sure to. God knows how long for. No computer. No phone. Like the Blue Moon all over again. Like a black jail. Only this time Sophie's trapped by the hurricane. I won't have a clue what's happening. And no chance to get things right with Zhou."

Pierre shook his head. "Won't work. They're expecting me. Not you."

"Where's the meeting?"

"In the library. Foreign books reading room. I'm to ask for *The Wealth of Nations*."

"So the contact might not know who you are. Unless they've got a photo."

"They're too careful for photos."

"Then they have to trust the signal. If they think it's trap they just won't make contact."

Pierre stared at the screen again. Then he stood up and reached for his jacket.

"Okay. I'll go first. Wait five minutes. Then go out the back. Get a cab to the library." He took a card from his wallet. "It's on Huai Hai Road. Show this to the driver. Hide what they give you in SkyeSlip right away. Then destroy it."

Nineteen

RED DOUBLE HAPPINESS MAN

DANIEL'S THROAT was dry. He sipped a glass of water and rolled it around in his mouth like wine. He reached to turn off the music. Then he had second thoughts. What they were doing, the listeners in the night? They must be bored, leafing through porn mags, dozing. Were they in contact with whoever was watching? Hard to imagine not.

Yet nothing could be taken for granted in Shanghai. Sometimes the high-tech glitter of maglev trains and soaring buildings overburdened the electricity supply and caused random blackouts. Not everything high tech worked, and not everything was high tech: he'd seen bamboo scaffolding on highrise construction sites, Flying Pigeons grinding along a ten-lane highway. And bitter rivalries set one faction against another at all levels of the bureaucracy. They always did. It was just possible the listeners didn't know Pierre had left the apartment. So why tip them off that he, too, was going out? Leaving the music and lights, he closed the door and stole down the stairs.

He picked his way through a clutter of bicycles to the back door and out to a stone-flagged courtyard with bonsai pines in pots. He passed lighted windows with intimate glimpses of other people's lives—a girl with a hairdryer looking at a large TV, a fat man in an undershirt practicing his golf swing—and came to a lane. As he emerged a taxi started up and nosed past. The driver looked across inquiringly. He shook his head, and made for Hengshan Road.

Clusters of early diners thronged the sidewalk, stopping to study the menus outside bars and restaurants. A cab came into view but a woman on the other side of the street got it first. She shouted something through the window and slid in with barely a pause in the heated argument she was having on her phone. As she slammed the door another one appeared, going the other way. Daniel waved and stepped into the road, causing the driver of an oncoming Toyota to stamp on the brake and mouth a string of obscenities.

"Library." The cabbie looked blank. The car behind honked, then the car behind that, the reflexive call-and-response that underpinned the city's constant bedlam. The driver pulled away slowly, muttering to himself. "Library." Daniel leaned forward and held up Pierre's card. The driver grunted. He glanced over his shoulder, then stepped on the gas and headed westward. Daniel turned. Were they being followed? All he could see was a blur of headlights speeding through the night.

White columns guarded the entrance to the library, an architect's nod to the learning of classical Greece. He found himself in an airy lobby, with open stairs at one side leading to five galleried floors. Security men in grey stood by the door, each dangling a radio. He felt their eyes on him as he walked past. One made a comment, and the others laughed.

At the reception desk he smiled his most engaging smile and asked a woman in thick-rimmed glasses if he could use the foreign material reading room.

"Identification." An order, not a request.

He gave her his passport. She settled down, brow furrowed as if studying it for an exam. She made careful note of his full name, his date of birth, his permanent address--the house outside Seattle; good luck with that--when he'd entered China, when he had to leave. She checked what she'd written. Then she double-checked. At last she handed the passport back and pointed to the stairs.

"Fourth floor." As he turned he saw her pick up a phone.

Institutional beige carpeting muffled sound in the reading room.

The stacks projected outward from the walls, so anybody between the shelves was hidden from view. Rows of tables formed ranks in the middle of the room and the dozen or so readers seemed mostly concerned with the thoughts of Western business gurus. A crop-headed boy in a Dallas Cowboys sweatshirt tapped his teeth with a pencil as he frowned over *What Millionaires Do to Get Rich*.

"I'd like to see *The Wealth of Nations* by Adam Smith."

The librarian, a lean-faced man in a short-sleeved white shirt, looked up from his desk. His gaze rested on Daniel, weighing him up.

"It has to be brought from storage. Please sit down." He gestured toward an empty table, then typed something into his computer.

The books were in order, but not numerous: the shelves must just be a holding area. He found a volume of black and white photographs of Chicago with text by Studs Terkel and took it to the table. He turned the pages, too keyed up to read. He was looking at a picture of cars buried under the great snowfall of 1967 when the librarian appeared at his elbow with *The Wealth of Nations*.

"Thank you." The librarian inclined his head and went back to his desk.

Perhaps there was a message inside. Using his laptop as cover, he opened it at random, seeing where the pages fell. He stood it on end and tapped it on the table. The boy in the sweatshirt glanced up, then returned to the more pressing question of how to get rich. Daniel riffled through the pages. Nothing. He waited, Adam Smith face-up beside him.

A girl with a straight nose and high cheekbones came in and sat down a couple of tables away. Even from behind she was beautiful, with glossy blue-black hair freshly cut. Was she the contact?

After some minutes a balding man with a book under his arm approached. He looked at Daniel, at *The Wealth of Nations*, at Daniel again. Then he disappeared into the stacks.

Daniel got up, as if to stretch his legs. He wandered over toward the window, glancing down the aisles. At the far end of the third row he saw the man. When their eyes met the man held up the book, showing its title: *Mirror for Man: An introduction to anthropology*. Then he placed it in the middle of shelf and turned away.

Daniel, dry-throated again, watched the traffic thread its myriad ways through the city. The TV tower pierced the sky, dwarfed by a new generation of skyscrapers that made the eastern bank of the Huangpu into an imperious declaration: *This is the new capital of the world*. He turned and sauntered toward the shelf, pausing to examine a well-thumbed copy of *How to Win Friends and Influence People*, attention suddenly caught by Houghton and Ross's *Statistics for the Social Sciences, 3rd ed.*

Glance around. Nobody looking.

When he opened *Mirror for Man* a sheet of folded paper fluttered to the floor. It was very thin paper, almost transparent, and bore six numbered paragraphs, handwritten in script so tiny it might have been inscribed with a pin. It looked like a woman's writing. Maybe the woman at the Blue Moon had collected the information but never sent able to send it. Had she been arrested? Met with an accident? Lost her nerve?

"*Gao Yutang, 57, book trader,*" began the first paragraph. "*I never finished school because of the cultural revolution. I taught myself to read. I always liked stories. I started selling books in our village, spreading them on a plastic sheet. I came to Shanghai. I sold books on Fuzhou Road. My wife was born in Shanghai. We had a house near the railway station. We lived there for fourteen years. Then we got a notice saying we had to leave because it was going to be pulled down. We didn't want to go. The chengguan said we had to. They threw rocks through the window. One of the rocks hit my wife. She became unconscious. The chengguan would not let me take her to the hospital. She died. While I was at my wife's funeral they padlocked the house and I could not go back in. I want to show the foreign reporters who is doing these things. I will stand under the Customs*

House clock at two o'clock every day. I will wear a yellow hat."

Each paragraph told a similar story of violence and dispossession. He took the paper back to the table. But as soon as he started typing a chime rippled through hidden speakers. The other readers stirred and stretched, closing their books. One by one they drifted out until only Daniel remained. He folded the note and slipped it in his pocket. As he did so two guards appeared at the librarian's desk. Seeing Daniel, one of them lifted an arm and tapped his watch. The librarian said something and they laughed. He said something else, apparently telling a story, or confiding a piece of gossip. As Daniel slipped past he dropped his voice so they listened more intently.

He walked down the four flights of stairs to the lobby. Where next? The apartment wasn't far. But the cops would be waiting. He couldn't risk going back until he'd got rid of the note.

He followed the crowds along a broad sidewalk until he came to a corner and spotted a familiar sign, a mermaid in a green ring with white lettering. There were tables and big umbrellas beside a wall whose grey brickwork was embellished with stripes of ochre. Less exposed inside. He pushed open the door.

Except for the tobacco smoke, he could have been in Seattle. Or Sydney or Singapore or Santander. In one corner a gawky redhead with a big nose and a New Zealand accent was addressing an audience of pale, skinny girls who looked like models. "St John's Wort. Much better than Valium. We're, like, brainwashed by the drug companies. I have some in my bag. Where's my bag? Ron, have you seen my bag?"

He ordered a cappuccino and looked around. The only free table was against the back wall. On one side two Japanese girls compared photos on their cell phones. On the other a solitary Chinese, sour-faced and slit-eyed, brooded over his Americano, which he sipped with a slurping noise. Daniel sat down and opened his MacBook.

"How much you pay?"

"I'm sorry?"

"Apple computer piece of shit. How much you pay?"

The Americano drinker fumbled with a pack of Red Double Happiness. His teeth were yellow at the front and brown further back. He blew a plume of smoke in Daniel's direction and coughed.

Daniel ignored him. The man leaned over.

"You want Rolex?"

"No. Go away."

"I get Apple computer best price. What you pay? Huh?"

He was peering at the MacBook. Daniel shut it quickly. The man cocked his head to squint at the piece of paper and Daniel pushed him away, harder than he intended. The man lost his balance. His flailing arms knocked over the display arranged on a shelf. Mugs and glass jugs shattered on the tiled floor. In the sudden hush he could be heard wheezing.

"Sorry." Daniel leaned over to help. The man shook him off, cursing. Two clerks in green aprons came out from the counter and started shouting. Others joined in. The red-haired woman said, "Serves him right. Little shit. He makes my flesh crawl. He's always hanging around. I said he made my flesh crawl, didn't I, Ron?"

A round-faced girl appeared with a dustpan and brush. The man pointed at Daniel and said something that made the two clerks turn and stare.

He tucked the paper in his pocket and picked up the laptop. A green-aproned figure with a shaven head blocked the exit. He indicated the girl with the dustpan and its glittering shards. "Hundred *yuan*." He held out a hand and motioned impatiently.

Fifteen dollars was ridiculous. But the Red Double Happiness man was gesticulating and the clerks were still staring. He took the sheaf of bills from his wallet and thrust five twenties into the outstretched hand. Then he pushed past into the street.

Two People's Armed Police officers were coming toward him. He looked around. At the edge of the sidewalk was a drain. Was there time to drop the paper down the grille while he went to cross the road? No. He froze. One of the officers glanced at him in passing. If they went into the coffee shop he would bolt down the first sidestreet. But they didn't.

His heart was racing. He thought of Sophie and the ultrasound and imagined their child's heart beating, hoofbeats galloping across some vast, empty steppe. Like his own.

A hundred yards down the road he found another coffee shop, a long, narrow place with booths along the walls. A spreading-ripples symbol on the door showed it had wireless access. It was half-empty. The sheaf of bills was thinner and he ordered an Americano. Then he slipped into the booth at the end so nobody could come up from behind. Again, he opened the laptop and smoothed out the sheet of paper. He typed in the other stories and contact details and hid the text in an image of the Yu Yuan garden, with leak windows and a lotus-covered lake. Then he opened a message to the address Beidermeyer had used.

"Sophie, I went to this place yesterday. Very crowded. Gangsters used to meet here to divide up the year's profits. Have you had the ultrasound yet? I was thinking about that. What's Leo doing? Your adoring husband, D." Well, what was he supposed to say? He understood now why actors sometimes stayed in character after the curtain came down.

A soft *whoosh!* and the message had gone. He took the paper to the washroom, tore it into very small pieces and flushed it away. Lightheaded with relief, he finished the coffee and set off back toward the park. When he turned into the lane he saw two cars outside the apartment. Neither had a license plate. He could make out shadowy figures and one of them was talking into a phone. But nobody tried to stop him.

In the apartment Miles's version of *Time After Time* hung on the air like the scent of autumn. Pierre nursed a tumbler of whiskey and

Daniel told him about the pick-up and the Red Double Happiness man.

"Did he see the list?"

"Must have done. But he wouldn't know what it was. Hard to read anyway. And he was more interested in the computer itself. What about you?"

"When I left three guys came after me. Didn't want to risk shaking them off so I walked. All the way to the Bund. Took some shots of the night view. I didn't go in anywhere. Didn't speak to anyone. Didn't pick anything up or throw anything away. Didn't even check in a store window to see if they were still following. Just meandered around. Then I came home."

Daniel took the orange juice from the refrigerator. He pressed the steel jug against his forehead, then drank. "So that's that. Excitement's over. Beidermeyer's got the names. All I have to think about now is Sophie getting swept away by a hurricane. And how to get back in touch with Zhou. And impending bankruptcy."

Pierre grimaced in sympathy. Then he turned to his own computer and the images of vanishing Shanghai. "Just got a call from Denny Marks. Wants to know how the book's coming. They want to put a preview on the website. Arriving tomorrow. We're having dinner."

"The Orbis website? What's it like?"

"Not as good as Magnum's. That's the gold standard. But getting better all the time. A lot of multimedia now."

Daniel found it and clicked on a photo essay about women in New York. The pictures were black and white, and they had a soundtrack. A woman with a frizz of grey hair was silhouetted against a window, eyes closed, listening to a Bach cello concerto. After a few bars the music faded and a voice began to intone: "If I told him, when I told him, if I told him everything, would he understand, would he understand everything ..."

He skipped around, looking what else was on the site. "And he's interested in old Shanghai. Okay if I join you?"

"Sure. Worth talking to, even if *The Riding Instructor* isn't quite his kind of thing."

"Right now it isn't anybody's kind of thing. That's why it's such a fantastic opportunity. Somebody has to be first."

Pierre moved to his bedroom. "I'll be out early. I want pictures of the daughter at the nail house. I can take that photo back. In the afternoon I'm going to Leander Byrne's gallery. The Amalgam. He's setting up a new show. Stop by around five and we'll go meet Denny."

TWENTY

KILLER PITCH

PIERRE RECKONED THAT Fugen Pan's daughter, Jinglu, would work from eight o'clock, when students finished the half-hour cleanup that began the Shanghai school day. At Hengshan Road subway station people trying to get on outnumbered the people trying to get off and he was swept along in the crush. Women with bullhorns harangued passengers to move further inside the car.

When the doors closed he was squashed face to face against a man in an orange ski jacket who had failed to elbow his way out. The man cursed. He'd missed his stop and now Pierre's camera bag was digging into his stomach. Too bad, *mon ami*. Pierre had years of pushing to the front of crowds. He would not have moved the bag even if he could. After one costly mistake at the start of his career he would no more lose sight of his gear than he would grab hold of an electric fence.

In the crater around the nail house concrete had been poured for the foundations, a grey jigsaw of right-angles and straight lines. He wanted to shoot the men harassing Jinglu with the house in the background. But if he climbed down near enough to use a wide-angle there was nowhere to conceal himself. The workers were already busy, trudging through the mud with bundles of rebars. He'd use a telephoto, and hope the goons followed her up to the street so he could get close-ups.

From the lane that ended at the construction site he had a clear view of the house, a hundred yards away. It was more alley than lane, two rows of brick tenements that faced each other across a narrow pavement. The houses blocked out what daylight there was and the lane was sunk in gloom. Two gossiping women brushed past with plastic buckets, heading for the communal stand pipe at the end of the block. A sign with the character for man was nailed above a doorless opening from which a white-shirted man emerged, zipping up his pants. He ignored Pierre, but hawked twice and spat a gob of phlegm not far from his feet. Was it an insult or just indifference? A show of *tong*? He found himself thinking about Zhou. Funny how he and Daniel, two of the most ambitious people he knew, had come into conflict. Like adversaries in some classical tragedy.

Somebody was lowering a ladder from the nail house. A figure in a pink jacket with fur around the collar came out of the door and started to climb carefully down. The zoom brought her closer; he could make out the band that held her hair in a pony tail, and the strip of mauve sock above a sneakered foot as she felt for the next rung. He saw the ladder move. Jinglu froze, clung on tightly. Three men stood around the foot of the ladder. Pierre shot one of them as he shook it again, violently, face twisted in a sadistic sneer. He switched to the wide-angle and photographed the whole tableau: the frightened girl, the man gripping the ladder, another lighting a cigarette, a third--in a green jacket--staring down at the ground. Back to the zoom, and Jinglu's face. She had closed her eyes. Her lips were moving.

Holy Mary, Mother of God, pray for us sinners, now and at the hour of our death.

She began to move again, reaching for the next step with infinite caution. Then the next. Then the next. He heard the men jeering. He kept his eye to the viewfinder as Jinglu's foot drew level with the hand of the man gripping the ladder. The man moved closer. Jinglu edged over to the side to avoid him, as she might avoid a poisonous snake. He shook the ladder again, and she almost fell. When she reached the bottom he leaned over and shouted in her ear, loud enough for Pierre to hear the obscenity, harsh and crude as a drill sergeant's.

She hunched her shoulders and set off toward one of the ladders up to the street. The man in the green jacket pushed past her and minced ahead, mocking her walk. She stumbled, and almost lost her footing in the mud. As she came closer Pierre could see the tears running down her face.

The man in the green jacket scrambled up the ladder. He emerged about ten yards from the end of the lane. When Jinglu reached the top he held out his hand, pretending to help her. She tried to ignore him but he stood in front of her and wouldn't let her pass. The other two pressed behind. The man who had shaken the ladder grabbed her bag and yanked it open. Exercise books and papers fell out, some onto the street, some back into the crater.

Jinglu bent to gather them up.

The man pushed her with his foot.

Fuck journalistic dispassion.

When Pierre's camera smashed down on his nose he staggered back with a cry and raised his hands to his face. Blood pumped out between his fingers. Pierre gripped the strap and swung the camera down again, as if driving back a tennis ball. With a thunk like an axe biting into wood, the edge of the body shattered the man's knuckles. Howling, he toppled backward into the crater.

Jinglu screamed.

The two women with buckets half-turned, staring back.

The man in the green jacket grabbed the camera strap and tried to wrest it away.

The other man kicked Pierre in the stomach, knocking the breath out of him and making him double over and let go of the camera.

The green jacket man jerked a knee into his face. Pierre felt a crunch like a tooth being pulled. Then he was on the ground, curled up in a ball of agony as the other two closed in.

DANIEL AWOKE amid disjointed scraps of a dream. It had something to do with the old Shanghai racecourse. Nikolai, the Riding Instructor, was part of it. But instead of a refugee's rags he wore the librarian's short-sleeved white shirt. As the last fragments melted away he tried to hold onto the image of the Russian's face. It was lean and dark, with deep lines from the nose to the corners of the mouth.

Footsteps on the ghost map lead past the racecourse. Chinese voices explode in furious quarrels. Shutters slam, playing children scatter like birds, a water seller shakes his bell. By the door of a tenement an old woman sits on a crate. She is skinning a rat.

Nikolai steps past her into a dark, narrow hallway and mounts the stairs. Open doors give glimpses of other lives: a woman clutches a bottle and weeps, children sleep four to a bed, two men try to distill a mash of rotten potatoes over fragments of smoking coal while another cleans a revolver. At the top of the stairs he comes to a blanket nailed across the opening to the attic. He pushes it to one side.

The room is empty. At first he is dumbstruck. Then he sinks to his knees.

"Petya! Oh, please God, no! Not Petya too! Don't take Petya!"

He had to get back to Zhou. It wasn't just calls from his own phone that didn't go through. He'd tried from the apartment landline and from Pierre's phone, both with the same result. He could feel the man's fury almost as a physical force, the eye of a storm that seethed and buffeted the air on the other side of the river.

Sophie.

Her phone was off. She wasn't online. He googled Hurricane Leo and found seven news stories, which turned out to be the same story seven times. Still heading northwest, could make landfall in forty-eight hours. He had to do something. But what?

The orange juice was cold enough to form beads of condensation on the glass. He opened the blinds and stepped onto the balcony. The skyscrapers stood against the sky like upended dominoes. Somewhere the eavesdroppers would be listening and watching. There was one car in front of the apartment, a black Audi. The other must have followed Pierre.

From the park came the sound of a flute. A squad of twenty or so figures slowly dipped, then rose majestically on one leg and turned. Watching them gather and fold some invisible immensity, Daniel remembered what it felt like to sail. If he could do anything he wanted this autumn morning he'd take Sophie for a stack of pancakes at Odlum's, then down to the quay where the sloop Golden Wind bobbed and dipped at her mooring. No sound in the world exhilarated him like the rattle of rigging against a mast. He'd been amazed how quickly she'd picked up sailing, as if she knew instinctively how the boat would respond. Like a skillful lover. But that was not going to happen, today or any other day. He'd sold the boat when things started to go bad, putting her in the hands of a broker down in San Francisco so he wouldn't see her skim across Puget Sound while someone else trimmed the spinnaker.

Instead, he took the subway under the river to Pudong. The flatness of the land and the brightness of the sky robbed the skyscrapers of the power that might have come from a sense of mystery. There was nothing hidden about them. They were immense, some of the biggest buildings ever put up anywhere, and the architects had given full rein to their imagination. But on a sunny morning like this their grandiosity and newness made them seem like the playthings of an unimaginably pampered child.

The glass door of Nan Tower 1 slid open. Seventy-second floor. To reach the elevator he had to pass the reception desk. But before he got that far the receptionist recognized him and picked up the phone. For the second time, despite his protests, his indignant invocation of the names of Renwen Zhou and Wenming Nan himself, he was frog-marched across the marble expanse and shown the street.

Fury surged through him. This was how Nikolai would have felt.

Humiliated. Utterly powerless. Shamed.

"IMMORTALITY" said Monica Trebone. A small, brisk, dark-haired woman of indeterminate age and sexual preference, she diced her filet mignon and transferred the fork to her right hand. "That's the killer pitch. Tell a Chinese you'll make them live forever and you can name your price."

"And throw in a warranty," Daniel said. "Death at any time entitles the purchaser to a full refund."

The restaurant was in a balconied mansion, once home to a French silk tycoon who'd established the first stable of Lipizzaner stallions outside Europe. The dining room was on the second floor and their table overlooked a garden with camphor and gingko trees and a path that curved away toward a lotus-covered lake. A good place to do business: everything that met the eye, from the oak beams of the vaulted ceiling to the single white rose in the middle of each table, whispered of success and its pleasures.

"Of course, it's not always possible." The fork speared a morsel of steak and raised it off the plate. "Sex toys, for instance. I thought about promoting them as a way to save male sexual energy. Preserve *chi*. But on reflection I don't think that's the way to go." She popped the meat in her mouth.

"I thought they were all made in China anyway."

"Half of them are. By people earning sixty dollars a month. But those are the Honda Civics of the vibrator world." She speared another piece of steak. "I'm bringing in the Ferrari Testarossa. The Sybian. The first container arrives Friday."

"Is there a demand?"

"The Chinese sex toy business is worth twenty-five billion. It's growing at thirty percent a year." She laid down the numbers like a poker player with a royal flush. "It's always been export-driven. Now the domestic market's taking off. Chinese women are discovering orgasms. There's about two hundred thousand sex shops in China. There's one near Suzhou Creek that's four floors high. You bet there's a demand." She chewed energetically. "Of course, where there's demand there's risk. Especially in China."

"What's the risk?"

"Piracy. The Sybian's not exactly high tech. Just a couple of motors and a few rods and a casing. Easy to take apart and copy. If it catches on some general will open a factory in Shenzen and sell knock-offs for a quarter of the price."

He lifted more of the flesh of his trout off the bones. "Immortality's a great idea. But I don't see how it ties in with *The Riding Instructor*."

"Where there's a will there's a way. Most of the time. It's how I did my biggest deal this year." Her eyes were so dark there was little difference between the iris and the pupil. They gleamed with enthusiasm. "This Frenchman came to see me. Patrick Ducros. Little guy in workman's clothes. But very clean. And glowing with health. He took out a map of Jiangsu province, northwest of here. The area around Lake Tai."

"Where the rocks come from."

"Right. Then he unrolled a geological chart and put them side by side. He got very excited. He kept jabbing at the chart and saying 'Greensand 'ere! Greensand! And under is chalk!'"

"What's greensand?"

"Crumbly sandstone. It's what Ducros grew up on. In the middle of the Champagne region. He'd found a place near Lake Tai with the same geology. Excellent drainage. South-facing slope. And just the right climate so the grapes don't ripen too fast. He wanted to buy the land, plant chardonnay and pinot noir, and build a state-of-the-art winery."

"Great idea. But who'd want Chinese champagne?"

"The Chinese." Again Monica reeled off the figures. "China's already the world's sixth largest wine producer. And that's with just four hundred wineries. Soon there'll be four thousand. Eighty percent of the product will be reds. But Chinese women have a proven taste for fizz. And as disposable income goes up so will demand."

"Especially if it makes them live forever."

She laughed. "Sure to. But it wasn't drinkers we were after. It was a backer. Pop quiz: if I say 'great champagne,' what comes to mind?"

"Veuve Cliquot."

"Exactly. A name. Not a taste. Phillippe Cliquot died in 1805. But his name lives on in the product. And for some people that kind of immortality is very appealing. We found one."

A waiter in a starched white shirt took their plates and she opened the proposal document on the iPad again. She flicked to the section headed *Concept*.

"This idea that it's the biggest innovation in movies since the talkies is interesting."

"Monica, it's more than interesting. It's revolutionary. Users don't just make their own movie. They compose their score, from scratch or pre-recorded loops. And they can show their work to other people. Anywhere. At any time. Can you imagine the cultural impact that's going to have? The creativity it will unleash? It's a completely new medium."

She looked up. "Do you have a name for it?"

"The software that ties it together's called SkyeWare. My company's name."

She pushed the computer away. "Has a lot of potential. Definitely. But I can't take it on myself. It's not my area of expertise. And I'm just too busy anyway."

"Know anyone else I could talk to? In the same line of business?"

"There's a few of us around. Mostly doing high-end stuff."

"Ferrari Testarossas."

"And single-malt distilleries. Things where there's a proven market. And not a lot of risk." She turned and caught the waiter's eye. With a barely perceptible nod he slipped away to get the bill. "Unfortunately *The Riding Instructor* doesn't meet either of those criteria."

She saw his expression and laid a hand on his arm. "Which doesn't mean you won't find a backer in China. Great gamblers, the Chinese. And things are changing so fast. But it might take time. Talk to Steffi Kleist. She goes for edgy stuff."

She glanced at the bill and took a credit card from her Hermes pocketbook. "If I was going to pitch it to a Chinese investor that's the angle I'd play up. The chance to get their name linked to something new. Something that will last."

"Like the daguerreotype. Or the Rubik cube."

"Or the peach Melba." She stood up and immediately the waiter was behind her, moving the cane-backed chair away. "Excuse me a minute."

"Could I use your phone? I left mine at home."

The number was on Zhou's business card.

A name that would appeal to Nan's vanity. NanoType sounded like something to do with printing. Too mechanical. Too twentieth-century. NanoSpace? NanoSphere? NanoVision?

This time he got through.

"Renwen, hi. Glad I caught you. Listen, about the other day. It was the cops. I didn't stand you up. I got caught in a raid. They took my phone."

Zhou began a torrent of Chinese. He switched from the handset to the speakerphone. Daniel felt they were talking across a chasm. But he still winced.

"Renwen... Renwen... I know you're angry... There was nothing I could do...."

More Chinese, strident, furious, foam-flecked. Then English.

"What you want from me? Huh? What you want?"

"Renwen, *The Riding Instructor's* going to be big. Really big. The biggest innovation in movies since the talkies."

"What do you want? Why you bugging me?"

"What you said. *Guanxi.* Pierre says you're well connected."

"I know people. Dong Xun. I know Dong. Married Nan's daughter. I asked him to the meeting, okay? Dong Xun. Then you don't show up. Make me look like a fucking piece of shit."

More Chinese. Then a single English obscenity, short and vituperative, spat out rather than spoken, followed by a click.

The dialing tone resumed its implacable hum.

TWENTY-ONE

ROMAN CANDLE

HE WENT to the Amalgam to meet Pierre and found Leander Byrne building a railroad. More precisely, he was watching half a dozen young Chinese in muscle t-shirts build it. They were bolting lengths of rail onto a row of sleepers that had been set on gravel in a shallow concrete trough. The track started thirty feet inside the immense double doors of the gallery and stopped in the middle of the room, if room was the right word for a space the size of an aircraft hangar. There was a smell of creosote from the sleepers.

Like many of the galleries around Moganshan Road the Amalgam was a converted warehouse and once stored chests of opium unloaded at Suzhou Creek. Now its walls were painted white and lit by spotlights on tracks suspended from the open ceiling. The spots fell on paintings, mostly big ones, in the style Daniel knew to be called Political Pop. The example in front of him was typical of the genre: it showed Mao holding up his little red book to ranks of workers all with the same blank face.

"*I bin workin' on de railroad,*
All de liblong day..."

Leander's tenor was strong and clear, powerful enough not to get lost in the space.

"Good voice," Daniel said.

"Had to sing for my supper. Mum and dad were actors. Dermott and Eleni Byrne. Stars of every church hall from Darwin to Sydney."

One of the boys grunted softly as he tightened a bolt with a long wrench. Sweat glistened on his arms. "That's right, Den," Leander called. "Put some back into it." The boy grinned.

"What's the track for?"

Leander went over to a table by the entrance and picked up a black binder. He flipped through photographs of paintings, some of which were on the gallery walls. Near the end he stopped.

"This little beauty. Isn't she a peach?"

The photo showed a train crossing a bridge, pulled by a locomotive that billowed clouds of dirty smoke like a diseased dragon. It was painted black, or perhaps blackened with grime. The driver could be glimpsed in profile, half-hidden by the wall of the cab.

"And this is what she looks like with her face washed." Leander turned the page. The second photo had been taken from much closer, so the engine filled the frame. This time it wasn't moving. It had indeed been cleaned, and a gold-painted slogan gleamed dully beneath the window of the cab. The driver and the stoker stood stiffly on the ground, like soldiers at attention. They were not much taller than the driving wheels, which were now red. Spoked disks of cast iron, these were connected by coupling rods that turned the in-and-out motion of the drive piston into continuous rotation. In front of one wheel Daniel could see what must be a brake, an arc of iron that clamped onto the rim and brought the whole juddering, reeking immensity of valves and pipes and boilers and scalding steam to a halt.

"Shanghai had the first railway in China," Leander said. "Built by a foreign trading company in 1876. But it only lasted a year. The government bought the engine and smashed it up. Thought it was a monster."

"That figures. This one doesn't look like a work of precision engineering, either." There was something primitive about the way the locomotive had been built. It looked lumpish and crude, beaten into shape by brute force on an anvil.

"A saltie," Leander said. "That's what it makes me think of. Meanest bastards on earth, salties. Big, too. Twenty feet long's not uncommon for a saltwater croc. Thing is, they've got that same look. Built for power, not aesthetic enjoyment."

There was a scraping as the railroad builders dragged a chest of bolts to the next sleeper. Leander's rheumy eyes lingered on Den. The back of the t-shirt was dark with sweat.

"And you're going to put it in here?"

"Coming by barge. Crane lifts it off the barge onto a heavy-load truck, a real whopper, tires like a 747. Truck brings it here and two more cranes pop it back on the track. Stick a flag in the funnel and bob's your uncle."

He folded his arms and slipped them inside the sleeves of his robe, a masterpiece of charcoal-colored silk, and stood watching the boys.

"What's the show?"

"Crass commercialism. Like most of them. Five years ago Shanghai artists were doing some really interesting stuff. A few still are. But you can guess what happened." He rubbed thumb and fingertips together. "Lots of it. Kids just out of school started selling for a thousand dollars. Then two thousand. Then ten thousand. In Shanghai you can live like a king on ten thousand dollars. For a while."

He turned to the paintings on the wall and moved slowly from one to the next, a stately, elegant figure with the nose of a Roman emperor. He stopped in front of a large portrait of a smiling Chairman Mao. This one, too, was holding up his little red book and pointing to it as if it was a bottle of hair tonic. Only it wasn't a little red book: it was a cell phone.

"Jia Laishun. Twenty-three. He wants twenty grand for this. And he'll get it. Which is just as well, since he's probably hoovered it up his snoot already."

Daniel examined a painting in mock social realist style of cheerful workers brandishing not sickles but laptops.

"Any problems with the censor?"

"As long as it doesn't call for the overthrow of the government they're cool. But this isn't for Chinese eyes. It's for foreigners. And not even foreign collectors. For tourists. They go apeshit over kitschy Mao stuff." He gestured at the track. "That's why I'm getting the engine."

The railroad builders had reached the end of the sleepers. Now they were setting up a buffer, a heavy iron bar they bolted onto legs that splayed out like a newborn foal's.

Daniel looked around as a side door opened. A woman in a corduroy cap stuck her head in, squinted at the pictures, then went away. He could see from the windows that ran along the top of the walls that night had fallen. He glanced at his watch again. Six twenty-five.

"Maybe he met someone," Leander said. "Shanghai's full of opportunities." His eyes held Daniel's, brow cocked. Daniel smiled.

"Maybe. His phone's turned off, which is strange." He couldn't help thinking about the man in the Yankees cap.

"Hang around a bit more. We can get something to eat. Fu Yen's just around the corner. Best drunken chicken in town. They use real Shaoxing wine."

"Thanks, but I have to find Pierre. I'll see if he went to the nail house."

"Fair dinkum. Don't miss the opening of Second Thoughts, though. My nephew's doing the music."

They shook hands, and Daniel saw his eyes slide back to Den.

MINDFUL OF THE CARBON CONFERENCE, the city government had ordered that all lights on construction sites be turned off at night. Seen from a plane, black pools lay amid the city's diamantine glitter like malignant growths on an x-ray. Had the plane been coming in low, watchers at the windows might have seen flames flicker in the middle of one of them.

The house was wooden and the wood was old and rotten. It burned quickly, the fire having started in three places at once. Flames shot up thirty feet and the blaze, on top of the column of earth, seemed to hang in midair like an enormous Roman candle.

As Daniel arrived at the end of the lane the door swung open, then half-closed again, flames licking along its edge. He saw a figure in the doorway, silhouetted against the conflagration. Fugen Pan's hair was on fire and he was beating at his head with his hands. There was a crash and a blazing beam fell behind him. Pushing it away with his elbow, he stumbled back inside.

Figures raced across the floor of the crater, carrying a ladder between them like a stretcher.

Pan reappeared, half-dragging, half-carrying a large bundle wrapped in cloth. The lower part was in flames and he flailed at them with one hand.

The rescuers reached the column and upended the ladder. One of them was already scrambling up. As he got to the top a hand reached from the bundle and tried to touch Pan's face. Pan leaned forward. Then the roof fell in, burying the teacher and his mother in an avalanche of tiles and blazing timber.

The fire sent a shower of sparks up into the night sky and roared in triumph.

TWENTY-TWO

AS OKAY AS HE EVER IS

WHEN HE GOT BACK to Pierre's apartment, stunned and appalled, the place was just as he'd left it. No camera bag, no scribbled message, no dirty plates in the sink. Pierre's MacBook was still on the table, Johnnie Walker on the counter. He poured a glass, downed it, poured another.

The old woman had looked into his eyes and made him soup. Only a couple of days ago. To see her and her son die such agonizing deaths was so shocking he could hardly believe it. Given what Pan had said, he had no doubt that the fire had been started by the developer's *chengguan*. As to who the developer might be... *Don't think about that.*

At least Pierre could not have been with them. He'd gone to the house early in the morning. If he'd still been there at five o'clock he would have called Daniel. And probably Denny Marks.

He opened the Orbis website and clicked on Contact Us. He glanced at the row of clocks on the kitchen wall. Eight-seventeen at night in Shanghai, eight-seventeen in the morning in New York. "I'll put you through to Consuela," said a languid voice in an office high above Seventh Avenue. Consuela wasn't in yet. He called again, and with a sigh the owner of the voice gave him Denny Marks's number.

"Said he'd be here two hours ago." Marks yawned, loudly. "Must have met a woman. Pilots get flights, bartenders get booze, shooters get more pussy than George Clooney."

"I don't think so. He'd have called. And his phone's off."

"Saving electricity." Marks yawned again. "When he shows up get him to call me. In the morning."

177

"Yes. Actually, I was going to come with him. I have a project I think will interest you. It involves Shanghai."

"Photography?"

"Multimedia. Networked."

"Pitch me, baby." He yawned a third time. "But make it quick."

Daniel heard some part of himself go through the elevator routine. When he finished Marks said, "Interesting. Ambitious. But out of the question at the moment. Orbis is pulling its horns in. One Shanghai project is enough. More than enough, the bean-counters say. If things get better, try again in twelve months. Sweet dreams."

He didn't like to think of what kind of dreams he would have. Sleep and waking had become equally hellish. He opened SkyeSlip and sent a message to Beidermeyer saying Pierre had disappeared and that he'd seen Pan and his mother burned to death. Then he poured another tumbler of whiskey.

SHANGHAI SNARLED its bestial nighttime snarl. He opened Skype and saw she was online. She didn't accept the call until he was just about ready to hang up.

"Sophie, I checked CNN. It's getting closer. You've got to be ready."

"We are ready. Got the last case of canned tuna from Escobar's. And some of those multigrain crackers you like. Too bad y'all won't be at the party."

"Water. You've got to have enough water."

"Don't believe lack of water's gonna be a problem."

He bit back an angry retort. Flippancy was her way of taunting him. Like the insolent cracker slur. He took a breath, let his anger subside. At least she was talking.

"What about Wayne?"

"Wayne's okay. As okay as he ever is. Making preparations. It's odd. He's pretty together in times of emergency. Rises to the occasion.

It's just the day-to-day stuff he can't handle."

"What's he doing?"

"Filling sacks with sand and putting them by the door. Been doing that all morning. Keeps taking his truck back to the beach for more. Filled some for the Fagins, too. Sharon says it's things like that keep her from leaving. Beneath the deep and truly shitty crust beats a heart of gold."

"You always said he's better when he has some physical work."

"It's about as much as he can handle. Of course, he doesn't have your education. Or talent. Always managed to feed his family, though."

"Sophie, we've been through this. I can't go and work for Rob Sheldrake. Or anybody else. Not when I'm so close. It would be giving in."

"And you'd rather lose me and the baby than give in."

"Sophie ..."

She changed tack.

"Know what Sharon said yesterday? Weird how so many women end up marrying their fathers. Couldn't understand why they don't have more sense. After what they've seen."

He stiffened. "Is that what you think? That I'm like Wayne?"

"You've both screwed my life up. Big similarity there."

Rage rose like a black fog. He wanted to hurl the laptop to the floor and smash his heel on the screen. Breathe. Breathe. Breathe.

She looked straight into the camera. "Tell me about the meeting, Daniel. Who was there? Did Pierre go?"

What would he gain by telling the truth? Forgiveness? Unlikely. She'd just add "liar" to his list of shortcomings. If he stuck to the lie it would be forgotten if he got the money. *When* he got the money.

"I went alone. To his office. The top guy and a bunch of underlings. We drank a lot of bad tea."

She said nothing.

"Listen, I have to go. I'll call again soon. Take care. Please. You have to. For the sake of the baby. Okay?"

Still she didn't say anything, just stared at the camera as if she was staring into his soul. After he cut the connection he felt he'd been talking with a stranger. Or an enemy.

TWENTY-THREE

PAGING LOVERBOY

"YOU WON'T BE so lucky again," the lieutenant hissed in Shuying Chen's ear. "Your American friends won't be able to help you next time. And this will still be waiting." He kicked at the tiger bench and its stack of bricks. "Remember what happened to that other little whore." He held up a photograph of Mayling Yu's battered face. "Too bad you won't get to share a cell. She won't be with us much longer." He glanced round. An officer waiting in the doorway stepped forward with Shuying's laptop. "Now fuck off."

She stumbled from police headquarters onto the square. Two thoughts filled her mind like the screams from the other cells. The first was to get clean, to wash off the dirt and vomit and try to scrub away the terror that had taken her over so completely. It had seeped from the walls of the cell like radiation and penetrated the pores of her skin to the very marrow of her bones. The second thought, equally urgent, was to get rid of the computer.

In one corner of the square was a park, with a stream that wound between the willows and maples and gingko trees. Green-painted benches stood on the path that followed the stream. She sank down on the first one she came to, the computer at her feet. Just the fact that they had put it back together and returned it was enough. They'd have put in a trojan to record every keystroke and let them see everything she did. And a microphone, so they could listen to her conversations. And a GPS chip, so they always knew exactly where she was.

She looked back. Three men in business suits strode along the path, voices raised in heated discussion. One of them threw her a contemptuous glance as they passed. Now a woman with a baby carriage was making her way slowly toward her. The woman stopped and leaned forward to adjust the baby's blanket.

When they eventually rounded the bend and disappeared Shuying stood up. Dizzy from fear and nausea and exhaustion, she clung to the bench to steady herself. Shakily, but as quickly as she could, she set off toward the subway station. She left the laptop under the bench.

HE CRAWLED BACK to consciousness in a tangle of sweaty sheets. Pierre had still not returned. Was he in a cell? A hospital bed? The morgue? With a sick feeling, he realized he could do nothing at all to help. Like the Riding Instructor, he was trapped in this infernal city with no money and no prospects of getting any.

He got up and went over to the French windows. The apartment was better sound-proofed than he'd thought. When he turned the handle and nudged the window open the soundscape snapped into focus. Two girls walked quickly past along the lane below, heels clicking in a brisk tattoo. A baby cried, doors slammed, an engine started, a woman screamed (whether in anguish or ecstasy he couldn't tell), another laughed hysterically, Sino-pop blared. And behind it all, the backing track stuck in a never-ending loop, was the constant revving, honking, rumble of traffic. He went on the balcony and looked down. The black Audi was still there. He'd been so horrorstruck when he came back that he'd forgotten all about it. He watched figures hurry through the park. He saw someone with a bag at his hip, heading in the direction of the apartment. But he didn't have Pierre's habit of looking around all the time to see what was happening.

When he went back inside and closed the door the apartment was very quiet. He became aware of its smell, the lingering trace of lives that had unfolded here for eighty years. Part of it was the pig's blood and poison ivy polish that made the pine floors gleam. What constituted the rest he could only guess. All the medicines and mushrooms and incense and unguents that passed through a Chinese household had mingled their aromas, sunk into the walls, and outlived their users.

He opened his MacBook. Sophie wasn't online. There was a message from her. Only it wasn't. This time Beidermeyer had used a photograph of a sailing boat. It was bigger than Golden Wind, a gaff-rigged ketch running before a stiff breeze. But given what he's been thinking the coincidence was uncanny.

"Darling, it's a beautiful autumn day here, perfect for going out on the water. Missing you. Hurry back, okay? Love, Sophie."

The real message wasn't much longer.

"*I've put the word out. Journalists look out for their own. Simple self-interest. They know if bad stuff happens they could be next. They'll ask the questions. Don't try and find Pierre yourself. That would draw attention. Just let me know if he turns up. Steve Holm says he'll be in touch.*"

On impulse, he opened the drafts folder. There was nothing in English. He still remembered the *kanji* he'd learned years ago, drawing them in the air while Elizabeth pretended to play the violin. But being able to read Japanese wasn't much help with Chinese. In the latest entry he recognized the ideograms for fire and death and a few others. He was trying to wrest some meaning out of them when the house phone rang. A high-pitched voice said something very fast in Chinese. A woman? He couldn't be sure.

"Pierre's not here. Do you speak English?" There was no reply. He thought the caller would hang up. Instead, there was silence.

"Hello? He might not be back for a while." It seemed to Daniel that whoever it was wanted to say more, but something was holding her back. There was a click, and the line went dead. A dissident wanting another meeting? One of Pierre's girlfriends? Maybe it really was just a wrong number. Yet that seemed unlikely.

Google showed nine stories about Leo. It was picking up speed. A hurricane watch advisory, meaning it could make landfall within thirty-six hours, was imminent. Sophie was still not online.

He was hungry. He looked in the refrigerator and scrambled the last three eggs, then toasted two slices of the multigrain loaf. There was milk and he made a latte, using as much of the fragrant black powder as the machine would hold.

A door slammed and footsteps faded away down the hallway. Then silence.

The phone rang again.

"Paging loverboy. Where the fuck is he?"

He almost told Marks he was probably in police custody, but stopped himself. It wasn't just the eavesdroppers across the park who'd be listening: he had no doubt the phone was monitored.

"I don't know. He didn't come back. His phone's still off."

"I've got a meeting in Tokyo tomorrow. Can't hang around here waiting."

"No. Something's happened to him."

"Accident?"

"Perhaps."

"When you find out call me. *Ciao*."

Even if he was sure Pierre had been arrested, what could he do? March into police headquarters and demand his release? He was trapped by insoluble problems. Couldn't help Pierre, couldn't help Sophie without money, couldn't get money without mending bridges with Zhou, couldn't mend bridges if Zhou refused to take his calls or read his e-mails.

A letter. An old-fashioned letter, written on paper. Hand-delivered? No, better if it arrived in the mail. Then at least he'd open it. Short rather than long. A single succinct page, part-apology and part-explanation of why to fund *The Riding Instructor* was to take a shot at eternal life. For a man like Wenming Nan, it was a once-in-a-lifetime opportunity. Nothing like it would come again. He'd mention Cliquot and Ducros's winery: there was sure to be rivalry among the mega-rich.

When he finished the letter he read it aloud. He cut the part about the Chinese being compulsive gamblers, hesitated, put it back but changed compulsive to enthusiastic. When it was as persuasive as he could make it, he ran it off Pierre's printer. He found envelopes and 60-*jiao* stamps in one of the drawers of the Chinese writing table Pierre used as a desk. The stamp didn't have any glue on the back; in a corner of the drawer was a pot of gum of the kind he hadn't seen since Grade One.

He'd noticed a green post box on the corner of Hengshan Road, five minutes' walk away. As he left the building the Audi started up and followed him, at the same pace. He slipped the letter in the box and turned back. The Audi stopped. The driver had mirrored sunglasses and his companion in the passenger seat was talking into a phone. Would they intercept the letter? No doubt they could. Please God don't let them throw it away. Or lose it forever in a file, some black jail for suspicious correspondence.

Back in the apartment he called Steffi Kleist and got her voice mail again. Her website said she specialized in finding Chinese investors for Western inventions. Successes included an infrared screening system to detect people with incipient fever symptoms and flying turbines to harvest wind power from the jet stream.

He'd just left another message when the buzzer went. Pierre's landlord had lavished money on frosted glass doors for the shower and brass taps and a ceramic-top cooker but cut corners on the buzzer. It could well be the original, its petulant fluttering rattle having announced every visitor since 1931. If it was Pierre he'd let himself in. Police? They'd smash the door down. The buzzer went again, a desiccated, old-fashioned sound like a cockroach in a coffee can. A friend of Pierre's? The woman who'd called?

He went to the hallway and spoke into the entry phone. "If you're looking for Pierre he's not here."

A burst of Chinese. Not a woman.

"Pierre. Mears. Not here."

More unintelligibility. Then a single syllable. Repeated.

"Skye? Is that what you're saying? Skye?"

"Skye! Skye!" Jubilant confirmation.

He wouldn't let a stranger into his house in the States. And this was Shanghai, a byword for coercion and sharp practice. Literally. Yet whoever it was knew his name. He might have a message from Pierre.

"Okay, come on up. Third floor." He pressed the button.

He opened the door and heard footsteps bounding up the stairs. Just one person, taking them two at at time. He peered over the wooden bannister into the stairwell and saw a figure in a blue baseball cap and yellow sweatshirt. He was swinging himself vigorously around at each bend, twisting upward at such speed he seemed to be coming up out of the earth like the bit of a drill.

In the crook of one arm he cradled a white carton. When he came to a stop at the door Daniel saw the sweatshirt bore the legend, Flying Tigers Fast Food. Below it was a graphic that might have come from a Japanese comic. It showed a motorcyclist leaning hard over into a bend, steering with one hand and holding aloft a stack of steaming boxes with the other.

"What's this?"

The delivery boy grinned and tapped the writing on his chest. He was surprisingly bulky, given his performance on the stairs. He held out the carton with one hand and unclipped a pen from the neck of his sweatshirt.

"I didn't order anything."

The boy said something incomprehensible and jabbed at a slip of pink paper taped to the carton. Daniel saw his own name, hand-written in blocky upper-case, and an empty square for confirmation of receipt. The boy proffered the pen, the toe of one scuffed sneaker tapping impatiently, keeping time to the city's frenetic beat. The space was too small for a signature, so Daniel scribbled his initials.

"How much?" That might be a problem.

But the boy just grabbed the piece of paper. Already he was racing back down the stairs. The door slammed. Moments later a motorbike snarled into life and pulled away, accelerating down the lane as if slashing it with a knife.

The carton was warm and smelled of something reminiscent of the smell of the apartment. He lifted the lid and found eight steamed dumplings the size of chestnuts, their wrappers crimped and twisted into points. To go with them was a pot of thin, reddish sauce. And tucked between them was a sheet of paper, folded in four.

Hello Daniel. I need to talk to Pierre. But you said he is away. I do not have computer to use. Please help us again. Please walk past the foreign languages bookstore on Fuzhou Road at exactly 2 p.m. It is opposite the hospital. Bring your computer. Turn your phone off. Thank you very much. Shuying Chen.

No more. He'd given them SkyeSlip. A gift from the gods, Beidermeyer had called it. If he hadn't gone to the Full Moon to help them he would not have made an enemy of Zhou. Their problems were not his problems. His problems were difficult enough already.

But Pierre. He had to find him. No matter what Beidermeyer said. Or what he'd tried to do with Sophie. Out of friendship if nothing else. People should always help each other. For one thing, if Denny Marks went back to New York without hearing anything it could jeopardize the book deal. And Shuying might be able to help find him. She was the only one who could.

He looked at the clock. Seventeen minutes past twelve.

He flattened the note on the table and studied it. A grease stain from the dumplings had replicated itself, a bloated comma in the middle of each quadrant. Was it really from Shuying? He couldn't tell. But if she hadn't sent it, who had? The police? They might have sent Pierre the video clip as a way to scare him, although it didn't make any sense. Were they trying the same thing again? Surely not. No point following him if they'd been the ones who told him where to go. He went out on the balcony. The car hadn't moved. They would have seen the delivery but they wouldn't know it was for him.

Yet of course they would.

He stared at the glass towers. He'd been facing away from the window when he said Pierre wasn't home. But they would have heard. If they were using a voice-activated monitor that would have triggered it.

And then he'd said he hadn't ordered anything.

He hurried back inside, snatched up the note, and tore it into pieces before he flushed it down the toilet. As the water swirled away his heart beat very fast.

TWENTY-FOUR

TANKS THE SIZE OF COFFINS

HE DIDN'T NEED to look to know the Audi was following. Take it easy. Just out for a stroll. Like any other tourist. He sauntered past the cafe tables on Hengshan Road and stopped to examine the menu posted in the window of Amici. He peered at the list of wines on offer at the wine merchant--not that he could even afford a bottle, let alone a case. At Herman Lazar's Galerie Cinq he gazed at a group of plaster mannequins in a scenario from an SM club, faceless figures with studs and cuffs and riding crops. One of them wore the kind of black leather cap the girl sported in the photo that launched Pierre's career.

"Like that? I knew we had something in common."

The belt of Fiona Schulman's trench coat was tied in a knot and the turned-up collar and black turtleneck framed her face, emphasizing her jaw.

"No, no, I was just ..."

"Of course you were. And what were you going to do next?"

He looked around. Beside the Galerie Cinq an artfully arranged pyramid of hessian sacks filled one window of Bertolucci's.

"Get some coffee. Beans."

"What a coincidence." She took a rust-colored package from her pocket. On the label aromatic wisps swirled around two cups. "I'd run out. So I ran out and now I've run back in again." She jiggled it a couple of times on her upturned palm.

"Then I was going to meet someone."

"You have."

"It's business."

She tapped the packet against her chin and looked at him thoughtfully.

"Something wrong, Daniel? You seem a little antsy."

"No, no, I just have something to do, that's all."

"Okay. Never let it be said I don't know when I'm not wanted. *Ciao*." She turned and disappeared into the crowd.

When he came to the subway station he ducked inside and ran. He threw three *yuan* in front of the poker-faced clerk, snatched the ticket, raced to the barrier and reached the top of the escalator just as the first passengers from the platform reached the bottom. He pushed his away through and managed to jam an arm in the door just as it closed. When it opened again, reflexively, warning light on, he shoved his way inside. As the train pulled out he saw two men run onto the platform and stare after it. One of them pulled out a phone.

He got off at People's Square and walked along Fuzhou Road toward the river. An alert would have gone to every station, along with his description. No way to know who was following him, not in this jostling crowd. But somebody would be. The street had a jumble of booksellers and printers and suppliers of paper and ink. He could see the hospital on the other side of the road, just past the traffic lights. He looked at his watch, which he had set to the second. For three and a half minutes he studied the fountain pens arranged on scarlet silk in a stationer's window. Fat, black, and ringed with gold, they bore price tags in four figures. Of course fountain pens would be big in Shanghai; they symbolized power.

As the Customs House clock struck two he arrived outside the bookstore. He barely had time to take in its four-story facade when a pale blue Volkswagen cab drew up. The rear door was already open. The driver leaned over and gestured for him to get in, quickly. As they pulled away Daniel twisted around to see if anyone looked as if they'd just been given the slip. He couldn't tell. Even in the small segment of the crowd visible through the cab's back window two men and a woman in a long leather coat were all making phone calls.

The cab turned left and sped north. The driver muttered under his breath and kept one hand on the horn, to the indifference of the flocks of cyclists who clogged the intersections. As they crossed Suzhou Creek Daniel saw a woman on a barge sprinkling barrels of golden chrysanthemums with a hose. They turned onto a street festooned with hanks of drooping utility cables. Long woolen underwear hung from bamboo poles above shops that displayed streamers, cans of kerosene, lychees, pillows, hair tonic. He looked back. Nobody had followed them.

The driver glanced in the mirror. He swung hard left, then right. They were in a lane that ran along the backs of the houses with the washing. An oncoming cyclist swerved and rang his bell. The cab stopped. The driver grunted and pointed to a doorway. The meter said 23 *yuan*. Daniel reached into his pocket. The driver held out a hand impatiently. Daniel gave him two notes and three coins and climbed out. The cab pulled away almost before he'd shut the door, and disappeared around the corner with a squeal of tires.

The lane was deserted except for an old woman in a headscarf who sat on an upturned bucket peeling yams. She didn't look up, but he could feel she was aware of him. He approached the doorway. Inside it, half-hidden in the shadow, was Shuying Chen. Even in the gloom he could see the strain etched on her face. She seemed to have aged ten years since they'd met in the park. When he moved forward to greet her she put a finger to her lips. Only after she had closed the door and bolted it did she offer her hand.

"Thank you," she said. "I knew you were a good man." Her eyes rested on the computer.

He handed her the bag. "Do you know where Pierre is? He went out yesterday morning and never came back."

She frowned. "Did he say where he was going?"

"To take pictures of a nail house. The guy who lived in it is dead. Burned to death. And his mother. Last night. I saw it."

She whispered something in Chinese. Then she lifted out the laptop and handed back the bag.

"I have to go out. I don't want to be seen carrying that. I'll use a shopping bag."

They were in a narrow hallway with cartons stacked to the ceiling. Some kind of grain had spilled from a sack at the end and been crushed underfoot. There was a strong chemical smell. Phosphate, perhaps, or fertilizer. He followed her up a steep flight of stairs that led into a dimly-lit room. Glass tanks the size of coffins stood against the walls, piled on top of each other. Each tank was full of fish, and buckets of fish food pellets littered the room. The stink, sour and overpowering, made his throat constrict.

Shuying appeared not to notice. "The shop's through there." She indicated a door in the corner. "Don't go in. You mustn't see the owner's face. And he mustn't see yours."

She looked around and gestured at a table and chair in the middle of the room. "You can wait there."

"Will you be long?"

"I have to go somewhere with a wireless connection."

"Internet cafe?"

"No. I'd have to register. That would set off an alert."

"Use someone else's card."

She smiled faintly. "Can't do that. They have iris recognition."

He felt very naive.

"There might be news of Pierre." She moved to the door. "If anything's happened somebody will know."

He wondered how she would find out. He remembered what Beidermeyer had said about the dissidents protecting themselves by ignorance. They must have ways of passing messages inside the country that even he didn't know about. Shuying hadn't said why she needed the computer. Better not to ask.

Left alone, he wandered from tank to tank. There were fish mottled orange and purple, flat fish, fish standing motionless on their tails like bored waiters, fish teeming in schools dense as subway crowds, fish striped like tigers and fish the color of the inside of sardine cans. He stared at half a dozen grey fish with perfect white-rimmed black circles on their sides like exhibits in an art gallery. All swam silently in the watery green light or drifted as they would drift until the day they were scooped out of the water dead and thrown in the garbage. He could hear traffic in the street, and distant voices shouting, arguing. But no sound came from the shop. Business must be slow; no customers, no deliveries. From time to time a white plastic cylinder in one of the tanks released a string of bubbles with a gurgle so faint he wasn't sure if he heard it or imagined it. The room had no windows.

Trapped in this reeking netherworld, he thought about Pierre. They wouldn't torture him. Not a foreign journalist. Not with the conference coming up. They'd have to let him go. But they might throw him out of the country. Pierre could go back to the house he'd bought on Bainbridge island. But where would that leave Daniel? He was still no closer to getting the money. In fact, he was worse off than when he'd arrived. He'd made an enemy of Renwen Zhou. And Zhou had been interested; he could tell. Fiona said he'd come around when he saw it was in his best interests. It all depended on the letter. If the letter didn't work he'd think of something else. He'd find a way. He always did. At least, he always had done.

But there was nothing he could do about Leo. Had it changed course? Blown itself out? Or was it still barreling across the Atlantic, gathering up its fury so it could snap off trees and overturn trucks and wash away houses like matchsticks? He saw it so clearly in his mind's eye, a swirling grey-green explosion of water. Sweat broke out on his forehead. His throat went dry. He had to drink something. Washroom.

There must be one somewhere. Through that door. He pushed it open.

Faces stared up: one woman, dumpy, indeterminate age, gold tooth, wearing a black baseball cap and plastic raincoat bundled around the waist with string; one man, scrawny, advanced in years, hairless skull with birthmark like the Apple logo; one small shark, steel grey, en route from blue plastic crate with yellow handles to vacant tank.

The couple dropped the shark into the tank, where it thrashed its tail and raced to and fro. The old man sprang forward, hissing at Daniel in a shower of spittle. He slipped, regained his footing, lunged forward again making vigorous shooing gestures. Daniel backed into the room and slammed the door.

WHEN SHUYING CAME BACK two hours later she used the lane entrance. He heard her footfall on the stairs and braced himself to her he'd seen the people in the shop. When he saw her expression he stopped.

"Pierre's in hospital. The *chengguan* beat him up. Then the police took him away. They must have been following."

"Oh, God. Is he badly hurt?"

"We don't know." Her face was drawn. "But he was luckier than the people in the nail house."

"How did you find out?"

She'd taken a subway to Longyang Road, then the maglev to Pudong airport. She went into a washroom where there were no surveillance cameras monitoring the stalls--a concession to foreign sensibilities--then bolted the door, opened Daniel's MacBook, and logged in to the drafts folder.

"Somebody at the hospital knew what happened. They're keeping him under guard. They must be interrogating him," Now she put her face in her hands and sobbed. Her shoulders shook. Daniel put his arms around her. Shocking how bony she was, how seemingly fragile.

After a few moments she pushed him away and wiped the tears with the back of one hand.

"They're sure he sent the execution video," she said. "They think he sent other things, too."

"But he won't say anything. They can't torture him. Not a foreign journalist."

"There are different kinds of torture." She looked away, as if in shame. "Torture that doesn't leave marks you can see. They lock you in a cell with the lights on all the time. There's no day or night. There's only screaming from other cells, and the tiger bench on the floor, and footsteps that run down the passage and stop outside your door. And wait."

The piping sent up another cluster of bubbles, to the indifference of the fish.

"The worst thing is if they find the list" She looked up. "Then they'll take everybody. All those brave people will just disappear. Like Mayling Yu."

He thought of the bookseller, waiting under the Customs House clock with his yellow hat and memories of his murdered wife.

"They can't get it from Pierre. I put it in a kind of code."

For a moment he saw relief in her face, a loosening of the tension in her forehead and around her mouth. Then it returned.

"But you have the key."

One of the purple and orange carp nuzzled the underside of its companion as if trying to roll it over in the water.

"So does Beidermeyer."

"Beidermeyer is in Chicago."

He could see where this was leading. But he couldn't leave. Not without the money. There was no way he'd find it in the States, not after going bust. Shanghai was the only option.

"Get out, Daniel. Now. For your own sake as well as ours."

She had no right to ask him.

"That's not possible. I have ... problems."

"So have we."

She put a hand on his arm, her eyes holding his in the watery gloom.

"They showed me pictures of Mayling Yu. They'd used an iron. Other things as well. Electricity. Cigarettes. Drowning."

He gazed around the room, as if a way out of the dilemma lay in one of the tanks or malodorous blue buckets.

"They will do the same to all of us if they find the list." She tugged his arm hard, forcing him to look at her. "They will do it to me. Do you understand?"

He thought of Sophie and the baby.

"Go. Right away. To the airport. Get the next plane."

Bicycle bells tinkled in the street.

"Please. Go."

A densely-packed school of fish took off like a flock of birds and made for the greener grass on the other side of the tank.

Daniel shook his head.

"I can't. I'm sorry. I just can't. My whole life is on the line here. My wife is going to have a baby. This is my only chance."

"Please." She squeezed his arm again.

"Shuying, I have to raise money. A lot of money."

"Where from?"

"Oh ... people. Rich people." He couldn't her about Wenming Nan.

She was silent, seeming to withdraw into herself. Then she said,

"Alright. You have helped us already. We are very grateful for that. I can't make you leave. But there is something else you can do."

She indicated the white plastic bag.

"Your computer. I need something I know isn't bugged. I'll get it back to you after the conference."

His hard drive was backed up on a remote server, so he could still get to *The Riding Instructor* and whatever else he needed. Anyway, he had the iPad. It was a small inconvenience. "Okay."

"Thank you. I have one more thing to ask. Show me how to use the code you sent the list in. I have to let Beidermeyer know about Pierre."

Twenty-five

TELL ME ABOUT DANIEL

When Pierre came around his left eye, the one he used to look through the viewfinder, wouldn't open. He couldn't tell if it was day or night. Blinds on the opposite wall were closed and the room was lit by fluorescent tubes. On a chair beside the door a man in the uniform of the People's Armed Police dozed over a newspaper on his lap. Pages of the paper had slipped to the floor.

He tried to move. The stab of pain in his side made him cry out. The police officer jerked awake with a start that sent more of the paper sliding off. He saw his charge was conscious and stood up and went to the door. Pierre caught a glimpse of a white-painted passage. "He's woken up," the man called. He came back, bent to pick up the paper, then sat down again.

The shallowest breath sent a jolt of agony from his ribs across his back. The left side of his face was numb; it felt like a slab of meat affixed to the side of his skull. From the smell of ether he assumed he was in hospital. His first thought was for his cameras. Then he remembered the fight. The man who'd kicked Jinglu had toppled backward into the crater, blood spraying from his face. Had he killed him?

The door opened. Two nurses bustled in, followed by a man in a white coat who was reading something affixed to a clipboard. He gave Pierre a perfunctory smile, more interested in the swelling of the face than its owner. He lifted a stethoscope and the nurses, who had stationed themselves by the bed, pulled down the sheets.

While the doctor listened, a woman came in and stood at the foot of the bed, looking down at Pierre. She wore a white shirt and dark skirt. The military crop of her hair made them look like a uniform. The doctor scribbled something on the clipboard and handed it to one of the nurses. "Severe bruising, X rays show two cracked ribs, but nothing else broken," he said to the woman. She nodded. He took a syringe from a steel bowl. "Don't worry," he said in English, seeing Pierre go tense. "Painkiller. Just painkiller."

As soon as he pressed the plunger Pierre felt warmth spread through his body. Tensions he had not been aware of eased. Muscles unclenched. The pain in his side began to ebb away. Morphine? Be careful. Don't get too relaxed. When the doctor and nurses left the room the police officer folded the newspaper, tucked it under his arm, and followed them out, closing the door.

The woman brought the chair over to the bedside. "I am Yang Chongshan," she said in American-accented English. She must have gone to school there. Another turtle. "What is your name?"

"Pierre. Kennedy. Mears." Speaking was difficult; his lips were numb.

"What do you do, Pierre?"

"Photographer."

"I thought so. You had a camera bag."

"Where is it?" His speech was slurred. His voice seemed to belong to someone else.

"Here. Beside the bed." She leaned over and held it up.

"Cameras there?"

She unzipped the flap and showed him the bodies and lenses snug in their rubber compartments.

He felt a wave of relief. It made him sigh. A sigh of relief. So there really was such a thing. A physiological response. Not just a turn of speech. Interesting. His thoughts were rambling. The drug. Must be careful. Not just pain it killed. Inhibitions too. Like whiskey. That's why they gave it to him. So he'd babble. He mustn't. Had to stay aware. Watch his tongue. Not get too loose.

"How do you feel, Pierre?"

He tried breathing a little deeper. The pain had almost gone. An image came to his mind of snow melting in the spring sunshine. He felt cocooned, protected.

"Feeling better," he mumbled. "Wish I could speak more clearly."

"I can understand you perfectly, Pierre."

A wave of goodwill rose in him. Must be the painkiller. Just like booze. Have to be careful.

"Can you? I'm glad. After you found my cameras. I want to thank you. Chongshan."

Some of the words were coming out a bit jumbled, a bit slurred, but it really didn't matter.

"What happened to you, Pierre?"

Yes, what happened? There was so much, when he came to think about it, that he hardly knew where to start. He shouldn't tell her. No. The painkiller was making him ramble. Bringing out the Catholic urge to confess. But why not? Why the big secret? They already knew he'd been at the nail house.

"I went to take pictures. It looked so strange, standing there in the crater. It made me think of a photo of a monk's hut somewhere in the mountains, all alone, completely isolated. It was a really dramatic photo, you could imagine what his life was like, this monk, never seeing anybody, you wondered what he did for food, where he got it from, did he grow it, he couldn't do that, not just on a spike of bare rock ..."

His mouth was getting dry as if he'd smoked a joint, all these thoughts pouring through his mind, all these beautiful thoughts like notes of music ...

"Are you thirsty?" She poured a glass of water from a plastic jug on the bedside table and raised it to his lips.

How cool the water was. Her face was close to his, leaning toward him so he could see the pores of her skin and the lines going out from the corners her eyes, crow's feet they were in English, Madeleine called them her *pattes d'oie* ...

"Why did you go to the nail house, Pierre?"

"For Shuying, after what happened with her father I had to help her, I could have stopped them but I didn't, maybe it was journalistic integrity but I was scared too, frightened of pain ..."

Chongshan laid a hand on his arm.

"Have you told anyone else about that? About being frightened?"

"I was too ashamed to tell anyone until Daniel, I don't know why I told him unless it was to do with some kind of premonition, I have those quite often, photographers do, they believe in them, like lucky accidents ..."

"But you can tell me, can't you, Pierre?"

Of course he could tell her, she made everything so easy. He tried to smile and he knew it was all lopsided because his face was swollen and felt like a slab of meat but that really didn't matter, she would understand, she would forgive him.

"I could tell you anything," he said.

A smile played on her lips.

"Well," she said, "why don't you tell me about Daniel? Is he a photographer too?"

DANIEL GOT THE CAB to drop him on the far side of the park and walked back along the lamp-lit path. He didn't want watchers tracing the number and finding where he'd come from. The Audi was back outside the apartment. Would this be when it happened, when the doors flew open and hands grabbed him and twisted his arms and bundled him into the car? The laptop wasn't in the bag. How would he explain that?

He could feel the driver watching him. The man in the passenger seat was jabbing the buttons of his phone again. The darkened windows hid whoever was in the back. He fumbled with the key, expecting a rush of footsteps. Then he was inside, locking the street door behind him.

They'd searched the apartment. An eerie feeling, knowing the forces he'd become aware of had come so close, intruded into his private space. He could sense their presence, like an echo. They hadn't turned the place upside down, presumably because they didn't want him to know. But the flask of irises on the table was no longer beneath the halogen spot where Pierre, picky to the point of obsession about how his apartment looked, always placed it. And he could see the wooden block that held the Japanese kitchen knives had been moved.

In the room where he'd been sleeping his bag was open beside the chair. He was sure it had been emptied out and repacked. If Pierre had talked, they would know the list was hidden in SkyeSlip, and that Daniel was the only one with the key. The easiest way to keep him in the country was to steal his passport. He patted his pocket and felt its reassuring flatness.

Six twenty-three in the morning on the east coast. Too early to wake Sophie. He undressed and put the shirt in the washbasin. He stared at himself in the mirror. Not a pleasing sight. The tan from sunny afternoons on Golden Wind had long since faded. There was something grim about the set of his mouth now, something tense and anxious. The face of a man whose luck had run out. He'd never imagined such a thing could happen. Not to him.

He stepped into the shower and turned on the cold water. The longer it ran, the colder it became. He counted slowly, forcing himself not to shrink from the icy needles until he reached twenty. Then he made it warmer and felt his body start to glow. The shampoo bottle showed bees buzzing around a hive. He poured a gob onto his palm and spent a long time massaging it into his scalp. He washed with the same thoroughness, then put on his last clean shirt and black jeans.

The Flying Tigers dumplings were still in their carton. He put them on a plate and found a pair of bone chopsticks. Cold, but edible. Which was lucky: Pierre's mother had instilled in him the French aversion to microwaves. He opened a beer. Shuying thought they would let Pierre go before the conference. But what if he was badly hurt? She'd told him the name of the hospital. Maybe he should just turn up and demand to see him. But then they'd know he'd been in contact with the protesters. That was the only way he could know where they'd taken him.

Pierre's MacBook was on the table. Must have been bugged with a trojan. Every keystroke he made, every website he visited, every message he read or sent would be watched.

Which could work to his advantage.

He opened the mail program and started a new message. "Steve, our mutual friend says you'll be here soon. I think he will have told you about a new development. I'll be in touch. You can count on that. If I'm not it means something has gone wrong. Let me know when you get this and I'll send more information."

Insurance. No guarantee that Holm would see it. But the prospect of more information should entice the authorities to let it through. If he heard back, then at least he'd know someone would come looking if he disappeared. So would the cops. And if he didn't, his situation would be no worse than it was at the moment. Which was about as bad as it could get anyway. He'd alienated Zhou. Now he'd probably alienated Fiona Schulman as well. A woman could reject a man's advances without lasting damage. But a man who turned down a woman risked making an enemy for life.

Everything depended on the letter. Would it arrive next day? Maybe not. He'd play it safe, and call Zhou the day after. From an external phone. Tomorrow he'd try to get in touch with Steffi Kleist again, and the TV producer, although she seemed to be ignoring his messages. Then he would look for the old Jesuit observatory at Ziccawei. Another hot spot. The Jesuits had provided shipping forecasts, and an approaching typhoon could delay the unloading of opium shipments. The storms were so powerful they'd been known to lift ships right out of the river and leave them stranded on the Bund.

Leo.

Seventeen minutes past seven on the eastern seaboard. She'd just be starting her day.

"Been up for hours." She was bundled in one of his sweaters, three sizes too big. "Mama makes me smell freshly-cut lemons but it doesn't do any good. Wake up, get up, throw up. Every morning."

"How are you apart from that? Any cravings?"

"Nothing stranger than usual. Yet."

"What about Leo?"

"Getting closer. They put out an advisory an hour ago."

"Oh, Jesus. You're got to get away from there. Remember Katrina. It doesn't have to be San Antonio. Just go anywhere inland."

She leaned closer to the camera. "New Orleans was all clapboard. We're in a new five-story building. Made of concrete."

"On the first floor."

"With two staircases up to the roof. I've checked."

That should have been his line. "Think of the baby."

"You haven't asked about the ultrasound."

He felt another jolt of alarm. "Was it alright?"

"More than alright. It was a miracle. It really was like hoofbeats. So strong. I felt I was listening to someone setting out on a very, very long journey."

He felt helpless, watching the expression on her face half a world away. She'd changed. There was something softer about her now. His phone rang. Let it.

"Sophie, I'm really happy about the baby. The more I think about it ..."

"Marks." A disembodied voice from his jacket pocket. "Looks like I've wasted a trip. Have to leave tomorrow."

He fumbled for the phone.

"Denny, I'll call you back. We should meet."

"Pierre's the one I should meet. That's why I came."

"Where are you staying? The Hyatt? I'll be there in an hour."

Sophie was blowing her nose with a tissue. "I know you're worried. But I'll be okay. Really. I'll stay online. You'll know what's happening."

He doubted if that would be possible once Leo arrived. But he didn't want to say so. "You've got to make sure you've got everything you need," he said. "Right away. Water. Batteries. Cans of food."

"Done that. Looks like Wayne's army training is finally paying off." Sharon hovered behind her. "Got to make sure the Fagins are okay. But I'll be around." The screen went blank.

He could tell she was afraid.

WAS SHANGHAI'S most prestigious hotel bugged? There'd be international outrage if it came to light. Yet he remembered what Pierre had said about a State Department advisory. He'd even looked it up. All hotel rooms and offices are considered to be subject to on-site or remote technical monitoring at all times. And even if it wasn't there was sure to be a mic in the computer.

He found the file Pierre had been working on when the warning video arrived and copied it onto the iPad. He put the speakers and the subwoofer in his shoulder bag. Would it work? In the apartment the screen of sound protected the window. In a hotel room the bug could be anywhere, in a light fitting or a door handle or under a table.

The Audi followed him to the subway. It was almost reassuring, in a way. They just wanted him to know they were there. Like surveillance cameras. Muzzled pit bulls. He didn't look back to see if watchers on foot came after him onto the subway; he had no doubt they did.

The hotel was in Pudong and took up the top floors of a skyscraper whose eighty-eight stories ascended step by step to the heavens. The atrium made Nan Tower 1's seem modest; it started at the fifty-fourth floor and rose for thirty-three vertiginous galleries, curling around the central building to a point of light far above. A tower within a tower. The receptionist wore the same smile as the one who'd had him thrown out. They could be sisters. The Hyatt version, though, gestured gracefully toward the elevator as she put down the phone down. "Eighty-first floor. Please go up."

He waited. People came in twos and threes and clustered behind him. When the elevator arrived he was the first to step in. He was tempted to turn around and step out again as the doors closed, to shake off whoever was following him. But that would be pointless. They only had to ask the receptionist where he was going. Which they'd know already anyway if they'd heard the phone call.

"Peon class," Denny Marks said, ushering him into a room with an orchid in a Lalique vase on the table. "The presidential suite's as big as a football field. But the view from this one's not bad." Outside the wall-sized window, far below, the city stretched to the horizon and beyond, an endless sea of light.

Marks was tanned and vigorous, forty-ish and starting to run to fat. As Daniel took out the iPad and the speakers he was aware of a pair of penetrating blue eyes that assessed him over half-moon glasses.

"I think karaoke night's Thursday."

Daniel put a finger to his lips and cupped a hand behind his ear. Marks fell silent. When he'd selected the Stones' *A Bigger Bang* for maximum noise Daniel leaned close enough to smell Armani Code and said, "Pierre got beaten up taking pictures of a property developer's thugs. The police took him to hospital."

"Badly hurt?"

"I don't know. He's been helping a group of protesters. The cops want to find out what he knows."

"Jesus."

"If he's okay they'll probably let him go before this conference starts. I couldn't tell you over the phone." He cupped his hand behind ear again. Marks nodded.

"Thing is, I didn't want you to think he'd blown you off. This is what he was going to show you."

Marks flicked through the photos, not spending much time on any of them. He went to his own laptop case and took a flash drive from one of the pockets. "Nice. I'll take these with me. When Pierre's back in circulation we'll go over the details. Thanks. Drink? There's whiskey, beer in the refrigerator. Or we can go up to Cloud 9. Highest bar on earth."

"I'd rather have some of your time."

"Then we definitely need a drink."

Daniel turned off the music and opened *The Riding Instructor*. "You heard the concept. But it's not something words can get across. You have to see it. Hear it. Engage with it."

For twenty minutes Marks followed the sound clues, conjured up places on the ghost map, spliced together video takes. Then he sat back and jiggled the ice in his whiskey.

"Cool. Totally. Never seen anything like it. My first thought is that maybe it is a bit too diffuse. A bit too crammed with different kinds of goodies. But the idea of users making their own unique movies and using real actors is wonderful. That really is revolutionary. If I was going to take it on that's the direction I'd point you in. Focus on that. But unfortunately, what I said still stands. Orbis just doesn't have the money. Perhaps next year, if things turn around.

"Then, maybe. Now, no."

Twenty-six

THE LIGHT'S WEIRD

NEXT MORNING he woke early. Not that he'd really slept. Fragments of dream entwined with spells of tense wakefulness, listening for footsteps to come thumping up the stairs. At one point during the long, restless night he remembered a photo he'd seen of Sophie as a child. She was nine or ten. It had been taken in the doorway of one of the anonymous clapboard apartments she grew up in and she was staring at the camera with haunted, wary eyes. Then he must have slipped into sleep. The face in the picture became the face of the child she was carrying, their child, a little girl with the same expression, eyes wide with anxiety.

As day broke the rumble of traffic grew louder, voices called in the street, doors slammed. They hadn't come to arrest him. They must still want to see what he would do next, hoping he would lead them to the dissidents. Or maybe Shuying was wrong to think that Pierre had told them about SkyeSlip. They surely wouldn't keep him much longer. There might be another message in the drafts folder. He logged on with the iPad. Nothing.

Sophie was online.

"Not here yet. Must have slowed down. But the light's weird."

"Weird in what way?"

She knitted her brow. "Like it's getting thicker. Oppressive. Like a thunderstorm. Makes me headachy."

He saw Wayne behind her, a coil of blue nylon rope over his shoulder. "How do you feel otherwise? How's the baby?"

She lifted her t-shirt and moved the camera so he could see her pat her stomach. "Baby's fine." She bowed her head. "Y'all happy as a clam in there, aren't you?" She looked back up. "But you sure look a mess. Been drinking with Pierre?"

"No. Pierre's... away."

"What's wrong? Backer backed out?"

"No, no, nothing like that. I should talk to him again tomorrow." Which was true, almost. "It's you I'm worried about. And the baby."

"We'll be okay. Wayne's got things organized. I think the idea of the baby is changing him. Almost like he feels he's getting a second chance. A new start."

"That's what I'd like."

She was silent. Then she turned on him. "How can you say that? Do you know how much you've hurt me? What it's like to get sucked back into that feeling of not belonging anywhere? That's all I ever wanted. All I ever worked for. To have roots. A home. Somewhere that's mine."

"Sophie, I'll do it for you. I promise."

"Don't promise. That's what Wayne does. Always promising. Just get the money. Because if you can't ..." Lacking any other way to make her point, she cut the connection.

Do something. Anything. He opened his e-mail. Jerry Hsieh wanted to know if he could get more photos of Dixwell Road and its Venetian bridges. Perhaps. But not from Fugen Pan. No word from Steve Holm. Had they blocked the message because they were going to arrest him?

He went on the balcony. The Audi was still there. He breathed deeply, letting his lungs fill and empty completely. He put his palms together, raised them over his head, then bent and put them flat on the ground. He extended one leg behind him, then the other, then stretched like a dog. After a dozen cycles he'd be better prepared to face what the day might bring. To have Sophie swept away by the hurricane.

To hear Pierre had been tortured. To run completely out of money. To be taken away and put in a cell with a tiger bench. Prepared?

Steffi Kleist had changed her message. Pressing personal business meant she would be unavailable for a few days and would return calls when she got back.

He toasted two slices of bread and peeled and quartered the last pear. The cheese was soft and he spread it on the fruit like butter. He ate with his fingers, savoring the creaminess and the juicy granularity. Then he scribbled a note and put it beside the computer in case Pierre came back. "Gone to see the Jesuit weather station. Careful with the laptop, you've had visitors."

He was about to leave when his phone rang. The display said Fiona Schulman.

"Fiona, hi, good morning. Listen, I want to explain about yesterday."

"*De nada.* Seems you're a lucky boy, Daniel. I just got a call from Zhou."

"What about?"

"Your project. Wanted to know if I was interested in it."

He gripped the phone tighter.

"Why would he want to know that?"

"He didn't, really. I think he was just using me to send a message."

"What message?"

"That you should call him. He couldn't make the first move himself. Not after you humiliated him. If he called first he'd lose even more face. But something seems to have changed his mind."

The letter.

"Fiona, thanks. Really. When this thing's a done deal I'll buy you the best dinner in town."

He hung up, then called Zhou, who answered on the third ring.

"Renwen, hi. It's Daniel Skye."

Zhou grunted. "Five o'clock this evening. Nan wants to see you, okay? You know what that means?"

"Renwen, thanks. I knew you'd be interested when ..."

Zhou cut him off.

"You got a second chance. Don't fuck up again."

"No, of course not."

"Be ready. I'll send a car."

There was a click. The dialing tone resumed.

It was happening. Not that he'd ever doubted it would. He'd known all along that someone in Shanghai would come up with the money. It was such an ambitious project, so in keeping with the city's aspirations.

Ten twenty-five. Sophie wasn't online; she must have gone to bed early. He'd send e-mail. Just to say there were promising developments, very promising, and he'd get back to her soon with the details.

He checked on Leo. Still heading toward Florida. The latest forecast said it would make landfall within twenty-four hours. He started to google the damage done by Katrina to see how ferroconcrete structures had fared. They must have survived the wind. But what about falling trees? Flooding? Then he stopped himself. What difference would knowing make? There was nothing he could do.

He went over his pitch again. Nan was unlikely to speak English so Zhou would translate. He turned back to the script, looking for places to tighten, things to cut, possible developments he'd overlooked. Was there a place for a Chinese friend, someone who would help Nikolai by doing something he couldn't do for himself? He'd fill in the details later. He just needed the seed of an idea. A water jar. Nan had hidden in a water jar during the massacre. Could he find a way to include that? No. Not something Nan would want to be reminded of. Might turn him off the project all together. Better to use some demonstration of business savvy. Some Chinese benefactor could save Nikolai by showing him a way to make money. Something connected to building and construction? He was wondering how far Nan could be swayed by flattery when his phone rang.

"Leaving for the airport pretty soon. Any news?" Marks's voice was faint; his battery must be running out.

"Nothing. I'll let you know when there is."

"Anything I can do? Anyone I can talk to?"

"No. The word's out. Just have to wait."

Marks started to say something else. But his phone died.

By two o'clock Daniel felt hungry. The sheaf of bills was pitifully thin. But he had to eat. He'd get a baguette from the bakery on Hengshan Road and a can of sardines.

He pulled the front door closed and walked past the Audi without looking at it. After he'd gone a few yards he heard it start up. Cyclists trundled down the lane, tinkling their bells as compulsively as drivers leaned on horns. An old man in a checkered Mickey Mouse cap and a stained pink jacket trotted past, pushing a wheelbarrow piled with cartons of radio-controlled cars. The sole was coming off one of his sneakers and made a slapping sound on the roadway.

As Daniel neared the main road he sensed that somebody else was following him, on foot. He glanced around. It was the balding man from the library. Their eyes met. He was carrying another book. He turned it so Daniel could see the title: Barbara Tuchman's *The March of Folly*. Then he was past, striding ahead in the direction of the subway station. After twenty yards he slowed down, evidently not wanting Daniel to lose him in the crowd.

No. No. No.

A few doors past Lazar's gallery a red, white and blue flag fluttered from a pole that jutted out above the Montmartre coffee shop. The man looked around and caught Daniel's eye. The anguish and desperation in his expression were inescapable. Then he went in. Daniel stopped and peered in the gallery window. For the second time, he confronted the faceless white figures. *No. Enough.*

Yet once again whatever it was that had possessed him since he saw the photograph of the Russian at the racecourse took him over. He made no conscious decision. But when he reached the Montmartre he found himself making a show of looking at his watch, assessing how much time before an appointment. Then he pushed open the door and set a cow bell swinging with a dull *clonk*.

The Montmartre had a Tour de France leader's yellow jersey pinned above the counter, and lots of black and white photos of cycle races. In the middle of the room was a soccer table, around which three men in suits seemed to be arguing about wrist technique. As he looked around one of them grabbed a handle and gave it a vicious twist to prove his point.

The balding man sat in a corner on the padded bench that ran around three walls. His arms were flat on the table in front of him, protecting the book like a schoolkid taking a test. Daniel took his Americano to the other side of the room. Beside him a woman in a low-cut red dress and a necklace of heavy silver disks murmured into a cell phone and stirred her café crème with a cinnamon stick. He watched the door. There were sure to be people following him on foot as well as in the car. But he had no way of telling who they were.

The man caught his eye again. He picked up the book and disappeared through a door marked Les Toilettes. A minute later he came back, without Tuchman. He walked straight past Daniel and out to the street.

Wait. Don't rush.

Just as he stood up one of the table footballers made for the washroom, moving at the usual inordinate Shanghainese speed. Daniel sprang forward, bumping the shoulder of the woman in the red dress and making her look up and hiss. He arrived at the door at the same time as the table footballer, who was yanking it open. Daniel pushed past, knocking the man off balance so he hit himself in the face with the edge of the door. His hand went up to his cheek. A moment later he started shouting. But a moment was all Daniel needed. He was in and bolting the door, aware of the pounding of his heart.

The washroom was little bigger than a closet. Against one wall were a basin and a mirror, and beneath the mirror was a shelf. There was a blue and white sake flask on the shelf, holding a bunch of violets. But no book. A long chain with a wooden handle dangled from the cistern, which was just below the ceiling. Daniel stood on the toilet seat and ran a hand over the top of the cistern. It was dusty. Something very light brushed across the backs of his fingers, and when he jerked his hand away a spider came with it, abseiling down a thread finer than a hair and scurrying behind the Guangzhou Liby toilet cleaner. He felt again, and dislodged the desiccated thoraces of three dead flies. And there, against the wall, was the book.

He lifted it down. For its thickness it was surprisingly light. There was no sheet of paper this time. Instead, pages 109--*Cardinal della Rovere fails to become pope*--to 448--*Nixon inherits the Vietnam war*--had been cut away to make a hole half the size of a cigarette pack. In it nestled a thumb-sized flash drive.

Leave it!

But it might have news of Pierre.

The table-footballer was on the other side of the door, pounding and cursing.

"Okay, cool it, I'll be right out."

He slipped the drive into his pocket. Then he reached up and put the book back. He pulled the chain and water swooshed out with a gurgling roar. He washed his hands to add further verisimilitude and get rid of the dust and weightless tangles of spiderweb. He opened the door and stepped out. The man shouted. He was pressing one hand to the side of his face and when he took it away and clenched it into a fist a red mark could be seen scoring his cheek like a dueling scar.

"Sorry about that. Had to go. Must have been the coffee." He moved closer so the man couldn't take a swing at him, put a pacifying hand on his arm, and peered sympathetically at the injury. "Ouch. That must hurt. Best thing is dab cold water on it. Look. See that?"

He pointed to the wash basin, and as the man looked he slipped past. Beside the football table the other two grinned. As Daniel hurried out to Hengshan Road one of them made a remark that sent his companion into a fit of laughter.

The Audi had gone from outside the apartment. But the Nissan SUV now parked in its place also had darkened windows and no license plate. He put a hand in his pocket and curled his fingers around the flash drive. If they leaped out he could flick it behind him over the fence. Maybe. But they didn't. As he shut the door behind him the dog began to bark and scratch and whine.

The tip of the Apple logo on Pierre's MacBook, Johnnie Walker's hat and the foremost iris were still perfectly aligned. He opened the iPad and made sure the wireless connection was off. Then he plugged in the flash drive. It held seventeen photos and a video clip. He looked through the photos. They were all of documents or pages of documents. Most were printed, but a few seemed to be notes or memos, written in a bold, vigorous hand.

He clicked on the video icon and knew immediately what it was. Whoever had been holding the camera was running, and the people around were running too. Shadowy figures swarmed down ladders into the crater and sprinted past the looming bulk of bulldozers and backhoes and diggers toward the giant Roman candle that sent gusts of sparks billowing up into the night. The camera swung away from the burning house and focused on three men running toward a ladder. They scrambled up and into a white van. As it pulled away the camera zoomed in on the license plate. Then it swung back to the house as Fugen Pan tried to beat out the flames that were consuming his mother. When the roof caved in the screen went blank.

He thought of that doll-like figure with wispy white hair making him the bowl of fragrant soup. Such a hideously painful death. A killing like that should not go unpunished. He didn't want to be involved. Even if it was just over-wrought imagination he couldn't forget the smell of burning flesh. Doing nothing would haunt him for the rest of his life and wait for him in the depths of every sleepless night.

He unplugged the flash drive and opened the wireless connection. Still no reply from Steve Holm.

Denny Marks. He could get it to Beidermeyer. He tapped on his phone. The number you have called is not available. Of course. The battery.

Two fifty-five. Marks had called about one-thirty. What had he said? He was leaving for the airport? Or leaving soon? Call the hotel.

Left an hour ago, sir. No, sir, we don't know what flight he was on. Orbis? It was the middle of the night in New York.

He couldn't screw up another meeting with Zhou, just couldn't. He'd get the video to Steve Holm. But the watchers knew about Holm. Any messages would be spied on or blocked. If they arranged to meet Daniel would be picked up before he got to the meeting place. Two fifty-seven. Two hours to get to the airport, find Marks, and get back. Would that be enough?

It had to be.

He dashed out of the apartment and sprinted to the subway station. The Nissan followed. So, he was sure, did watchers on foot. No point in trying to shake them off. They'd think from the phone call to the hotel that he was going to the airport anyway. He changed lines in the noisy, overlit jostle of People's Square and by three twenty-three he was at Longyang Road, waiting for the maglev. It accelerated away like a departing jet, except that the only sound it made was a hum. For the first time in days he saw open country, bleak marshland cut up by waterways and dotted with electricity pylons. It was all a blur; the digital display on the bulkhead said four hundred and thirty kilometers an hour. After seven minutes they pulled into the great beached whale of Pudong airport.

In the check-in lobby's vaulted immensity he saw four Tokyo flights on the departure board. As he looked the status of a JAL flight changed to departed. An ANA plane left in an hour, the other two not until evening.

On his way to the ANA check-in he stopped at the washroom. Third stall on the left. He bolted the door and lifted the lid of the cistern. From his pocket he took a condom from a box he'd found in Pierre's bathroom. He put the flash drive in it, blew it up, tied the end in a knot and dropped it in the water, where it floated like a jellyfish. It was bound to block the flushing mechanism and be discovered. But with luck that wouldn't happen in the next few minutes. It was less of a risk than handing it over in public.

At the desk, he asked in his politest Japanese if Denny Marks was on the passenger list. Equally politely, the clerk said she was not allowed to disclose personal information. He said it really was very important. She said she really was very sorry. Was it just the Japanese customer relations training that made her sound as if she meant it?

"Of course. I understand. It's rude of me to ask. But perhaps you might just tell me if he's *not* on it?"

She furrowed her brow, pondering. She ran a finger down the names. Half-smiling, she gave a barely-perceptible shake of her head.

The only other thing was to have him paged. It was just possible he was taking a later flight. The PA system was crystal-clear and the message filled the vast space without booming or distortion, an intimate murmuring of the name of Denny Marks into the ears of thousands. He waited three minutes. No response.

He hurried back to the washroom, picked up the flash drive, took it out of the condom and caught the next maglev back into the city. The unsmiling, unspeaking couple who got in behind him had been on the platform at Longyang Road.

He reached the apartment with ten minutes to spare and googled Leo. The National Hurricane Center rated it a category three but expected it to reach four soon. A radar image showed it poised above the Atlantic, waiting for the moment to attack. It looked like a monstrous, unblinking, evil eye.

Twenty-seven

CHEZ NAN

HE WONDERED if this was the Mercedes that had ferried Pierre to photograph Nan's jailbait. Instead of heading in the direction of the cathedral, though, they went the other way, toward the Bund. Night was falling, and the traffic inched forward, stopped, inched forward again. As they crossed the river a tourist boat, its bow shaped like a long-clawed dragon, sped past the container ships waiting to unload.

When the driver got out and opened the rear door Daniel half-expected him to salute. Nan Tower 1 seemed to climb forever into the darkness. Guards watched without expression as he crossed the marble plain. Behind the desk his nemesis the receptionist ignored him but picked up a phone. The express elevator lofted him to the seventy-second floor without stopping, and when it did he was prevented from stepping out by Renwen Zhou, who stepped in.

"Going up," Zhou said, and pressed the top button on the panel. His phone purred, saving him further explanation. He listened intently, eyes never leaving Daniel. When they reached the roof he put the phone back in the pocket of his cashmere jacket.

"Taking a ride. Wenming Nan's *bieshu*."

At the end of a short passage of grey-painted concrete blocks and heating pipes was a double door, held shut by a metal bar. Zhou pressed down on the bar and they stepped outside. Nan Tower 1 was high, but newer buildings were higher. He wondered how many people worked in them. What did they do all day, up here in the sky?

The rumble of the city came from far away, drowned out by the thudding of the helicopter that stood in the middle of a white-painted circle, rotor flicking. Zhou, bent low, tugged at the door handle, rotor-wash whipping his dark hair. He turned, and gestured for Daniel to get in.

The helicopter lifted into the air and hovered, as if waiting at an invisible stop sign. Then it shot upward. One moment the gritty bitumen of the roof was beneath them; the next it was tossed away like a giant frisbee, turning on its axis, dropping, sinking back among the diamonds strewn from one horizon to the other. The Huangpu lay across the landscape like a bloated black snake. Everything else was light--silver light, orange light, the red and blue neon light that lined the highway. Far below Daniel saw the flickering of the bus-sized video screen that was towed up and down the river, displaying ads. Launch night he'd get one of those off Battery Park.

The racket of the engine made speech impossible. Zhou pulled out an iPod. What was on it? Sino-punk, the kind he'd heard playing from Pierre's apartment? Wagner? Willie Nelson? He had no idea.

He knew about the scale of Shanghai's building boom, about the new sub-cities mushrooming on its fringes. But to see it spread out below him and going on and on and on gave him a new sense of how much money Nan must have made. Not that he could put a figure on it: the wealth, and what it must make possible, were on a scale beyond his imagination. Highrises were followed by patches of houses that were as rigorously ordered as the skyscrapers. He thought of Tokyo and its sprawl. Jumbled and chaotic and impromptu, that city's organic growth made it feel human despite its size. But Shanghai looked untouched by human hand. It could have come off some unimaginably vast assembly line and been snapped together by robots.

Soon after the first patches of darkness appeared the helicopter began to lose height. Below them stretched an airstrip, edged with sodium lights. There was a control tower, and a hangar with three private jets by the open door, ready to roll out. Instead of landing, the helicopter skimmed over the treetops. The moon appeared beneath them, three-quarters full, in the black waters of a lake. And there beyond the lake, lights ablaze in the darkness, stood Nan's *bieshu*. It was more estate than villa, with a cluster of outbuildings laid out along the meandering course of a river. Beside it stood a windmill, blades turning at unexpected speed given the stillness of the night. He wondered if it was driven by electricity.

The pilot set the helicopter down in the courtyard, staying clear of the Rolls and the Maybach Exelero that gleamed in the shadows. Zhou had barely slammed the door before it lifted off again, sliding crabwise across the sky and disappearing back toward Shanghai. The house was modeled after a French château, an immense five-story pile with steeply-pitched roofs surmounted by a bell tower. As they crossed the courtyard Daniel counted twenty-four windows on the main floors and half a dozen others in the turrets that flanked the house like bookends.

He found himself in a richly-paneled entrance lobby, facing a wide marble staircase that swept upward and then forked into two. At the point where the stairs divided stood a black horse. It was looking back toward the door as if disturbed by whoever had just come in. So bright and alert were its eyes that Daniel did not at first realize it was stuffed. A woman in a cheongsam waited inside the door, hands folded. In a low voice she said something to Zhou. They both turned and stared at Daniel. "Nan is in a meeting," Zhou said. "Wait." He disappeared down one of the passages that led from the lobby.

The woman took Daniel down another corridor, its walls hung with paintings of the French aristocracy, and ushered him through a door. She said something he didn't understand. When he made no reply she turned and left. The room was the size of a tennis court. This, too, was paneled with wood, some kind of mahogany that exhaled a faint spicy perfume. In the middle of the Aubusson carpet, so deep he could feel its quality even through his shoes, two long sofas faced each other. They were covered in silk with a pattern of yellow flowers. Two windows, their lavish drapes gathered at the waist, overlooked the lake. As he gazed out and wondered how long he would have to wait, a police car pulled up on the gravel. Two officers got out and came to the house.

Clouds hid the moon now. Was the hurricane gathering speed? He remembered New Orleans, desperate people on rooftops screaming HELP US! at the news helicopters while alligators feasted on the dead and dying. He opened the iPad and found the house had a wi-fi network. Password? Could be anything. He typed "guest," and to his surprise it worked. Must be so Nan's minions could see what his visitors wanted to find out. He googled Leo. Landfall expected in six hours. The National Hurricane Center now rated it category four. Sophie wasn't online. Again, the image of swirling water rose in his mind, threatening to overwhelm him. He forced himself to breathe deeply, to concentrate on running over the presentation in his mind.

The door opened. "You're on," Zhou said. He led Daniel up the stairs, past the horse on its marble platform. A plaque on the wall said, *Obsidian, 1978-2004. The only horse to win the Japan Cup, the Dubai Cup, and the Kentucky Derby in the same year.*

"So Nan's interested in horses."

"Interested in everything." Zhou didn't look around. "Bought that one for his daughter."

At the top of the house its character changed. Facing them was an ornate table of dark wood with elaborately curved legs. On it stood a jade carving of a laughing immortal with a topknot and curling goatee. He was playing with a dragon which had clambered up like a kitten, eyes on the peach in his hand. At each end of the table stood a chair with footrests that made Daniel think of a dentist's office. Zhou opened a door and beckoned him to go in.

The room, four times the size of the sitting room, felt less like a room than the lobby of some grand hotel. Two things struck him immediately. One was the indoor garden, a traditional Chinese scholar's garden with a purling stream and a waterfall. A miniature mountain could be glimpsed through a moon window in the surrounding wall. The other was a Mitsubishi Zero. The plane's fuselage was dark green, its underside grey, and the canon in the wings protruded from strips of egg-yolk yellow. The Japanese flag was ringed with white. The Zero sat next to an immense black desk, resting back on its tailwheel like a well-trained dog waiting for its master. And behind the desk, like the core at the heart of a reactor, sat Wenming Nan.

He was skimming through a pile of documents, pen poised. Some he annotated with characters which he drew at the top in a bold, powerful hand. Others he put to one side. He seemed to spend the same amount of time on each one, working in rhythm like a farmer winnowing rice. The impression was of relentless, churning activity.

Zhou embarked on an introduction in which Daniel heard the words Riding Instructor. Nan continued to winnow through the papers. Zhou motioned Daniel to start the presentation.

"Monitor?"

Zhou pointed to a huge TV mounted on the wall. Daniel hooked up the iPad and it sprang to life. Nan paid no attention. The first screen was the ghost map of Shanghai, with an audio collage of ships' sirens and chanting coolies and hoofbeats. The sound faded and Daniel launched into his pitch. He'd put the presentation together to make the most of the pictures. Some were images he'd scanned from magazines of the time. The Sino-French Institute's archive had a set of *Shanghai Manga*, a splashy weekly that used the work of Chinese and Russian artists, perhaps even Olga Derieva's father. He had photos, too, of cafes and clubs and Mme. Litvinoff's Salon of Love.

Zhou translated. Nan didn't look up. He gave no sign of listening.

The last screen, Daniel thought, was the clincher. An archival black-and-white photo of Du Yuesheng, the Godfather of Shanghai and kingpin of the opium business, changed into a dramatized video clip. He'd spent days getting the photo to morph smoothly into the frozen frame of the actor, then into color, then into video. They'd shot the scene at a rundown pier in west Seattle, with Jack Yip in a yellow gown as Du. He is watching chests of opium come ashore, cigarette held vertically between his fingers. When the shipment is almost unloaded he tells his men to open one of the chests. Someone has substituted low-grade local opium for the more valuable Indian variety. Du orders his White Russian bodyguards to dismember the handling agent and send his body back to the ship, piece by piece.

"The ability to make your own movie is completely new." He emphasized the extent of this innovation with an expansive spread of the hands. "*The Riding Instructor* is the next step in the evolution of the movie business. As I said in the letter, whoever has his name associated with it will be remembered for all time. Like Phillippe Cliquot."

Zhou frowned, apparently puzzled by the reference, but carried on. Nan wrote something at the top of the document he was reading, put it aside, picked up the next.

"Interactive entertainment is the way of the future. It's going to be immensely profitable." He looked around. The cockpit of the Zero was open, as if the pilot would appear at any moment and climb in and the engine would clatter into life with a puff of exhaust. "Not even the Japanese are doing anything like this."

Nan looked up. His eyes, set in dark sockets, showed the remote disgust of a man who'd achieved his ambitions long ago and arrived at a place where nothing could touch him, somewhere very cold, with only his own momentum for company. When he spoke his voice conveyed power the way a *sumi-e* painter conveys a mountain range.

Zhou translated. "How much?"

"Twelve million dollars to finish the proof of concept." Leave some wiggle room for the house. "Full investment to be negotiated later. It's going to be on a par with a major Hollywood production."

Nan said something else. Then he turned back to the documents. He had an odd way of holding the pen, gripping it between the first and second fingers of his fist with his thumb on top.

Zhou said, "For sixty percent of the return." Daniel's heart jumped. "With conditions."

"Listen, I understand you want to be involved. But the only way I can do this is with complete editorial control."

Zhou waived a dismissive hand.

"A package."

"Distribution rights?"

Zhou shook his head. "Nan gives you twelve million dollars for the proof of concept, okay?"

He could keep the house. He had a vision of Sophie and the child on the beach on a summer afternoon, collecting shells, bending to watch crabs bury themselves in the sand.

"Okay."

"You give him sixty percent of the net income from the finished production."

Haggle? Not one of his talents. Don't kick a gift horse in the teeth. "Right."

"You also give him the list of names you sent. And the video of the nail house fire. Okay?"

TWENTY-EIGHT

YOUR FRIEND WAS HAPPY TO TALK

NAN STARED at him, motionless.

"China has too much politics," Zhou said. "Politics is the past. Business. That's the future. Making money."

Daniel, stunned, said nothing. For a moment he might have said he didn't know what Zhou was talking about. What list? But after his initial dumbstruck reaction it would have been pointless.

"To get rich is glorious. That's what we're doing." Zhou gestured toward the window, to the lake and what lay beyond, the silver haze that suffused the eastern sky. "You saw. From the helicopter. You saw what we've done. What we've built. Ten years ago all that was just fields."

As a boy Daniel liked to take a magnifying glass and focus the sun's rays on a piece of paper until it curled and smoked and burst into flame. He thought Nan's stare might have the same effect. It wasn't just his eyes. His whole being communicated. He had a patina like rock star's, a burnished aura that reflected back all the expectations people had of him. Except that people didn't look at Nan with adulation. They looked at him with fear.

"Losers make trouble," Zhou said. "But losers don't matter. Winners matter. Winners don't want shitty old houses." He took the iPad and studied the screen. "Where are they?"

There was contempt in the way he asked the question. And arrogance. *Tong.* An assumption of innate superiority.

"Where's what?"

Nan spoke, in a voice that would sharpen knives. He did understand some English after all.

"Don't bullshit, Daniel. That's the worst mistake you can make." Zhou stood close, almost touching. Was it a conscious adoption of the classic bad-guy interrogator's technique, or just Shanghainese body language? *Tong*? He reached across and picked up something from the desk. The Tuchman book. He held it in front of Daniel's face and flipped though it like a fan.

"Don't think we don't know what was in it. Your friend was happy to talk." He took out his phone, tapped the screen and thrust it at Daniel. A photograph showed the balding man hanging by his thumbs from a hook in the ceiling. His face was a barely recognizable pulp and someone was holding an electric baton to the soles of his feet. Daniel looked away.

"Give Nan the video and the list and he will give you twelve million dollars, okay?"

"What's the alternative?"

Nan made no move. His face had the color and hardness of olive wood.

"Nan doesn't answer questions. Do you want to find out?"

Daniel looked around, at the grotesquely-fissured rock of the miniature mountain, at the fighter plane. He remembered the view from the helicopter. Nan existed on a level far beyond the reach of any social constraint. He could do anything he wanted and nobody could touch him.

"When can you make payment?"

"When you give us what we want."

"Can you transfer that much out of the country? In dollars? What about the foreign exchange regulations?"

Zhou glanced at Nan. Nan looked impassive.

"Don't you realize?" Zhou's voice was thick with contempt. "Nan does what he wants." He leaned closer. "Where are they?"

Buy time. Not that he could see what to do with it. "On my laptop."

Zhou picked up the computer bag and took out the MacBook. He'd brought it in case he wanted to plant another message. *Shooters always think ahead.* "Not that one. That's Pierre's." Zhou opened it anyway, looked at the Recent folder, looked in Documents, looked in Movies. Then he snapped it shut and pushed it back in the bag.

"Where is yours?"

God knows. "Pierre's apartment."

Zhou translated. Nan nodded, a faint inclination of the head.

"Come." Zhou moved to the door.

He wanted to see Nan's eyes again, to find some hint about what went on behind them. But Nan had gone back to the documents, working his way through them with the implacable persistence handed down by a hundred generations of peasant ancestors.

As they descended the stairs they passed a tough-looking man with the grizzled demeanor of a soldier. He gave Daniel a hard look, as if committing his features to memory. The woman in the cheongsam opened the door without speaking. As they stepped outside a black BMW pulled up. Zhou opened a rear door and gestured for Daniel to get in. The driver, either unaware of what churned-up gravel did to glossy paintwork or just not caring, accelerated across the courtyard toward an architectural extravagance modeled on the Arc de Triomphe. Then he turned onto a paved road, and put his foot down hard.

Nan's chateau fell away, and the windmill and shadowy outbuildings. The road was lined with poplars, so they seemed to be rushing through a tunnel. When the trees stopped the headlights showed they were in farmland, dotted with shacks. For all its glitter, for all the over-sized buildings whose illumination tinged the night sky ahead with silver and crimson, Shanghai was still an aberration. Most

Chinese thought themselves lucky to own a mud-spattered cart and a bullock to pull it.

The interior of the car smelled of leather. Zhou took out his iPod. The road became a six-lane highway. The sky grew brighter.

His head throbbed. He thought of Sophie and the baby. In the house. Then he thought of Gao Yutang, the yellow-hatted bookseller, waiting under the Customs House clock every day for the opportunity to bring his wife's killers to justice, however slim the chance, however great the danger.

The traffic was heavier now and the driver changed lanes constantly, jigging in and out, leaning on the horn. In Daniel's head the voices of Sophie and Shuying rose in strident conflict, pleading, insistent, irreconcilable.

Just bring the money. That's all you have to do. Just find money.

He could still do that. All his e-mail was archived on a remote server and that included the photo with the list. The drive with the torching video was in his pocket.

He could see the twin spires of the cathedral ahead. They'd turn right onto Hengshan Road at the next intersection. Then they'd be at the apartment.

They will do it to me. Do you understand?

The BMW stopped at a light. The driver drummed his fingers on the steering wheel.

Daniel brought the point of his elbow down hard into Zhou's crotch. Zhou howled and doubled over, smashing his face into the back of the driver's headrest. The driver's foot slipped off the brake and onto the gas pedal. The BMW shot forward and rammed the truck in front, burying its hood under the bumper. The truck's load of old bicycles shifted and half a dozen of them fell onto the BMW, shattering its windshield.

He flung the door open and hit the side of a taxi. He had just enough room to squeeze past. The taxi driver lowered his window and yelled. The trucker jumped down to see the damage and yell at the driver. The driver looked stunned. Zhou sobbed, hands squeezed between his thighs. A trail of spittle dropped from his open mouth.

The signal changed and drivers further back began to honk. So did drivers nearby, a blaring cacophony of aggression and short temper, all directed at Daniel. In the chaos he dodged behind the cab and onto the sidewalk. Then he pushed his way further and further into the crowd until he could no longer be seen from the road.

Twenty-nine

GUANXI

HE HEADED AWAY from Pierre's apartment, weaving as fast as he could through the late-night crowd. A woman in front of him slowed to take a phone from her purse. He careened into her and sent it flying onto the road, where it was flattened by a truck loaded with watermelons. The woman, smartly dressed in a blazer and tan skirt, unleashed a torrent of invective. Daniel stumbled, almost dropped the laptop bag.

When he reached an intersection he looked back. He couldn't see anyone following. He ducked around the corner and came to a halt, panting, beside a pharmacist's store with a blue neon cross in the window. Most passers-by kept to the main street. After a minute the woman in the blazer hurried past, just a few feet away, shouting into a phone. She must have had two.

He had a phone. He just couldn't use it. He was in a strange city, surrounded by speakers of a language he didn't understand. He had no money, and no prospect of getting any. At the same time, he had enemies whose resources were as limitless as their brutality. It wasn't just Nan's men who would be looking. So would the police, who would have told him about the list and the video. The two he'd seen arrive at the house must have brought the Tuchman book. They saw him make the pickup at the Montmartre. But the only way they could have found out about SkyeSlip was from Pierre. Had they tortured him? Shuying saidtorture didn't have to leave marks on the body. He would not have told them unless he had been coerced in some way.

Guanxi. Connections. He realized, with a sickening sense of emptiness, that it wasn't the letter that had changed Zhou's mind. It was a deal with the police. If protesters told the foreign media about Nan's business methods he would get bad press abroad, just as he was extending his operations into Laos. The police knew Daniel had sent the names in SkyeSlip. But they couldn't arrest him because of the conference and the e-mail to Steve Holm. So they'd persuaded Nan to make a deal. That was why they hadn't grabbed him after he picked up the torching video. They knew he was going to meet Nan, and Nan would buy them what they wanted.

Or appear to. He had a second realization, even more unwelcome than the first. It was all a scam. There never was any money for *The Riding Instructor.* Nan and Zhou had simply tricked him, like the fool he was. They had shanghaied him.

The first thing was to see if Pierre was back at the apartment. But if he turned on his phone they'd pick up his whereabouts from the GPS chip. He'd seen a few red iron call boxes around the city, refurbished relics of the days of British influence. But he couldn't remember where. There was fifty *yuan* in his wallet, and some coins in his pocket. About eight dollars. He'd find a coffee shop with a phone. But where? Hengshan Road was covered by surveillance cameras. They were sure to spot him. Better to borrow one. There would be plenty of foreigners around, even this late. All he had to do was wait at the intersection. He went back a few steps and hung around by the corner, staying close to the wall.

The people passing might as well have been on another planet. A man pedaled past on a unicycle, wearing yellow overalls and a clown's whiteface makeup. He honked a horn to clear a path through the pedestrians ahead. Two students swaggered past eating hotdogs, one of them half-hidden behind ski goggles. A girl in a green coat clung to the arm of her companion, a tough-looking youth in sunglasses. White socks peeped between his black jeans and Reeboks.

Two foreigners who looked like businessmen hurried toward Daniel, talking animatedly in German. "Excuse me," he said, stepping forward a pace. The one with the receding hairline and glasses waved him away with the dismissive flick of the fingers he would use for any panhandler, and they strode on without pausing in their conversation.

A pair of Chinese girls stopped at the crossing, arm in arm. One had a polka-dot scarf tied loosely around her neck. She looked at Daniel and smiled faintly, not quite in his direction.

"Hello," he said. "Do you speak English?"

Before she could reply a stocky youth in a leather jacket and baggy jeans came up and started shouting in his face. Half a dozen others appeared and clustered around. The meaning was clear: foreigners should not try to pick up Chinese girls.

"Okay, no need to make a fuss." He raised both hands, palms turned out, the universal gesture of conciliation. "I just wanted to borrow a phone." He pushed imaginary buttons on his hand and held it to one ear. The signal changed and the girls started across the road. The youths straggled after them, while the one in baggy jeans mimicked Daniel's phone play and added some ribald comment that made the others laugh.

A siren wailed. Had to get away from Hengshan Road. He hurried back past the pharmacy and ducked down the first turning. He remembered the day laborers. Lots of people slept in doorways. If he found somewhere dark and covered his head he should be safe until morning. He was in an alley between office buildings. He was aware of furtive movement, the purposeful shuffling and scurrying of rats. Lights shone in a couple of the windows but the alley itself was dark despite the silvery haze behind the knife-edge of the rooftops. Pierre had called Shanghai a place of dark Expressionist shadows; now he could see why.

A bench in the park would be more comfortable. But day laborers were being kept out of sight because of the conference. Parks would be the first places to be cleared. He would have to take his chances with the rats. And the snakes. He remembered the photo on Pierre's wall, kids on a construction site grinning as they held up a sinuous, yard-long rope of life. Was he still in custody? The first reporters would arrive soon, if they hadn't already. Beidermeyer would have told them Pierre was being held by the police. They'd have to release him. Or charge him.

He found a large doorway for deliveries, set back in the wall like a window in a frame. With one foot he scraped away what he could of the grime and filth decomposing in the corner. The concrete was too hard to sit on. He squatted with his back against the door, hugging his knees. His elbow hurt from its sharp contact with Zhou's crotch. He hoped Zhou's crotch hurt more.

Eight thousand miles away Leo would be making landfall, uprooting trees, washing away houses. He couldn't even call Sophie; if he turned on his phone they'd find him immediately. He ran a finger under his watch strap. What would his father do? Be smarter than to get into such a situation to start with. For the first time in his life he felt utter despair.

For a long time he kept slipping toward oblivion but jerking awake just as he reached it. When sleep stole over him like patchy fog it brought nightmares, or perhaps it was all one nightmare. The snake man letting a snake slither out through his mouth turned into Sophie, walking down a catwalk in rags. Kamikaze pilots with silk scarves stood around Nan's desk and drank a final cup of sake, while Gaowen's executioner looked back over his shoulder with a smirk. The flock of seagulls that followed the Steinway through the air hurled curses that groaned like an instrument of torture.

The seagulls vanished as he jolted back into consciousness. But their cries did not; they became more rhythmic, more mechanical. He opened his eyes. In the darkness he made out a shadowy figure creaking past on a rusty bicycle with a trailer. The cyclist, whose only discernible feature was a broad-brimmed straw hat, stopped with a grinding of brakes and bent to pick up some scrap of paper that he added to the pile on the trailer. Then he stood to push down on the pedals. The creak of the bicycle faded as he vanished into the darkness.

Daniel's knees ached. He stood up, stretched, massaged his calves. He thought about walking somewhere, anywhere, to pass the time. But staying where he was, among the rats and the refuse, was safer. As the night dragged on it grew cold, making him abandon all attempts to sleep. He tried jogging on the spot, arm throbbing where he'd hit Zhou, face contorted in a grimace. His shoulders stiffened and grew tense. He squatted down again, huddled in the corner, and waited for the darkness to pass.

THIRTY

CATEGORY FOUR

AT DAYBREAK, when he heard traffic start to build on Hengshan Road, he went to the end of the alley and watched for a cab. The first three he waved at speeded up when they saw him. Twice he had to duck back around the corner and flatten himself against the wall, out of sight of prowling patrol cars. The hard-faced man coming up Nan's staircase would also be hunting him. But that was something else he could do nothing about.

Eventually a shaven-headed driver stopped. He sucked a tooth and muttered to himself as he pored over Leander Byrne's business card. At last he threw the Volkswagen into gear and set off, still muttering as he peered around at every intersection. Daniel huddled in the back. They headed north and crossed Suzhou Creek. Each jump of the meter took him closer to the point where he wouldn't be able to pay. Would the driver start a fight? Call the police? Maybe both. He braced himself for another quick getaway. Even that was probably futile; the driver knew his destination and he had nowhere else to go. But after the cab turned down a backstreet and followed a small canal and stopped outside the Amalgam the meter said only nineteen *yuan*. As he pocketed the single coin from his last twenty he felt relief, almost exhilaration.

The gallery was closed. He curled up in the doorway. It was no more comfortable than the last one, despite being painted a welcoming sky-blue. But he was too tired to care. Oblivious to the stares of passers-by on the canal bank, he slept.

An hour later Leander purred up on his electric scooter, robe flapping behind him like a priest's soutane. Seeing Daniel, he cocked an eyebrow.

"Banana peel boiled in water," he said. "That's the Chinese cure for a hangover. I'm a hair of the dog man, myself. C'mon in. I'll put you right."

"Sophie. My wife. I have to see if she's okay."

As Leander busied himself with a red Bugatti espresso machine Daniel went to the iMac in his office. It stood on a large pine table amid a clutter of letters, ink cartridges, scribbled notes, a box of blank disks, photos of boys, catalogs, a well-thumbed copy of Robert Hughes' *Shock of the New*. He opened Skype, and without much hope typed her name. The internet connection would surely be down, knocked out by wind and rain or crashed by the volume of traffic. But he saw with relief that she was online. Moments later her face filled the screen in front of him. She was very pale.

"We're okay. But all hell's breaking loose. It's a category four. God knows what a five must be like. The end of the world."

Around midday the wind had taken on a feral aspect, pouncing, wrenching, roaring. It made palm trees along the waterfront bend in abasement and traffic signals dangling at intersections tug at their lines like kites, desperate to escape. Wayne had boarded the windows up. On the TV news they watched a sheet of corrugated iron cartwheeling down the street outside in pursuit of whatever its jagged edges could lacerate in passing. Careening garbage cans bumped and skittered, contents dumped or spilled or strewn behind them, a race through the torrential downpour to finish in shards of shattered storefront glass, or a levee's tumultuous churn, or bobbing against the wall of a flooded alley with pizza boxes, a doll's arm, a dead armadillo.

"Have you got everything you need? Food? Water?"

"I told you. Wayne got that. While he could still go out."

She turned the laptop to show the survival kit. From his last foray he'd brought back more batteries and cans of sardines and added them to the pile on the kitchen table: the coil of rope, candles, a case of bottled water, an axe, a bow saw, three flashlights with watertight rubberized bodies, a can opener, a camping stove and canisters of propane. Now he stood guard, as if someone might snatch them away. Daniel saw that his eyes, forever shifting in his thin, sallow face, had the fevered brightness of a man on the run. Like his own.

"Thank God I could reach you," he said. "I was sure the power must be down. It sounds like the apocalypse over there."

Leander had speakers and a subwoofer attached to the computer. Daniel could hear the chaos on the other side of the world in sound so rich and bass-heavy it made him flinch. Anything that had not been secured blew down or blew off or blew away and outside the condo was an infernal cacophony. The wind roared like a jet taking off overhead. When there was a momentary lull while Leo gathered its strength for the next assault a gate or door could be heard swinging back and forward and smashing into its frame in a violent, unpredictable rhythm. And it all seemed to be happening in Leander's office.

"A couple of times it's crashed. Then it's come back again." Her face was taut and drawn. "After the first time I got your e-mail. Daniel, you're not lying to me are you?"

A particularly savage gust was followed by a thud from the roof. The impact was audible above the roar and battering of the wind. Daniel saw Wayne's lips move in prayer or entreaty or whatever he had turned to when the man beside him stepped on a mine or got impaled on a shit-smeared bamboo spear or had his head blown off by a rocket-propelled grenade.

"Jesus, what was that?" Daniel gripped the arms of the chair.

"Could be anything. On the news there was a truck tossed off the road. Like a candy wrapper."

In the background he saw Sharon go over to Wayne and put her arms around him, as if comforting a child who has had a nightmare.

His fingers gripped her shoulder.

"It's not just wind," Sophie said. "Wind can't be a strong as this. It's something else. Something more powerful. I think it's the devil."

He saw fear etched in her face. He didn't need to imagine what it was like in that room, with the roaring and the crashing and Wayne getting ever closer to snapping point, whatever that meant. He could see it. And hear it. From eight thousand miles away, he could feel the terror. He was going to tell her it wasn't the devil and it would all be over in a few hours, a day at the most, and that she must stay calm and not panic and remember how much he loved her. But the screen went blank.

He rattled the keyboard and came close to picking it up and smashing it down on the table. After few moments Skype no longer listed her as being online. He called from Leander's phone and got a message saying that adverse conditions were affecting service, try again later. He logged onto the National Hurricane Center. The most recent entry in the storm archive, posted fifteen minutes previously, said Leo had crossed the Florida coast. Wind speeds of 147 miles an hour had been recorded and a storm surge of twelve feet was possible. Wayne and Sharon's condo was a pink concrete low-rise. It wouldn't blow away. But the unit faced the street. How high above sea level? He couldn't remember.

When he tried to google news for updates about the effects of the storm the iMac's screen went blank. Then it showed a message saying Server not found. He tried again, with the same result. Reuters, AP and the *New York Times* were also unavailable.

"Tactic one," Leander said, looking over his shoulder. "They tell you what you're looking for doesn't exist. Usually it's temporary. It'll come back. You just don't know when."

Daniel felt a fresh jolt of anger. He had to know what was happening, even if he was powerless to do anything about it.

"Most likely because of the conference," Leander said. "My guess is there's some big story about how everyone is pissed off with the Chinese. The government doesn't want that to get around. Not when they know they're going to have to make concessions. It would make them look like they're backing down. And looking weak is the one thing they dread."

Daniel tried CNN. He couldn't get that either. "This is ridiculous. What if foreign reporters can't even reach their own sites?"

Leander sipped his espresso, saucer on the palm of one hand. "Journos are a different kettle of fish. Most of them will have virtual private networks. The great firewall won't exist for them. And even if they don't have VPNs some hotels have unfiltered access. The government doesn't give a toss about foreigners. They just want to control what their own people see."

"I can't go to a hotel. There must be another way."

"Try *People's Daily*, English edition. It's bookmarked."

He scrolled past a picture of three laughing girls playing with a puppy. In the world news section he found a story from the Xinhua agency. But it was old, saying only that landfall was expected in a few hours and the National Hurricane Center warned people to stay inside.

Tweets. He found three tagged with Leo and damage. But they just linked to the NHC site. There were no accounts of what was happening.

"Hungry?" Leander opened the refrigerator. "There's yogurt. And honey. Fu Yen opens at eleven if you want proper tucker."

He realized he hadn't eaten since he finished the bread in Pierre's apartment, eighteen hours ago. He needed energy. Even if he didn't know what for.

"Thanks. Yogurt's good."

"Help yourself. Use the couch if you want some shuteye. Make yourself at home. I'll be as busy as a cat burying shit with the show opening."

The container bore the claim, Genuine Balkan Yogurt. At the first taste his appetite came back, and he scraped the pot clean. Rather than filling him, it made him realize how hungry he was. Again, he thought of Nikolai, the Riding Instructor, and his constantly growling belly. He looked from the iron-framed window at the canal and the warehouses on the other bank. This must be one of the few parts of Shanghai that had not changed. Nikolai himself could have stood in this spot and seen the same October light, the same scummy water, the same blackened and decaying brickwork. And felt the same anguish.

He couldn't help Sophie. He couldn't help Pierre. The only thing he might do was to pass the torching video to Steve Holm. Yet that, too, seemed impossible. Holm's phone would be monitored. As soon as Daniel called the police would know where he was and pick him up within minutes. If he left the drive somewhere they'd get to it first.

His head was pounding and his elbow throbbed. He pulled up his sleeve and found a plum-colored bruise the size of a golfball. Leander must have some painkillers. He gazed around the office. Canvases leaned against the walls. Some, presumably intended for Second Thoughts, were ironic portraits of Mao: Mao with an iPod, Mao as obsequiously grinning doorman at the Hyatt hotel, Mao as a strap-hanging commuter on the subway, nose buried in his own Little Red Book. The skull of some large animal, possibly a tiger, stood on a chest. There were shelves of art books and prints of Robert Mapplethorpe's muscular naked black men. There was the refrigerator. But no sign of a medicine cabinet.

He went into the gallery, feeling the acoustic change from somewhere small and confined to somewhere open and spacious. Kelly Broome had set up the suitcase and the cymbal on a riser opposite the door. Now he lifted the guitar out of its case and took a Y-shaped steel bar from the pocket that held strings and picks.

"Come on, Petunia, give me an A," he called to his daughter, who was arranging the display of CDs on its bleached branch. She ran over and took the tuning fork. Kelly brushed a thumb across the strings, which shivered on the air. Petunia struck the tines of the fork on the concrete floor and pressed it against the guitar, next to the iguana climbing out of the soundhole. It hummed. Kelly plucked a string and twisted the tuning head. The note rose, and merged with the hum. He played it again. "Spot on."

Petunia set off on a circuit of the Amalgam, making the fork vibrate against the wall, the heating pipes, a paint can, an aluminum stepladder, a bronze sculpture of a rearing horse that awaited relocation to the storeroom. The locomotive, now in pride of place in the middle of the gallery, made it boom like an organ. Her eyes widened. She struck the note again. She ran over to the riser, picked up the didgeridoo, carried it back to the locomotive and looked around.

"Den!" she shouted. "Come here! I'm going to give you a sound bath."

Den ambled over, grinning ruefully. He put one foot into the boiler of the locomotive.

"Not *that* way. Head first."

Leander glanced across from where they were hanging a portrait of Mao holding a Starbucks cup. "Just like your mum," he said to Kelly. "Wouldn't take no for an answer. Not from man or beast. Ever tell you how she got a carpet snake out of the dunny? Twelve feet long if it was an inch. First she grabs it by the tail and pulls. The snake digs its heels in. So Aggi hikes up to the other end. She takes one shoe off and starts hitting it over the head. A little girl, same age as Petunia, bashing this monster serpent. Pretty soon it just gave up and slithered away. Dad was laughing so much I thought he'd pop his cork."

"All the way in," Petunia commanded. Den's feet vanished. She scrambled up on the tender and gripped the didgeridoo between her knees, its mouth pointing at the boiler, Her playing didn't have the rolling mellifluence of Kelly's. It was more a series of quacks and farts. But the Amalgam was cavernous enough to create echoes, and the sound bounced from wall to wall, crisscrossing as if woven on a loom.

A loose barn door on one of the rows of spotlights rattled empathetically.

When she finished the echoes left a tingling silence. Den backed out of the boiler, grinning more than ever and shaking his head in amazement. Scattered laughter burst out among Leander's crew as they piled up cases of Yellow Tail shiraz. The best Daniel could manage was a taut smile.

Petunia went back to setting up the CD display.

And in a flash he knew what he had to do.

Thirty-one

MADELEINE

An hour later he sat on a bench in the park Alex Orlovski remembered from his boyhood. A worker in a green cap and overalls trimmed dead leaves from a bush and stuffed them in a plastic sack, then stepped back to consider what to cut next. A runner loped past, a tall Chinese woman with hair gathered in a pony tail that stuck out of the back of her Mariners baseball cap. Birdsong came from cages in the trees, little blue-roofed boxes with delicate wooden bars that housed finches and jays.

His palms were sweating. He'd just made a call. They wouldn't take more than a couple of minutes to pick him up. This would be his last chance to talk to Sophie for a while. He touched her number, just in case. To his surprise, he got through.

"Ten minutes ago," she said. "Everything suddenly came back on. Weird. The wind's as strong as ever."

"What about flooding? The NHC's expecting a twelve-foot surge."

"Wayne and me went up to the roof half an hour ago. There's water pouring down the street. Cars are floating past. Bumping into each other like dodgems. People in boats." Her laughter edged close to hysteria.

"At least you can get up there. If you have to. Don't leave it too late. Keep warm. You have to keep warm. And have enough drinking water. That's the most important thing."

"I told you. Wayne's looking after us. It's like he's become a real father. Taken responsibility."

The park had four entrances. Daniel saw People's Armed Police officers running toward him from different directions and assumed there were squad cars at each of them. His insides turned to liquid.

"Sophie, listen, this is important. You might not hear from me for a day or two. Call Beidermeyer. Ben Beidermeyer. In Chicago. He'll tell you what's happening."

But she wasn't paying attention. "Hear that? Sounds like someone banging on the door. Must be a body in trouble. Unless it's the Jehovah's Witnesses." Her laugh was hysterical.

"Sophie ..."

Hands gripped his elbows.

"Daniel Skye." An accusation rather than a question.

He took a deep breath and nodded.

THEY TOOK AWAY the phone and the laptop bag and frisked him, patting down his body and under his arms and between his legs. He felt a hand on the inside of his right ankle. The cop said something, reached into the sock, and took out the flash drive that held the torching video.

Two of them gripped his wrists and pushed them together while a third pinioned him with plastic handcuffs. The cuffs cut into his skin. With an officer holding each elbow and another grasping his collar he was hustled along the path that followed the stream to the main gate. They strode quickly and without speaking, the phalanx of hard-faced cops and their *waiguoren* captive. People stepped aside as they approached and looked away. Some turned their backs. He wondered what they wanted to avoid, seeing or being seen to see. Lack of curiosity was not a Shanghainese trait. But clearly there were some things in which it was unwise to display too keen an interest.

The cops pushed him into the back seat of one of the cars waiting at the main entrance. The process sent a jolt of pain through his arm and made him gasp. The officer in the front seat, a horse-faced man with big yellow teeth, turned around and said something that made the others laugh. The cars pulled out and other drivers were quick to make way. With sirens wailing and lights flashing the convoy went halfway around the square. Then it pulled into the underground parking of an immense concrete and glass tower. A steel barrier crashed down behind them and shut off the outside world. The ride had taken less than a minute.

The car stopped beside a set of glass doors. He winced as he was pulled out. A radio squawked and tires squealed as someone in the echoing concrete cavern pulled away at speed. He was frogmarched through the doors, past a guard who stared over the top of a newspaper, and down a short corridor. The wait for an elevator took longer than the car ride. Muttering, the horse-faced officer jabbed irritably at the button. They went down, not up, and emerged in a narrow passage which had the anonymity of an ant's nest with bare concrete walls, fluorescent lights, unmarked doors. Was this where Shuying had been kept? Where Mayling Yu's torturers worked? Where the balding man told everything he knew? He listened for screams but heard only their footsteps.

Horse-face opened a door like all the other doors and pushed him inside. His first impulse was to look if there was a butcher's hook in the ceiling. There wasn't. Instead, there was a metal desk with two laptops, from behind which a man in a lieutenant's uniform scowled at him. A short-haired woman in a white shirt and black skirt stood beside the desk. His escorts shoved him onto a chair and kept hold of his arms, which they forced over the chair's back.

"Hello, Daniel," the woman said. "I am Yang Chongshan. I've heard a lot about you."

"Me? I don't think so."

"Yes. We know a couple of the same people. Renwen Zhou is one.

We went to grad school together. In California."

The lieutenant had not taken his eyes off Daniel. He gripped a pencil in both hands.

"Renwen's very angry, Daniel. So is Wenming Nan. You're lucky we found you first."

He remembered the hit man coming up the stairs at Nan's *beishu* and thought she might be right. Not that it was any comfort.

"Why did you throw away twelve million dollars, Daniel? Wasn't that why you came to Shanghai? To get money?"

He'd asked himself that question, huddled in the doorway while the rats scuttled. He hadn't come up with an answer. Not that he could put into words, anyway. It all came down to a bowl of egg soup with spearmint.

The lieutenant grunted an order. The officer with Pierre's MacBook stepped forward and put it on the desk.

Yang opened it and turned it toward him. "Show us SkyeSlip."

"SkyeSlip? What's that?"

The lieutenant hissed.

Yang pressed a button on a recorder that lay on the desk. The sound was tinny and the voice dreamy and languorous. But there was no mistaking whose it was.

"... *hid a whole book in one photograph ... a book by his mother ... she's a writer ... that's where his imagination comes from ...*"

"Pierre told us, Daniel. Everything."

"Where is he?"

She didn't answer, just picked up a flash drive off the desk and put it in the MacBook. On it were all the e-mails he'd sent and received since he came to Shanghai. Including the photos he'd sent to Beidermeyer.

"Show us."

"What if I don't?"

"We wouldn't like that, Daniel."

"I don't give a fuck what you wouldn't like." One of the guards jerked his arm, wrenching it in its socket and making him cry out.

"Your wife won't like it either."

He froze. "What's Sophie got to do with it?"

Yang turned the other computer to face him. There was a blur of movement on the screen. Then Sophie's face appeared, close up, eyes wide with fear and staring into the camera.

"Daniel. Oh God. One of them's got a gun. Do what they want. Please, Daniel. Please."

She had to shout to make herself heard above the roar and clatter of the hurricane. A man in the yellow oilskin peered into the camera and brandished a pistol. Then he pointed it at Sophie.

"Show us," Yang said.

"Oh, Christ. Oh Jesus. Leave her alone. Leave her alone or I'll ..."

"You'll what, Daniel?"

Another crash from the roof of the condominium made Sophie and the man with the gun look upward, both equally frightened.

"Daniel, tell them. Please. Please!"

The man was holding the gun to her head. He looked very young and very nervous.

"I can't!" He swung around to confront Yang. "You've got to stop this. She's pregnant. Understand? She's going to have a baby. Tell them to stop. Right now."

The horse-faced officer wrenched his arm, making the cuffs bite harder.

Sophie was sobbing.

Yang said, "When you open SkyeSlip."

"I can't! This is Pierre's computer. I can't open SkyeSlip on it."

"Don't lie, Daniel. We know you gave it to him."

"Yes. I gave it to him. But I don't know his password."

Yang conferred with the lieutenant.

"Ask him."

"Where is he?"

She turned the other laptop so he could see the screen. It showed a Google map in street view. A red dot blinked in the middle of one of the streets, jerked forward, blinked, jerked again.

"He's on Hengshan Road," Yang said. "Just passing La Boheme." She picked up Daniel's phone from the table.

He shook his head. "Tell him to stop pointing the gun at Sophie."

The cop jerked his arm again. But the pain didn't stop him staring at her eyes, red-rimmed and wide with panic, staring back across eight thousand miles.

Yang leaned toward the laptop and shouted some peremptory command. The man lowered the gun.

"Call." She handed a pair of black-handled shears to one of the guards, who snipped the bands of plastic. Blood trickled down Daniel's palm from where they had cut into the skin. Yang thrust the phone at him. He scrolled to Pierre's number and tapped it with a bloodstained finger.

It took Pierre a long time to answer, and when he did his voice was slurred.

"Daniel. Been looking for you. All over."

"What's your password for SkyeSlip?"

Yang and the lieutenant listened intently.

"Password? Daniel, is that you? Says it's your phone. Sounds like you. But you can never be sure ..."

"Pierre! It is me. I have to get into SkyeSlip. On your computer. Right now. They've got Sophie."

Across the Pacific she buried her head in her hands. Her shoulders shook, but the sound was lost in Leo's infernal howling.

"Okay. Password. My mother's name. Madeleine."

Daniel turned to the keyboard. His hands were numb and swollen. When he tried to type it felt like hitting the keys with sausages. Blood dripped onto the spacebar. The SkyeSlip logo appeared, the image of a cloud whose folds partly hid an assortment of letters. Sophie had designed that. Beneath the cloud was a box which said Enter Code. He began to type, slowly, agonizingly:

M-a-d-e-l-

Before he could finish, a different sound came from the condo, rising above the storm's chaotic din. It, too, might have been made by a beast in torment, the roar of a bull as the matador's sword sank deep.

Sophie screamed, and vanished from the screen. There was another scream, from the man in the oilskin. He was no longer holding the gun, or anything else. His hand dangled by a single tendon and blood spurted from the yellow sleeve. Wayne's face appeared, a gore-spattered mask of savagery. He bellowed as he swung the axe, again, and again, and again. Then the screen went blank.

In the stunned silence Daniel could hear the horse-faced officer behind him. He was breathing through his mouth. The lieutenant's face was frozen in horror.

After a few moments Yang gestured at the MacBook. "Open it," she ordered. "Madeleine."

Daniel typed "*i-n-e*." He paused, and seemed to collect himself, as if making sure of his footing before diving from a very high board. Then he hit the enter key.

That screen, too, went blank.

"Do it again," Yang said. "Madeleine."

"It's gone," Daniel said.

"Start again." Her face hardened even more. He shook his head.

"Can't. It's really gone."

"What do you mean?" She spat out the words. The horse-faced cop grabbed his arm, the one he'd hurt elbowing Zhou in the crotch, and twisted it. The pain was like an electric drill on the joint.

"Dead. Poison pill."

"Open it!"

Another savage twist. Eyes squeezed shut against the pain, he shook his head. Under torture he would say anything, true or made up, no matter who he betrayed. How lucky he no longer had anything to keep secret.

"Didn't Pierre tell you? Destroys itself if you use the wrong password. Overwrites itself with zeros. Can't bring it back. Ever."

"Pierre gave you his password. Madeleine."

"Yes." The pain in his arm turned his expression into a mask of agony. There was something triumphant in it nevertheless.

"*M-a-d-e-l-e-i-n-e.* I misspelled it. Left out the second *e.*"

THIRTY-TWO

THE BIGGEST STORY IN MEMORY

ALONE IN A CELL, he remembered the petitioners in black jails. Would he, too, simply disappear? He told himself the cops knew that if he vanished Steve Holm would come looking, along with the massed ranks of the foreign media. And Pierre knew. Anyway, nothing that happened now could be as bad as the events of the last few days. Then he remembered the baby, that tiny being with a heartbeat like galloping hooves. What if the double trauma of the hurricane and the hostage-taking caused Sophie to miscarry?

And what about Sophie herself? Wayne had saved her from physical danger. How far he could protect her against emotional damage, though, was anybody's guess. Yet Daniel knew that, deep down, she was tough, one benefit of having come through a turbulent childhood. She would survive, even though the immediate future held one more unpleasant shock: she thought he had indeed found a backer. He dreaded telling her he hadn't.

But at least he no longer had to agonize over which would be worse, losing Sophie or letting go of his dream of making *The Riding Instructor*. The dream had been crushed. He wondered if it would come back to haunt him, if he would grow old embittered by failure. No. Compared to the yellow-hatted bookseller he was lucky. If Sophie would forgive the lies and the pain he'd caused he would work on Sheldrake's museum project.. They'd have the baby. And perhaps one day he'd have another brilliant idea as brilliant as *The Riding Instructor*.

He curled up on the mat which was presumably meant to serve as a bed. His elbow throbbed and his head was pounding. No way was he going to sleep, no matter how exhausted he felt. But the next thing he knew a cop was bending over him and shaking his shoulder. Another, standing by the open door, held his phone and computer bag. He said something and jerked his head toward the passage, indicating Daniel was free to go. It was like a rerun of what had happened at the Blue Moon. There was no sign of Yang or the lieutenant.

Outside, night had fallen and traffic clogged the square. He called Sophie, not thinking he'd get through. But she answered right away.

"Guess I'm in shock," she said. "But I'm okay. The cops got us out in a boat."

"What about the baby?"

"The doctor says trauma can sometimes cause a miscarriage. But I'm healthy. It should be alright."

"How about Wayne?"

"The police are talking to him. Before they arrived he hugged me. He asked me to forgive him. He said he'd always loved me and he was sorry he hadn't given me a better life."

"That's how I feel."

Silence. Then she said,

"Opposites attract. I love you, Daniel. I really do. But I can't live with someone who's going to throw everything away because of the voices in his head. I just can't do that."

"Sophie, listen. I didn't get the money. It was all a scam. But I'm coming back. I'll call Sheldrake. We'll lose the house. But we'll get another one. We'll survive."

"That won't make you happy, Daniel. You know it won't."

"I don't have any choice."

"BEDLAM OVER HERE," Beidermeyer said from Chicago a couple of hours later. "For the media it's the most perfect storm imaginable.

Anybody not in Shanghai covering the conference is in Florida covering the hurricane. And this huge story breaks about Chinese agents in Boca Raton. Which ties in with the Shaowen Gen execution video. Biggest story in memory. Not that memories are very long these days."

"How did they get there in the hurricane?" He couldn't imagine anybody going anywhere in that wind.

"Very capable people, the Chinese. Run the largest espionage operation in the States. By far. And they have their own style. Instead of a few highly-trained agents in Washington they use a huge number of amateurs, spread all over the place. My guess is these guys were students. Already living in Florida. They'd have been in position before the hurricane struck."

Daniel had the phone to one ear and a hand covering the other. Leander had hired a local rapper to harangue guests at the opening of Second Thoughts, and Kelly was adding to the backing track on suitcase-drum and didgeridoo. The rapper's torrent of Shanghainese was punctuated with bursts of English, mostly obscene. The whole thumping din reverberated around the Amalgam, drowning out the popping of corks and the clink of glasses.

"When they locked me up I thought I might be there forever," Daniel said. "Like the petitioners. In a black jail. But they let me go without a word. No deportation order, no threats, nothing."

"Complete denial," Beidermeyer said. "That's how they'll spin it at first. For as long as they can. Still not very hip about public relations. And when that fails to take the heat off they'll massage it. Bury it in investigative committees. Say it was the work of a rogue element. Or a set-up by Falun Gong. Or the Tibetans. Or Muslims."

Beside Daniel in Leander's office Jia Laishun was stretched out on the couch, murmuring obscenities of his own into the ear of the willow-slim girl beside him. Shaven-headed, he wore baggy blue shorts with a pattern of gold chrysanthemums. The girl bent over a mirror and scraped his advance, already converted into pharmaceutical-grade nose candy, into neat white lines.

"Good news for Mayling Yu," Daniel said.

"Good news for everybody," Beidermeyer said. "Except Wenming Nan. Not that the Chinese themselves will do much. Way too much *guanxi*. But reporters will dig out the owner of the van in the torching video. Ten to one there'll be a link to some Nan-owned enterprise. Which could mean some kind of justice for Pan and his mother. Even if it is an underling who takes the rap. The Laos thing was already in trouble. UNESCO was freaking out. Gross cultural insensitivity. Now it'll be dead in the water."

He thought of that cold, dark-eyed man, winnowing through papers in his fake château and dreaming of vengeance on his own mother's murderers. How many millions would he lose? He remembered the nail house, burning in the night. Some people lost more than money.

The girl held the mirror on the palm of her hand and offered him a rolled-up hundred-dollar bill. He shook his head.

"What are you going to do now, Daniel? Still want to make *The Riding Instructor*?"

"That's not going to happen." He felt a numbness as he spoke, much as he had felt the first time he told somebody his father had just been killed. Part of himself had died, too. "I have to get some money to live on. That's the priority. I'll be working with a friend who's got a contract to redesign the Smithsonian's website."

"Interesting."

"Sure. A lot of people would give their right arm to work on that project."

"But not you."

He laughed to mask his discomfort. "No, no, it's fine by me. It means I can support Sophie and the baby. That's more important than anything else."

"*The Riding Instructor* will mark the biggest change in how we look at images since the Lumière brothers made their first jerky movie of workers leaving a factory. Backers who act now will be in line for an as-yet unimaginably profitable return, just as the first investors in the personal computer saw their money grow by many orders of magnitude beyond even their most optimistic expectations.' I quote."

"Did I leave the proposal on that thumb drive?"

"Didn't need to. I saw it when you showed me SkyeSlip. I have a photographic memory. I got the impression it was more passion than hype. And passion is the key to a good pitch." Daniel could sense him adjusting his bifocals. "Still want to do it? Or has the enthusiasm withered on the vine?"

"It's not enthusiasm that's the problem."

Jia Laishun, having availed himself of the rolled-up banknote, beat out a fast tempo on the back of the leather couch. The girl ran her tongue around his ear. Daniel turned away.

"Could you do something with less than ten million?"

"That's not an option. Not anymore."

There was a pause. Daniel imagined him fiddling with the signet ring.

"Thing is, I owe you, Daniel. When you reach my age paying debts is important. Have to do it while you can. Luckily, I think this time I'll be able to."

"How?"

"Helen Belvedere Lefkovitch. Grandpa made a killing in hogs. She set up the foundation back in the seventies to help victims of the Khmer Rouge. Very hands-on, even if she is pushing eighty. Bit of a loose cannon when it comes to investing. But very smart."

"You really think she'd be interested in backing *The Riding Instructor*?"

"Not the whole nine yards. Not to begin with. But I think I could get something in the mid-seven figures. The funding committee meets next Friday. I have some pull. I'll have a word with Helen. She's been talking about raising the profile of the foundation. And you'll be flavor of the week with the media. That's a big plus."

For the second time in the day, Daniel was speechless. Then he said, "Ben, I can't believe this. Are you sure?"

"Nothing's ever sure. Let's just say I know what I'm talking about. Give me a couple of days, okay?"

He sat back, dazed, while Jai Laishun and the girl writhed on the couch. Five million. Yes. He could do something with that. Hire actors. Programmers. Hire someone who could leverage five million into ten million, ten million into twenty.

So *The Riding Instructor* really did have a will of its own, an urge to take form and come into being, to take the world by storm. Just when he thought the dream was dead it came back to life, as tantalizing as ever. It wouldn't let him forget. He'd still have sixteen-hour days and a to-do list in triple digits. Wouldn't have it any other way. But he would not become obsessed again. He'd learned that lesson. He'd get someone else to take care of the finances. And he'd spend time with Sophie. Every day.

Skype said she was offline so he called Pierre. "What do you want first?" Pierre said when he heard the news. "Warm congratulations or abject apologies?" He still sounded groggy.

"Forget the apologies. Except for calling me an asshole."

"Sorry about that. Asshole. And about the other thing. With Sophie. Got the feeling you didn't believe me when I said it before. But I am. Really."

Get mad, then get over it. His father's maxim. He touched his watch. "Okay. Case closed."

"That was pretty nice dope they gave me. Like opium. You'd love it. Sends you floating off on golden clouds. I'm going back in the morning to see if I can get some more."

"Get some sleep, Pierre."

"Have to book a ticket to Thailand first. Full moon in a couple of days."

"Think the Chinese will let you back in?"

"Shuying says keeping me out would just be more bad publicity. Another angle to keep the story alive. The howler monkeys of the media are always snuffling around for fresh kibble. But who knows?"

"She alright?"

"She's okay. Keeping out of sight. Doesn't want to get picked up again before she can talk to the reporters about Mayling Yu. I took advantage of the afterglow of Yang's dope to say sorry I didn't stop her father getting his legs broken. She cried. I cried. We howled into our phones like dogs at the moon."

"So no more nightmares."

"Not about the baseball batsmen. Now I'm haunted by the guy falling back into the pit when I smashed his face with the camera. That one will run and run."

Daniel went into the gallery. Petunia sat on the front buffer of the locomotive, swinging her legs. At her feet was the card table, with its display of CDs.

"Your friend Big Steve," she said. "Know a lot about music, does he?"

"I don't really know. Why?"

She tapped the branch with her foot, making the CD cases jump. "He didn't buy any of Dad's CDs. But when I said you'd asked me to give him yours he grabbed it. Then he left."

"Well, I wouldn't take it personally. He probably had something on his mind."

"He said he was going to see Lilly. Is she your girlfriend?"

"No. Just a friend. I have a wife. Sophie."

Petunia unzipped a green purse with a fading picture of a goblin and emptied it onto her lap. Among the coins were a few notes which she'd folded as small as she could. She picked through them and smoothed out a twenty-dollar bill.

"He gave me this." She considered him soberly. "You must be very good. It didn't even have a label." She held out the money.

Daniel laughed, and folded it back in her fist.

"You keep it," he said. I don't think I'll be needing it."

Then he went back to the office to Skype Sophie again.

About the Author

Michael C. Boxall was born in England and studied English and American literature at Warwick University, after which he became a trainee editor with a documentary film company in London. When he won the Eisaku Sato Foundation prize for a paper on Japanese-European relations he was invited to Japan and subsequently became a journalist. After winning the United Nations University Prize for writing on the impact of new media he studied communications in graduate school at the University of Washington. An internship at *Harper's* confirmed his interest in magazines and he later returned to Tokyo as editor of *Intersect*, an English-language monthly about Japan. As well as writing for print he has worked in multimedia and Star Sites, about the significance of archaeoastronomy in five different cultures, was named educational CD of the month by Newsweek Interactive. In 2003 he was one of two joint winners of the $25,000 Lupton New Voices in Literature award for a proposal for a non-fiction book entitled *Driven by Desire: Sex and the Spread of New Media*. He has also won prizes for short fiction. *The Great Firewall* will be followed by a second China-related thriller, *Final Cut*.

Made in the USA
Charleston, SC
27 April 2012